HOT PURSUIT

BOOKS BY STUART WOODS

FICTION

Insatiable Appetites†
Paris Match†
Cut and Thrust†
Carnal Curiosity†
Standup Guy†
Doing Hard Time†
Unintended Consequences†
Collateral Damage†
Severe Clear†
Unnatural Acts†
D.C. Dead†
Son of Stone†
Bel-Air Dead†
Strategic Moves†
Santa Fe Edge§
Lucid Intervals†
Kisser†
*Hothouse Orchid**
Loitering with Intent†
Mounting Fears‡
Hot Mahogany†
Santa Fe Dead§
Beverly Hills Dead
Shoot Him If He Runs†
Fresh Disasters†
Short Straw§
Dark Harbor†
*Iron Orchid**
Two-Dollar Bill†
The Prince of Beverly Hills
Reckless Abandon†
Capital Crimes‡
Dirty Work†
*Blood Orchid**
The Short Forever†
*Orchid Blues**
Cold Paradise†
L.A. Dead†
The Run‡
Worst Fears Realized†
*Orchid Beach**
Swimming to Catalina†
Dead in the Water†
Dirt†
Choke
Imperfect Strangers
Heat
Dead Eyes
L.A. Times
Santa Fe Rules§
New York Dead†
Palindrome
Grass Roots‡
White Cargo
Deep Lie‡
Under the Lake
Run Before the Wind‡
Chiefs

TRAVEL

A Romantic's Guide to the Country Inns of Britain and Ireland (1979)

MEMOIR

Blue Water, Green Skipper

**A Holly Barker Novel*
†A Stone Barrington Novel
‡A Will Lee Novel
§An Ed Eagle Novel

STUART WOODS

G. P. PUTNAM'S SONS *New York*

PUTNAM

G. P. PUTNAM'S SONS
Publishers Since 1838
Published by the Penguin Group
Penguin Group (USA) LLC
375 Hudson Street
New York, New York 10014

USA · Canada · UK · Ireland · Australia
New Zealand · India · South Africa · China

penguin.com
A Penguin Random House Company

Library of Congress Cataloging-in-Publication Data

Woods, Stuart.
Hot pursuit / Stuart Woods.
p. cm.—(Stone Barrington ; 33)
ISBN 978-0-399-16916-8
1. Barrington, Stone (Fictitious character)—Fiction. 2. Private investigators—Fiction. I. Title.
PS3573.O642H69 2015 2014040673
813'.54—dc23

Printed in the United States of America
1 3 5 7 9 10 8 6 4 2

BOOK DESIGN BY NICOLE LAROCHE

This book is for Bill Bratton and Rikki Klieman.

HOT PURSUIT

1

STONE BARRINGTON STOOD on a wide expanse of tarmac, leaning into thirty knots of icy wind, holding his hat on his head, his trench coat inadequate to the task of keeping his body temperature in the normal range. It was January in Wichita.

He watched as a thing of beauty made a turn and rolled toward him. It bore his tail number, but not on the tail—on the engine nacelles. Its white fuselage bore stripes of blue and red, sweeping back to a night-blue tail, emblazoned with stars. It was his brand-new Citation M2, for which he had waited two years. The form of the delivery pilot, a man named Pat Frank, could be seen in the pilot's seat, having flown the twenty-minute flight from the factory, in Independence, Kansas.

A lineman ran forward and chocked the nosewheel, and the pilot cut the engines, their dying whine leaving the howl of the wind as the only noise on the ramp.

Stone had spent the past sixteen days in the classroom and the simulator; the content of his life had shrunk to sweating out instruction all day, then ordering room service at night and falling asleep in front of the TV. He wanted the real airplane and he wanted New York. Now.

The door of the airplane swung open and a figure kicked the folding steps down, and Stone got his first surprise of the day. The ferry pilot descended onto the tarmac, and her blond hair streamed with the wind. "Hi," she said, holding out a hand. "I'm Pat Frank. Can we get out of this wind?"

"Follow me," Stone said, running for the airplane and climbing the steps. He glanced into the cockpit, which was completely familiar to him, since the three fourteen-inch screens of the Garmin 3000 avionics and the accompanying switches and throttles were identical to those in the simulator. He sank into one of the four comfortable passenger seats and waved Ms. Pat Frank to a seat facing him. "So you're the hand-holder my insurance company sent to make my first flight with me," he said.

"I am that," she replied. "At the very least. You may recall that you paid me to do the acceptance flights and inspections for you, too."

"And I thought I was signing checks to some grizzled veteran of the airlines, corporate flying, and, maybe, FedEx."

"I'm all that, except the grizzled part," she said, smiling, revealing perfect teeth set off by her red lipstick. The soft, goatskin leather jacket, zipped up against the weather, could not conceal her ample breasts. "All we need is fuel and a flight plan filed."

"I've taken care of both."

"I hope to God you don't want to do the walk-around inspection in this wind," she said. "I've already done it this morning in a nice warm hangar, and if you want to get me off this airplane you're going to have to drag me."

A lineman stuck his head into the cabin. "Fuel's on the way," he said. "You want me to stow your bags, Mr. Barrington?"

Pat Frank handed him a key. "Up front, please, and kindly remove the ten bags of lead shot first."

"Lead shot?" Stone asked, baffled.

"Weight and balance," she said. "My hundred and twenty pounds weren't enough to get us into the envelope. With you aboard, no problem, unless you have plans to have some slip of a girl fly the airplane alone."

"Can't think of one," Stone replied.

"Well, if you've already been to the can, let's button this thing up, then climb into the cockpit and see if we can make it fly."

"After you," Stone said, stripping off his trench coat.

She pulled up the steps, closed the door, and swung the lever that locked it. In a moment, she was in the copilot's seat.

Stone went forward and, with some difficulty, managed to get his six-foot-two frame into the pilot's seat.

Pat helped him with adjusting the seat. "It's snug, but you'll get used to it," she said. "For some reason, Cessna puts all the room in the rear, where the passengers sit—not where the owner-pilots for whom this airplane was intended fly the thing."

She read out the pre-start checklist, he flipped the appropriate switches, then he turned on the power and the three glass panels slowly came to life, along with the two smaller screens just ahead of the throttles, called the GTUs. These were the iPad-like units with which most of the airplane's systems were operated. Stone had spent a week playing with a computer-simulated version, memorizing the patterns and trying to forget the old G-1000 in his former airplane.

"Did you have a Mustang before?"

"Yep, I gave it to my son."

"I hope he's older than eight," she said. "That's quite a toy."

"He's twelve, or so, and he's already type-rated."

She shook her head. "I never heard of a father giving his son a jet airplane." She watched as he managed to tap a flight plan into the GTU, then run the system checks. "Not bad for a first flight," she said.

"They drilled me well in class. Don't worry, I'll need your help before long."

Outside, the fuel truck drove away, and the lineman signaled that the chocks had been pulled. Stone pulled the hand brake and started the engines. When all systems were running smoothly, he listened to ATIS, the tower's recorded weather report, then called clearance delivery, adjusting the microphone attached to his Bose headset. "Wichita clearance delivery, November One Two Three Tango Foxtrot is IFR to Tango Echo Bravo. Do you have a clearance for me?"

They did, and Stone copied it down and read it back. It included a departure procedure, and he inserted that into his electronic flight plan, then called for permission to taxi. "Thank God that wind is right down the runway," he said. "I don't feel like fighting it." He taxied to the end of the runway, and Pat read out the pre-takeoff checklist. With every switch in its proper position, he asked permission to take off and was cleared. He rolled onto the runway, lined up with the centerline, centered the heading bug, flipped on the pitot heat switches, and pushed the throttles to the firewall.

"Airspeed's alive," Pat said after a few seconds, then, "Seventy knots . . . aaaand rotate!"

Stone put both hands on the yoke and pulled back until two V-bars on the display in front of him mated, showing that he had achieved the proper climb angle.

"Positive rate of climb," Pat said

Stone raised the landing gear flaps.

"Four hundred fifty feet," she said.

He pressed the button that turned on the autopilot, then removed his hands from the yoke. They were given an initial climb to ten thousand feet, and he was told to switch to Wichita departure. The frequency was already entered into the G-3000; all he had to do was tap the glass panel at the proper spot. "Wichita departure, N123TF with you out of three thousand for one zero thousand."

"N123TF, cleared on course. Climb and maintain flight level 410."

Stone repeated the instruction and pressed the NAV button to tell the autopilot to follow the flight plan, then he dialed forty-one thousand feet into the computer, pressed the Flight Level Control button, and sat back.

He put behind him the claustrophobic previous two weeks and room-service food, and reveled in his new airplane as it climbed quickly to FL 410.

"Does your wife fly?" Pat asked.

"I'm a widower," Stone replied. "For some years."

"My condolences."

"Thank you. Why don't you delay your return to Wichita, and let's have dinner tonight?"

"I'm moving into a new apartment tomorrow in New York," she said, "and I'd love to."

2

THE FLIGHT was predictably smooth for the first hour. They grilled each other, this being more of a first date than a qualifying flight for the insurance company. Pat was from a small town in Georgia, Delano, which somehow had a familiar ring for Stone. She had started flying after college, had flown air taxi and package delivery, then corporate jets, then for an airline. By the time that went bust, she had made captain, and she took herself to another airline. Finally, she had made the break.

"I'm starting a business," she said. "I'm calling it The Pat Frank Flight Department, something that the charterers and the corporates have as a matter of course, but not the owner-flown jets. I'll do all the paperwork, keep the maintenance schedule, update the logbooks weekly, et cetera, et cetera."

"I could use a service like that," Stone said. "My secretary has been doing all the work, but since she knows nothing about airplanes, it's hard for her. You're hired."

"Great! My first client! Of course, I can't have dinner with you tonight, for professional reasons."

"You're fired," Stone said.

"Well, I guess I can make an exception, your being my first client and all."

"You're rehired." Stone looked at the multi-function display before him. "There's the weather the forecast predicted," he said, pointing at a green mass ahead of them that was dotted with yellow areas. "We'll fly over the bulk of it, but when we start our descent on the arrival procedure, we'll have to contend with it and maybe with some ice, too. And we'll need an instrument approach."

"Your airplane is equipped to deal with it," she reminded him.

Stone tapped an icon or two and brought up the weather at Teterboro. "Six-hundred-foot ceiling, six miles of visibility, wind 040 at twelve, gusting twenty," he read. "No problem. We'll keep an eye on it, though."

"There was some light snow in the forecast, too," Pat said.

They entered into the arrival procedure, a loop to the north, then back to the south, that the air traffic controllers used to line up and keep distance between the conga line of airplanes that would be landing at TEB. ATC gave them a lower altitude, and Stone turned on the ice prevention systems that heated the leading edges of the wings and tail and the windshield. Five minutes later they were in Instrument Meteorological Conditions and blind, except for their instruments. They continued their descent on the arrival, and at the end of it they were vectored to the Instrument Landing System for runway 6 at Teterboro. ATIS told them that the weather had deteriorated to three hundred feet and two miles of visibility, with blowing snow.

Once established on the ILS, Stone watched the indicator for the glide slope and put down the landing gear. The three green lights that indicated that the tricycle gears were down did not come on. "Uh-oh," he said, then recycled the gear switch. "I guess we're going to have to blow the gear down." There was a tank of nitrogen aboard that could be used to force the gear down in the event of a hydraulic failure.

Pat reached forward and twisted the knob that selected night or day flying to "day," and the three green gear lights appeared. "Some ass turned it to 'night,'" she said. "And the daylight washed out the dimmed lights."

"That's a relief," Stone said.

She read out the landing checklist, and the autopilot flew them down the glide slope; all Stone had to do was control the airspeed. At three hundred feet they broke out of the clouds, into light snow, and the runway lay directly ahead of them. At 160 feet, Stone turned off the autopilot and landed the airplane smoothly by hand.

"And your first landing is a greaser!" Pat said. "You've just passed your insurance check ride!"

Stone called ground control, requested taxi to Jet Aviation, where he kept the airplane, and was given the route. Five minutes later Pat was reading the shutdown checklist, and he was shutting down the engines and switching everything off. He noted the flight time on the Hobbs meter and entered it into his logbook. "We're home," he said.

Pat left the cockpit, opened the airplane's door, and kicked down the steps, which lowered themselves gently into place. Stone went to the rear luggage compartment, switched off the battery to conserve power, and handed a lineman the engine and pitot covers for installation. He locked up and went to the forward luggage compartment, removed his and Pat's bags, and handed them to another lineman, who put them onto a cart.

"Put her in the barn," Stone said to the other lineman, then he and Pat followed their luggage through the Jet Aviation terminal and out to where Stone's factotum, Fred, waited with the Bentley.

"Good flight, sir?" Fred asked.

"A great one, Fred. This is Pat Frank."

Fred tipped an imaginary cap, and they got into the car.

Pat produced her phone. "I didn't book a hotel for tonight," she said.

"Don't bother," Stone replied. "I have guest rooms."

"How kind you are!"

"Saves picking you up for dinner."

Half an hour later they were in the garage, and while Fred dealt with the luggage, they took the elevator to the third floor. "We'll put you in here," Stone said, showing her to the largest guest room. "I'm right down the hall." He looked at his watch: "You've got two hours to get gorgeous," he said. "We'll meet in my study for a drink at seven—it's on the first floor."

"How are we dressing?" she asked.

"You mean you have more than one dress in that little bag?"

"The option is jeans."

"Wear the dress. See you at seven." He walked down the hall to the master suite.

AT SEVEN he was reading the *New York Times* in his study when she walked in, clad in a tight LBD and sporting pearls and very high heels.

"You got gorgeous," Stone said. "What would you like to drink?"

"What are you drinking?"

"Bourbon. Knob Creek. I have gimlets and martinis already made and in the freezer, and most other drinks, but I can't make a banana daiquiri."

"I'm a Georgia girl," she said. "I'll have the bourbon."

He poured them both a drink. "Some friends are meeting us at the restaurant," he said. "Dino and Vivian Bacchetti. She's called Viv."

"Fine."

"In my extreme youth I was a cop, and Dino was my partner. Now I'm a failed cop, and Dino is the police commissioner of the City of New York."

"How did you fail?"

"I got shot in the knee, and I disagreed with my betters on the handling of an important case. They used the knee as an excuse to dump me."

"And how did you go about becoming a lawyer?"

"I was already a law-school graduate. I took a cram course and passed the bar, and an old school buddy had a job waiting for me."

"You make it sound so easy."

"I was lucky. I had inherited this house from a great-aunt, my grandmother's sister, and I was renovating it, doing most of the work myself. I was more than a year into the job, my savings were gone, and I was in debt to the bank and a lot of building suppliers, when I ran into my old friend Bill Eggers, of Woodman & Weld. The rest, as they say, is history."

"A pretty successful history," she said, looking around. "The place is beautiful."

"Fairly successful. When my wife died I came into some money that had been made by her first husband."

"Thus, the gift of a jet to your son."

"Thus. How do you happen to be moving into an apartment in New York tomorrow?"

"My sister got married and moved to the suburbs. She owned an apartment and rented it, until I could clear the decks for the move. The tenant's lease is up tomorrow. I'll probably buy the place from my sister, eventually."

"Good idea." Stone wrinkled his brow. "What's your sister's name?"

"Greta Frank."

"The Greta Frank who was recently acquitted of murdering her husband?"

"Her first husband."

"I followed the trial in the media."

"She was completely innocent, of course."

"Of course. And she was lucky enough to have a very smart attorney."

"Yes, Herbert Fisher. Do you know him?"

"He's a partner in my law firm, and was a protégé of mine."

"Then I suppose Greta has you to thank, as well."

"In a roundabout way, I guess. She didn't lose any time remarrying, did she?"

"Nope. I think they were an item before her husband's untimely death."

"Whom did she marry?"

"Larry Goren, a hedge-fund zillionaire."

"Her late husband was also one of those, wasn't he?"

"Greta has always been attracted to money."

Fred appeared in the doorway. "The car is out front, Mr. Barrington."

They both polished off their drinks and left the house.

3

THEY BEAT DINO and Viv to Patroon and ordered another drink. A jazz group was playing, a new wrinkle of which Stone approved.

Mike Freeman ambled over. "Good evening."

"Hi, Mike," Stone replied. "Pat, this is Mike Freeman, an old friend and business associate. Join us, Mike."

"I'm stag tonight. Sure you don't mind?"

"Not in the least."

Mike signaled to Ken Aretzky, the owner, that he was joining Stone, then sat down and ordered a drink.

"Dino and Viv will be here soon," Stone said, looking at his watch. "I think."

"I thought you were in Wichita," Mike said, "and yet here you are with a beautiful woman."

"She's not a woman, she's a pilot," Stone said. "Pat did the acceptance for me at the factory, and the insurance company okayed her to do the first flight with me. We just got in this afternoon."

"How's the new Citation M2?"

"Wonderful. It's already parked in your hangar. Pat, Mike is the head of Strategic Services, a large security company, and they own a hangar at Teterboro."

"How convenient," Pat said.

"Pat is starting a new business, running the flight department for owner-operators, like me."

"Good idea."

"I'm her first client. I had to fire her to get her to have dinner with me."

"What's your business called?" Mike asked.

"The Pat Frank Flight Department."

"Catchy."

"I thought so, too."

Dino and Viv finally arrived, and introductions were made. They had just ordered drinks when another man approached the table. Dino introduced everybody to Everett Salton, who was the junior senator for the state of New York. Stone had never met him but was usually impressed with what he heard about the man in the news.

"Will you join us, Ev?" Dino asked.

"Thank you, but the senior senator and I are having dinner, as if we don't see enough of each other. Another time, I hope." The senator said good night and wended his way to his table.

"Good guy," Dino said. "I think."

"You think?" Stone asked. "Don't you know?"

"He's a politician—you can never really know a guy like that, you just know what he's for and against, issue by issue, and sometimes even that changes with the wind."

"You know, since becoming commissioner, you've also become a cynic."

"I'm a realist, that's all. You, however, are a pushover for anybody who's nice to you."

"Nonsense."

"Name somebody who's nice to you that you don't like."

Stone thought about that for a moment. "Well . . ."

"A pushover, like I said."

"I think that's a good personal trait," Pat said.

"Do you like Pat?" Dino asked.

"Of course, she's nice to me."

THEY WERE BACK at Stone's house by eleven, and he kissed her good night at her bedroom door. "I don't suppose you need tucking in?"

"I can handle it, thanks."

"Do you have an early start tomorrow?"

"Not so early. The movers are supposed to show up at noon."

"Then wander down the hall around seven and have breakfast with me."

"Sounds good."

"What would you like?"

"Whatever you're having."

"See you at seven." He kissed her again and went to the master suite, undressed, and left a message about breakfast for Helene, his housekeeper. He turned on the news, but there was nothing much new since the early-morning shows, and he fell asleep quickly.

He was awakened by a soft hand on his cheek and a light kiss on the lips.

"Good morning," she said. "I'm early."

"How early?"

"Half an hour."

"Then join me," he said, reaching over and turning down the covers on the other side of the bed.

She shed her robe, giving him a glimpse of a curvaceous body, and pulled the covers up over her breasts. "I don't think I've ever started a day like this without an intimate evening before."

"Best time of day," Stone said, raising an arm and offering her a shoulder. She moved over and nestled against him. Things moved quickly along, and they were resting in each other's arms when a chime rang. "That's the dumbwaiter," Stone said. He got out of bed, opened the door, and removed a large tray, setting it on the bed.

"Wow," Pat said. "That's what I call room service."

"Helene is always punctual."

Stone switched on the morning shows and saw an interview with the two senators on the sidewalk outside Patroon.

"Salton is pretty slick," Pat said.

"He is, isn't he?"

"You didn't know him before last night?"

"Only from television."

"He seemed to know who you were."

"I didn't notice that, and there's no reason why he should."

"But he knew Dino."

"Dino's the police commissioner."

"You have a point," she said. "Still . . ."

Stone's bedside phone rang, a rare event at this hour. Stone picked it up. "Hello?"

"This is Ev Salton. I hope I haven't called too early."

"Not at all, Senator."

"Will you have lunch with me today?" He didn't ask if Stone already had a date.

"Yes," Stone said.

Salton gave him an address. "Just ring the bell," he said. "Twelve-thirty?"

"That's fine."

"Good morning to you, then."

"Good morning." They both hung up.

"That was Senator Salton," Stone said.

"I told you he knew who you were," Pat replied.

4

STONE ARRIVED at the address, a double-width town house in the East Sixties, and rang the bell. He noticed a security camera high and to his left. Almost immediately a man in a black suit and green tie opened the door. "Your name, please?"

"Barrington."

"Please come in, Mr. Barrington, and follow me." The man took his overcoat, then led him to an elevator, and Stone was ushered in. "Press five," the man said.

Stone pressed five, the doors closed, and when they opened, Senator Everett Salton stood waiting in a small foyer. He shook Stone's hand.

"Good to see you, Stone."

"And you," Stone replied.

"This way."

Stone followed him to one of several doors opening off the foyer, and into a sort of sitting room with a table set for two.

Salton indicated where Stone should sit. "I hope you don't mind, I've ordered for us—saves time."

"That's fine," Stone said, taking a seat. His place was set with elegant china and crystal and a huge, starched Irish linen napkin.

"Would you like a drink?" Salton asked.

"Thank you, just some fizzy water."

Instantly, a waiter entered the room and took their drink orders.

"What is this place?" Stone asked.

"It's a sort of club, I suppose," Salton said.

He supposed? "Does it have a name?"

"It does not. The members refer to it vaguely as 'the club' or 'the association' or 'the East Side House.' To what clubs do you belong, Stone?"

"Only a small golf club in Washington, Connecticut, where I have a house."

"No city clubs?"

"None."

"I find that remarkable," Salton said.

Stone didn't ask why. "Are all meals taken in this setting?" Stone asked, indicating the room.

"No, there is a proper dining room downstairs, but only members are permitted to use it. As a group, they guard their privacy jealously. Guests are received in these private rooms."

"I see," Stone said, overstating his understanding.

"I've wanted to meet you for some time," Salton said.

Stone wrinkled his brow. "Why now?"

"Because, until last evening, we had not been introduced." He smiled. "I realize that's a bit old-fashioned of me, especially since I'm a politician, but it has been my experience that the means by which one makes acquaintances is almost as important as the acquaintance."

"That's not only old-fashioned, it's very selective," Stone said.

"Yes, it is, isn't it? Last evening you were in the company of two men I know fairly well, and that spoke well of you."

"Is either of them a member of this club?" Stone asked.

"One is. I proposed the other this morning, along with you."

Stone was dumbfounded. This man, who professed to be so selective, had proposed a man he didn't know for what was obviously an extremely exclusive club. "I'm not sure I have the qualifications for membership," Stone said. "What are they?"

"Substance, character, and to a lesser extent, cordiality," Salton replied.

"And influence?" He thought he was beginning to see what this was about.

"Sometimes. Many members acquire more of that here than they bring to the party. And we are more inclusive than you might imagine. There is an unspoken rule—virtually all the rules here are unspoken—that no candidate is discriminated against for any of the usual exclusionary traits—race, religion, et cetera. The membership is quite broad in that regard."

"Is it also large?"

"Given that the membership is worldwide, not terribly. There are no more than a couple of hundred members who have their main residence within a fifty-mile radius of the city, and you know more of them than you think you do. Several of them joined you in a group whose contributions started Katharine Lee's campaign for the presidency."

And that, Stone thought, is why I am here. Their lunch arrived—

a fish soup, followed by poached salmon and a glass of a flinty white wine.

"You're going to the inauguration, of course," Salton said.

"Of course."

"Will you be staying at the White House?"

"No, I wouldn't want to impose on the Lees at such a frenetic time for them. I'll be at the Hay-Adams Hotel." He didn't mention that he had declined an invitation to stay at the White House because his date was his friend Holly Barker, who ran the New York station of the CIA. Holly had felt it was inappropriate for her to stay there because of her position.

"My wife and I would be delighted to have you stay with us at our home in Georgetown," Salton said.

"That's very kind of you, but there will be four in my party."

"Then perhaps you, your companion, and the Bacchettis would be our guests for a buffet dinner before the Inaugural Ball?"

"We'd be delighted," Stone said. They ate in silence for a few minutes.

Finally, Salton spoke up. "I suppose you're wondering why I'm not pumping you for more information about yourself, but you see, I already know a great deal about you—your background, parentage, education, police service, and law practice. There are at least a couple of members here whose fat you pulled from the fire during your early career."

Stone laughed. "I used to do quite a lot of that," he said.

"And you did it well and discreetly," Salton replied. "I admire that."

"I know a fair amount about you, too," Stone said. "You're that rare person whose first public office was the United States Senate.

I liked, when you first ran, that you didn't seem to scramble for the seat."

"Oh, I consumed my share of rubber chicken," Salton said, "but my way was eased somewhat by members of this club."

The waiter returned to take their dishes.

"Would you like dessert?" Salton asked.

"Thank you, no."

The waiter came back and poured coffee. Shortly another man in a black suit and green tie entered and handed Salton an envelope, then departed.

Salton opened the envelope, took out a sheet of stationery, and read what was written on it. He tucked the paper into his inside pocket. "Congratulations," he said. "You have been elected to membership, as has Michael Freeman."

Stone blinked. "Do you mean that Dino Bacchetti was already a member?"

"Dino was your co-proposer, as was Bill Eggers. You mustn't blame them for not telling you. Another of our unwritten rules is that we may not tell any non-member that we belong, or even confirm that the association exists."

Stone laughed. "I'll blame them anyway."

"This is how it works: for a year you will not receive a bill from the group. After that, you'll be billed annually for a sum that is the cost of our previous year's operating expenses, divided by the number of members, plus a sum—usually around ten percent—to account for inflation and new expenses. Occasionally, the board will authorize an assessment to cover some large expense—a new roof, renovation, et cetera. There is no initiation fee. If you do not receive a bill on the first day of your thirteenth month of membership, then enough of the membership will have thought ill of you to cancel it, and no more will be said."

"How often does that happen?" Stone asked.

"Rarely. There have not been more than two such cases in any year."

"How long has the club existed?"

"Since 1789," Salton replied, "more than a century in this building, which was purpose-built from a rough plan drawn by Thomas Jefferson, who was a member, along with Washington and Benjamin Franklin. Now, come, and I'll give you a tour of the house."

5

SALTON LED the way to the stairs. “We’ll walk down,” he said. “By the way, there’s a lovely roof garden above us, but it won’t open until spring.” They didn’t pause at the fourth floor. “There are some rooms here, which are sometimes used by out-of-town members—or members who have found their domestic arrangements temporarily inhospitable.”

“Are there women members?”

“About twenty percent of us,” Salton said, “and the number is growing. Kate Lee is among them, elected many years ago, as is our future first gentleman.”

They came to the dining room, which, at that hour, was thinly populated. Stone spotted a couple of familiar faces there, lingering over coffee.

Another floor down and they entered the most beautiful library Stone had ever seen, paneled in American walnut with white accents and two stories of bound volumes. "We have a very fine collection of American history," Salton said, "including some volumes from Jefferson's library." They continued past the first floor and emerged into a garage, albeit a very elegant one.

"I didn't notice the garage door when I entered," Stone said.

"The garage extends into the building next door, where our administrative staff are located and which provides the entry for cars. We find it convenient, because driving in means that members won't be seen to come and go so often. We wouldn't like to encourage curiosity." They approached a slightly stretched Lincoln town car, where a chauffeur stood with the rear door open. "Come," Salton said, "I'll give you a lift home."

They got into the car, and Stone found it had a non-standard interior of tan Nappa leather and burled walnut.

"I can't be seen in a Bentley or a Mercedes," Salton explained, "so I bought an old town car and had it renovated. There are so many in the city, no one notices."

They drove up a ramp to street level, and Stone noticed that there were two garage doors: one closed behind them before the other opened to the street. Now, *that* was discreet, he thought.

"The building is open twenty-four hours a day," Salton said, handing him a gold key. "This will get you in between midnight and six AM, should you feel the need for a quiet drink or just to remove yourself from the world for a few hours." He reached into a compartment, withdrew a handsome envelope, and handed it to Stone. "This will tell you something of our history and perhaps mention a few of those unwritten rules. If you wish to bring a guest, call the front desk and book a dining room on the fifth floor. It's a privilege best used rarely."

The Lincoln drew up at Stone's front door. "Would you like to come in for another cup of coffee?" Stone asked.

"I'd love to another time, but I'm expected downtown for a meeting," Salton said. He handed Stone a card. "Here are my private numbers in both New York and Washington, along with my Georgetown address. Drinks at six on Inauguration Day, dinner early. If you decide you won't attend the ball, there'll be entertainment at the house."

"Thank you, Senator," Stone said, shaking his hand.

"From now on it's Ev," Salton replied. "We're very happy to have you among our number."

"I look forward to it," Stone said. He got out of the car, and it drove away. He entered the house through his office door.

"Good afternoon," his secretary, Joan, said as he walked past her office. "Would you like your messages, or would you prefer a nap?"

Stone took the pink slips from her hand. "I'm wide awake, thank you." He handed Joan the senator's card. "Put all these numbers into the system, please." The system would populate his iPad and his iPhone, as well.

"Oh, was he your lunch date?"

"He was."

"He's such a handsome man," she said. "And so well spoken."

"He's all of that and more," Stone said, and went into his office. Dino's call was first. He dialed the private number.

"Hello, new boy," he said.

"You son of a bitch," Stone said. "You never said a word about it."

"That's because I know how to keep my mouth shut," Dino replied, "when it's desirable to do so. You should work on that."

"How long have you been a member?"

"I guess that's not classified: since shortly before I made commissioner. By the way, I was having lunch with Mike Freeman next door, while you and Ev were talking. He's very pleased to be among us."

"So am I," Stone said.

"It's a good place to lunch when you're alone," Dino said. "There's a big table where the stags sit. You'll meet some interesting people."

"That's good to know. Ev didn't mention it."

"There's too much to mention in one lunch. Did you like the guy?"

"Very much. He seemed very like what I thought he'd be. He invited us all to dinner inaugural night."

"I know."

"Tell me, Dino, have you been much put upon for favors from other members?"

"Hardly ever," Dino said. "That's frowned upon, unless a member has invited you to call upon him. I try not to offer that courtesy to many people. Listen, I gotta run—speaking date."

"Talk to you later."

His next call was to Holly Barker.

"Well, hi there," she said. "Are we still on for the inaugural?"

"You bet your sweet ass we are. And you should wear that green dress you bought in Paris. It's perfect for a ball."

"How'd you guess?"

"Oh, and we have a dinner invitation before the ball: Senator and Mrs. Everett Salton, at their house in Georgetown."

"That sounds very grand."

"It should be."

"I have some news, but I'm sitting on it until we're in D.C.," she said.

"You're being secretive."

"I'm secretive for a living, remember?"

"Well, there is that."

"I'll send Fred to pick you up: Home or office?"

"What time?"

"Ten AM?"

"Oh, home, I guess. How much luggage can I bring?"

"As much as you need, and not a bit more."

"Oh, shoot, I wanted to bring a selection of things."

"Select before you pack."

"If I have to."

"See you tomorrow."

"Bye."

Stone hung up and made his other calls. Finally, he got to Pat Frank and dialed the number she had left.

"Hello?"

"It's Stone."

"How was your lunch?"

"Very interesting. First time I've had lunch with a senator. How was your move-in?"

"Not bad. I had the movers take everything out of the boxes and then take them away. I'm already half done with putting things away. When do you leave for Washington?" He had told her about the trip.

"Tomorrow morning."

"Need a copilot?"

"I've got to fly the thing alone sometime—when better than when a thousand other private airplanes are simultaneously diving on the capital?"

"Try not to bump into any."

"You betcha. I'll be back in a few days. I'll call you."

"You'll be only one of a hundred clients by then."

"Yeah, but I'll still be the first, and deserving of special attention."

"And special attention you will get."

He hung up laughing.

6

STONE MADE his first landing as a single pilot in the M2 without incident, in spite of the inaugural traffic in the area. He flew the ILS at Manassas, Virginia, and taxied over to the FBO. The stretch limo he had reserved months ago awaited on the ramp; the driver introduced himself as Benny, and he quickly had their luggage in the trunk.

"Where to, Mr. Barrington?"

"The Hay-Adams Hotel, please."

Traffic was heavy, and they had to wait in a line of cars to unload at the hotel's front door. Stone got everybody out and left Benny to deal with the luggage. He was warmly welcomed at the front desk, and they were immediately taken up to their suite, which Stone and Dino had once used before Dino's marriage. The spectacular view of the White House was still there.

They ordered from room service, and while they waited, Holly broke her news. "Kate is going to appoint me assistant to the president for national security affairs, which means I'll sit on the National Security Council," she said.

"Wow!" Stone shouted. "Good going, Holly!" He added champagne to their lunch order.

"Then you're going to resign from the Agency?"

"I'll take an unpaid leave of absence," Holly said, "in case it turns out I'm not a good enough politician."

"Does Lance know?" Dino asked.

"I told him yesterday. If he'd had to hear it on the news he wouldn't have liked it."

"When do you start?"

"One second after Kate takes the oath, so I won't be flying back to New York with you. I've got to find an apartment here as soon as possible."

Stone had a thought. "How about in Georgetown, on Pennsylvania Avenue?"

"Sounds good. Do you know somebody?"

"I do. Let me call him." Stone took his cell phone into the bedroom and called Bruce Willard, who had briefly been his client. Bruce had an antique shop on Pennsylvania Avenue, and he lived in an apartment above the store. He had also recently inherited a house in Georgetown from his lover, so he would be moving soon.

"Hello, Stone," Bruce said. "You in town for the inaugural?"

"I am, and I've brought a friend along who is going to be serving in an important job on the White House staff. She needs a place to live. Are you moving out of your apartment?"

"I moved a week ago, and I need a good tenant."

"I recommend her highly. When can she see it?"

"I'll be here all afternoon."

"I'll send her over in a couple of hours. Her name is Holly Barker."

"I'll look forward to meeting her."

They hung up, and Stone went back to the living room. "You can see the place after lunch."

"Tell me about it."

"I've never seen it, but the owner has very good taste—he owns a high-end antique shop, and the apartment is over that. He inherited a Georgetown house from his friend, and he's already moved out of the apartment. Benny will drive you over there."

"Any idea how much the rent is?"

"None at all. Make sure he likes you."

"I'll try."

HOLLY'S LIMO PULLED UP before the shop, and she took a moment to look it over before she went up the steps. The building was wide, and she took that to mean that the apartment would be, too. She walked into the shop and a handsome, middle-aged man greeted her and introduced himself. "Hi, I'm Bruce Willard. I expect you're Holly Barker."

"I am," Holly said, looking around. "What a beautiful shop."

"Thank you—we try. Would you like to see the apartment?"

"Yes, thank you."

He took her into the hallway to the elevator and pressed a button. "There are two apartments. My shop manager lives on the second floor, and the third and fourth floors were my apartment until last week. The house I'm moving into is fully furnished, so I can leave whatever of my things you might like."

The door opened into a foyer, and that into a beautiful living room. A spiral staircase rose to the floor above.

"The elevator goes to the fourth floor, too, which will make it easier to move in. Stone says you're going to work at the White House. In what position?"

"I can't say, until the president has announced it publicly," Holly replied. "It happened only yesterday."

"I'm ex-army," Bruce said.

"So am I. I commanded an MP company and later was exec of a regiment."

Bruce grinned at that and showed her the well-equipped kitchen and the study, then he took her upstairs, where there were two bedrooms with baths.

"It's all wonderful," Holly said. "Can a government employee afford it?"

Bruce mentioned a number.

"That's very generous of you," Holly said.

"I want the right person. How can I not fall for an ex–army officer with a White House job, who arrives in a limo?"

Holly offered her hand. "Done, then."

"When would you like to move in?"

"I've already packed some boxes in my New York apartment. I'll call the movers and tell them to start moving me. Stone and my other friends are going back to the city the day after tomorrow. I'd like to start sleeping here then, if that's all right."

"I'll have the housekeeper clean it within an inch of its life," Bruce said. "Oh, the rent includes cleaning, electricity, and gas."

Holly couldn't help it; she hugged him. "Promise not to let me buy too many things in your shop."

"I'll promise you no such thing, only good prices." He took her downstairs and gave her the keys to the building and the apartment, and she wrote him a check for the first month's rent. Bruce said her lease would start the first of the month, and he wouldn't take a security deposit.

Holly burst into the suite at the Hay-Adams and threw herself at Stone. "It's perfect! How did you do that?"

"You did it. I just referred you."

"I'm moving in the day after tomorrow!"

"I'm delighted for you."

"I can't tell you how much trouble this is going to save me. I won't have to sneak off work to hunt for an apartment."

They dined in the hotel's restaurant that evening. The place was choked with Democrats from all over the country, with a sprinkling of senators and congressmen thrown in for spice.

Then, the following afternoon, a sunny and cold one, they sat in good seats down front and watched as Kate Lee took the oath and made a very good inaugural address, keeping it brief. They went back to the White House and attended a very crowded reception in the East Room. Kate glowed and hugged everybody, and Will shook their hands. "Nobody will pay attention to me anymore," he said to Stone, with mock sadness. "Will you come see me sometime?"

"I'll take you flying in my new airplane," Stone said.

"Is there room for a couple of Secret Service agents?"

"There is. I'll even let you fly it."

"Sold!" Will said. "I'm going to New York in a couple of days. Want to have dinner?"

"Sure. Would you like to fly up with us?"

"Would I ever!"

"We'll leave at your convenience."

"I'll call you."

Then they went back to the Hay-Adams to get dressed for Senator Salton's dinner party.

7

EVERETT SALTON'S HOUSE was more imposing than Stone had imagined. Set back from the street on an acre or more, it had a curving driveway to the house and back to the street, and there were a dozen cars ahead of them.

Finally, Benny deposited them at the front door and drove away, to a side street, to wait for Stone's call. The door was opened by a butler before they could ring the bell, and Ev Salton and his wife greeted them in the foyer. "Good evening, Stone, and this must be Holly Barker." Holly shook his hand, and he leaned in. "Congratulations on your appointment. You'll do well, if everything I've heard about you is true." He straightened. "Everybody, this is my wife, Alexandra, and welcome to our home."

Alexandra Salton was nearly as tall as her husband, and she was dressed in a gorgeous, floor-length gown and wearing spectacular diamond jewelry. "I look forward to getting to know all of you," she said to the group, then they were herded into a large drawing room, where there was a bar set up and several waiters circulating with drinks and canapés.

"The Saltons live well," Holly said.

Dino spoke up. "Ev comes from very old, very large money."

"And he spends it well," Stone said. He had already spotted half a dozen senators he knew from the Sunday morning political shows, and a couple of them were at the opposite end of the political spectrum from Salton. One of them was a first-term, firebrand right-winger from Arizona, the sort who had no trouble speaking ill of his own party when he ran out of lies about Democrats. His name was Trent Barber, and he was said to have presidential aspirations, but then that was true of most of the senators Stone had met.

"You're staring at Barber," Dino said. "Don't start any arguments here."

"Me, argue?"

"I wonder how Senator Salton knew about my appointment?" Holly asked.

"He probably got it from the horse's wife's mouth," Stone replied. "She didn't swear herself to secrecy, did she?" He began to notice a few single men and women, appropriately dressed for the occasion, but each wearing the same lapel pin. "There's somebody here with Secret Service protection," he said to Dino.

"Wonder who that could be?" Dino said. "Senators don't rate that."

"Ladies and gentlemen," Everett Salton said in a voice loud enough to shush the room, "the president of the United States and the first gentleman!"

The room burst into applause as Kate and Will entered, smiling.

The two immediately walked over to Stone's party and greeted them.

"The first of many stops this evening," Kate said to Stone.

She and Holly air-kissed. "It's okay to tell people about your appointment," she said. "After all, you don't need Senate confirmation."

"I found an apartment," Holly said, "and it's on Pennsylvania Avenue, though not exactly in your neighborhood."

"I want to hear all about it," Kate said, but then the Saltons intervened and started moving her around the room.

Will Lee was left standing with Stone's group. "I'm going to have to get used to being the least interesting person in the room to talk to," he said. "It will be worse than being vice president."

"Not as long as you're sleeping with the president," Stone said.

"I suppose that having the president's ear will get me a little attention now and then," Will replied. "We'll see."

Then dinner was announced, and the Lees made their exit, bound for the next party and, eventually, the four inaugural balls that were being held around the city.

Stone's group got plates and stood in one of the two buffet lines, then made their way to the room next door, which turned out to be a large library, not unlike the one in the house on the East Side. They captured a sofa and a couple of chairs, and a waiter brought them wine.

"It's funny," Holly said, "I worked out at Langley for all those years and lived in Virginia, too, and the only reasons I ever came to Washington were to testify at committee hearings when Kate didn't want to come, or to have dinner at a good restaurant. Do you suppose everybody here lives like the Saltons?"

"Everybody doesn't live like this *anywhere*," Stone said. "Only those with money and the taste and style to spend it on beautiful things for a few generations—long enough to hand it down to their descendants."

"This is my first visit to Washington," Viv said, "and what a nice way to start!"

"Most of the senators and congressmen here tonight are committee chairmen or ranking members," Holly said. "There's enough power in this house to make it explode. How did you get invited here, Stone? You're not exactly a Washington figure."

"Dino introduced me to Salton a couple of days ago, and he asked me to lunch. We seemed to get along well, and he invited me—all of us—for tonight. In fact, he offered me a guest room, but I had already made other arrangements."

"Was that one of those power lunches at the Four Seasons?" Holly asked.

"No, it was at a place on the East Side. I didn't get the name."

They finished their dinner and waiters took away their plates and offered cognac and coffee.

"Another half an hour, and we can be fashionably late for the ball," Stone said.

AS HE SPOKE a very handsome man came into the room, looked around for a moment, then left. Holly was transfixed, and she couldn't figure out why. He was tall and dark, with fairly long hair and a short beard, and perfectly dressed, right to the large diamond in one earlobe. She began to rack her brain for some clue as to where she had seen him before.

"Holly," Stone said. *"Holly!"*

Holly snapped back to attention. "I'm sorry, I was lost in thought."

"About what?"

"Did you see the man who came in? About forty, short beard, tuxedo?"

"Holly, every man in the house is wearing a tuxedo."

"This one had a diamond earring. Did you see him?"

"No, I don't think I did."

"I know him from somewhere, and I can't remember where."

"Was your impression positive or negative?"

"Negative," Holly said. "But I don't know why."

Shortly, they left for the ball, and after another limo-line wait, got inside the huge armory, where an old-fashioned big band was playing Basie and Ellington. This, he figured, was the establishment ball.

Then the president and first gentleman arrived, and the crowd was moved back on the dance floor to allow them to start a waltz together. Then, to Stone's surprise, they danced over to where he stood. Kate took his hand, and Will took Holly's, and they moved onto the floor with them while Kate waved to everybody else to join them.

"Are you having a good time?" Stone asked Kate.

"A better time than I thought I would," she said. "I keep thinking about tomorrow, and all I have to do."

"Don't try to do it all on the first day," Stone said. "After all, you have eight years." She laughed, and he looked over her shoulder and saw his former girlfriend, Ann Keaton, dancing with a man he assumed was her new beau. He gave her a wave, and she waved back.

They got back to the hotel, exhausted.

"I can't believe I waltzed with a president," Holly said. "Even if it was a former president!"

"Starting tomorrow," Stone said, "you're going to be dancing with a president every day."

8

HOLLY WOKE STONE before dawn by running her fingernails down his back. He rolled over into her arms.

HALFWAY THROUGH, Holly said, "This is probably the last time I'll get laid for eight years!"

"Not if I have anything to say about it," Stone said, continuing to enjoy his duty.

When they were done, Holly got out of bed and started laying out clothes.

"What are you doing? It's six o'clock in the morning!"

"I've got to get into a shower and some clothes and get to the White House!"

Stone rolled over and went back to sleep, until she was shaking him at six-forty-five. "Will you please drop off my bags at Bruce's antique shop on your way to the airport?"

"Of course," Stone groaned.

She gave him a big kiss and ran from the suite. Stone went back to sleep.

He was awakened again a little after nine. "President Lee for you," a woman's voice said. "Will you speak to him?"

"Oh, *that* President Lee. Of course."

There was a click on the line. "Good morning, Stone," Will Lee said. "Is your offer of a ride to New York still open?"

"Of course."

"I had to get Kate to order the Secret Service to let me do it. How about that?"

"You'd better get used to it, Will."

"I guess I'll have to. Are you flying out of Manassas?"

"We are."

"Is one PM all right?"

"That's fine. We'll get into New York ahead of rush hour."

"Only one Secret Service agent will be coming along."

"Traveling light, huh?"

"Lighter than I've traveled for, what, nine years, including the first campaign. I feel weightless. See you at one."

Stone got himself into a shower and dressed, then found Dino and Viv reading the papers and waiting for breakfast to arrive.

"I ordered for you," Dino said. "Bourbon and Alka-Seltzer."

"I'm not in the least hungover," Stone replied. "Are you?"

"Police commissioners aren't allowed to drink enough to get hungover."

"I'm hungover," Viv said, "but it's a champagne hangover, so not so much."

The doorbell rang, and a waiter pushed a rolling table into the living room and set it up.

"Stone," Viv said, "that was a sensational evening. Thank you so much for setting it up."

"I enjoyed it, too," Stone said.

"Where's Holly?"

"At the White House, at work. She left at six-forty-five."

"I guess it's going to be like that for the duration."

"She says she won't get laid again for eight years."

Viv laughed. "I expect she'll turn up at your doorstep from time to time."

"I hope so."

HOLLY HAD SIGNED a lot of documents and been given her White House and NSC ID, which she wore on a ribbon around her neck, and now she was being shown to her new office. She was surprised to find that it was in the West Wing, where the president and higher staff worked, not in the Executive Office Building across the street. It wasn't huge, but it was comfortably furnished with an antique desk and a seating area, along with a small conference table and some nice paintings, and it was within spitting distance of the Oval Office. As she sat down, her phone rang, as if her ass had pressed a button. She picked it up. "Holly Barker."

"Good morning, Holly," Lance Cabot said. Lance was the director of Central Intelligence and her boss until this morning.

"Good morning, Lance."

"I wanted to welcome you to Washington," he said. "I saw you across a crowded room at the Saltons' last evening, but I was held prisoner by the director of the NSA and couldn't get to you."

"I didn't see you at all."

"That's because the director of the NSA is a very large man, the kind who blocks views—landscapes, even. Did you enjoy the party?"

"I did, and at the ball I danced with President Lee—Will, I mean."

"Then you had a better evening than I. The NSA produces lousy dance partners."

"Lance, I saw somebody at the Saltons' who rang a bell, but I couldn't place him. He's about forty, dark hair and short beard, and he was wearing a diamond earring. Do you know him?"

"I believe that must have been Ali Mahmoud, who is a Saudi diplomat—well, 'diplomat' is too strong a term, but he carries a D passport. Handsome, charming, ladies' man. That's all I know about him."

"None of it helps me," Holly said. "The sight of him induced dread in me, and I don't know why. It's driving me crazy."

"I haven't cut off your computer access here. Shall I leave it in place? You could check him out, and I expect the computer would be an asset in your new job."

"Yes, please."

"Done. Your codes will remain the same. Must run." Lance hung up.

A middle-aged woman in a business suit rapped on the door and walked in. "Hi, I'm Margery Lyon—Marge—and I've been assigned as your secretary, until you get sick of me and ask for somebody else. Got a minute?"

"Sure, Marge, come on in."

Marge sat down, tossed a file folder onto the desk, and began flipping through her steno pad. "The folder contains the résumés for half a dozen people who want to be your assistant. You start seeing them at eleven, one every fifteen minutes. I'll arrange call-backs for the ones you like. You're not bringing someone from the New York station with you, are you?"

"Nope. I haven't even had time to think about it."

"Your staff ID card is good for the White House Mess. Anything else you need, ask me. I'm pretty good with computers, too, if you need help. Yours will be delivered"—she consulted her watch—"right now." There was a knock at the door and a young man wheeled in a cart containing a computer and a printer. "Where do you want this?"

Holly pointed at the shelving behind her. "Go."

He went to work.

"Oh," Marge said, "you have your first NSC meeting in the situation room in"—she consulted her watch again—"three minutes. Come on, I'll walk you over there."

Holly followed Marge down the hallway to what appeared to be simply a rather cramped conference room. "This is it?"

"Disappointing, isn't it? You were expecting something more Hollywood, with lots of screens and high-tech stuff, right?"

"Right. My situation room in New York was more impressive." People were pouring into the room and taking chairs, so Holly grabbed one before they were all gone.

Marge crept up behind her and whispered in her ear, "You're senior here—it's your meeting. Have fun!"

The room settled a bit and everybody looked at Holly.

"Good morning," Holly said "I'll get to know you all as soon as I can. The president's first intelligence briefing is not until two o'clock this afternoon, so I have nothing right now. Let's meet again at four, and I'll pass on whatever I can. Starting tomorrow, those briefings are at eight AM, and we'll meet right after that to pass on information in both directions. Anybody have anything pressing for us right now?" She looked around; nobody spoke. "No world crises? How disappointing. See you at four."

Holly got up and walked out.

9

HOLLY INTERVIEWED each of the applicants for her assistant's job, and it depressed her that the academic records of every one of them exceeded her own. Not the practical experience, though, which was mostly internships.

The first four of them were from the same mold—two men, two women—she tried not to think of them as boys and girls—freshly scrubbed, fashionably dressed, bright as new pennies. The fifth applicant was their antithesis: model tall and slim, but poorly dressed, bordering on slovenly. Her hair was too long and close to being a mess, and she wore heavy black glasses and no makeup. Her record was astonishing: six years at Harvard, with a major in international affairs and a PhD at the end and a straight 4.0 average. This was the kind of woman who had probably alienated her peers, because she always knew the answer and always got the highest grade on her papers. Her name was Millicent Martindale.

"Why do you want the job, Millicent?" Holly asked.

"I don't want the job," she replied. "I want the secretary of state's job, but I realize I'll have to do something else until I'm old enough." Acerbic, too, not to say arrogant. All right, arrogant.

"I see you interned on the staff of the Senate Foreign Relations Committee for two summers. Did you learn anything there?"

"Less than I'd hoped. One or two of the interns, including me, seemed to know more about foreign relations than some of the committee members."

"What do you read?"

"American history, biography, and every relevant monthly magazine."

"Do you read any political magazines?"

"No. I despise politics."

"What sort of family background do you come from?"

"Wealthy and Republican. My father is CEO of a large, family manufacturing concern."

"So you're not short of a few bucks."

"Nope. I have an income from a very substantial trust fund."

"I'm considering hiring you, Millie, but if I do, you're going to have to go through what will be a very difficult learning process."

"I've never met a learning process I couldn't master. And I prefer Millicent."

"This one is going to be new to you. You start Monday morning at seven AM. Between now and then I want you to find a makeover artist. Do you know what that is?"

"I know what a make*up* artist is. I don't know *over*."

"You don't read women's magazines, do you?"

"They make me want to vomit."

Holly picked up the phone and buzzed Marge.

"Yes, ma'am?"

"Marge, I want you to find the best makeover artist in D.C. and block out all her/his time between now and Monday for Millicent Martindale."

"Give me half an hour," Marge said.

"Wait a minute," Millicent said. "I think I'm beginning to get this: you want me to change the way I look, and I'm not up for it."

"Then I chose the wrong assistant." Holly closed her file, picked up another one, and pretended to read it. Millicent sat in stunned silence. Holly looked up. "Why are you still here?"

"All right, all right! I'll do it!"

"This isn't just about appearance," Holly said. "Of course, when you come in here Monday morning I want to see somebody dressed the way your mother would approve of. I want to see a hairdo and appropriate makeup, but I want a lot more than that: I want to see an attitude that is cognizant that you are the lowest form of life on the White House staff, and that *everybody* knows more about *everything* than you do. And I want to see you smile at least a third of the time. Another thing: ask Marge to find you an optometrist—get some contacts, and I don't ever want to see you in those fucking glasses again. And that's not all, there'll be more every day, and you'd better learn fast. You don't report to me, you report to Marge. Got it?"

Millicent seemed to have shrunk. "Yes."

"Yes, *what*?"

"Yes, ma'am."

Marge breezed in and handed Millicent a sheet off her steno pad. "His name is Terry Tift. He's just what you need, and he knows the White House drill. He's expecting you in half an hour. You need an optometrist, too. His number is at the bottom of the page—you have an appointment tomorrow morning at nine."

"I'd better not recognize you Monday morning," Holly said. "Get out."

Millicent fled.

"Marge, tell everybody she likes to be called Millie."

Marge beamed. "Got it!"

Holly had been surprised to be included in the president's daily intelligence briefing. She found herself seated at the long table in the Cabinet room with the vice president, the secretary of state, the chairman of the Joint Chiefs of Staff, the director of Homeland Security, the director of Central Intelligence, the director of the National Security Agency, and the director of the Federal Bureau of Investigation, each of whom had brought a minion, all of whom were seated in chairs around the perimeter of the room. Place cards had been put out for the participants, and Holly found herself next to a chair with no place card.

Suddenly, everyone leaped to their feet, and Katharine Lee swept into the room, a bound legal pad under her arm. "Seats, please," she said. As they sat down she leaned over and whispered to Holly, "Remember, you're not briefing, you're *being* briefed. Come with me when the meeting is over." Then she sat down next to Holly.

"Homeland Security," Kate said, and the director stood up. "Remain seated, please, all of you. What do you have, Stan?"

The man sat down. "Madam President, good morning. Overnight we have had strong hints from three sources, two of them electronic, that an important Al Qaeda figure has been infiltrated into Washington, perhaps even into our government. His purpose looks to be—using his position to glean intelligence—the organizing of a major terrorist attack against the city, with a government building or facility at its center."

"Do you have a name?"

"Not yet, Madam President. We are working backward to determine that. We've sent out word to the appropriate operatives to locate the top twenty Al Qaeda officials. We'll work from a list of those missing from sight. That will give us a short list, then we can turn the attention of all agencies to finding him."

"That seems a logical procedure. Anything else to report at this time?"

"No, Madam President."

"Don't send out any broad alerts," Kate said. "We don't want to get his attention. I hardly need say that no one is to mention this to anyone outside this room." She patiently worked her way through those present; nothing else rose to the level of the first report.

When they were done, Kate left the room first, and Holly trailed her to the Oval Office.

"Well, that was fun, wasn't it?" Kate said, flopping down on a sofa. "Hot stuff, right off the bat. I wonder if they've been saving it for a few days, just to start my administration off with a bang?"

"I wouldn't be shocked to learn that."

"It will be interesting to see how quickly the press picks up on the story and who leaks it. Did you find an assistant?"

"Yes, ma'am, but she won't start until Monday—she needs work."

Kate laughed. "Let me guess: an Ivy League drudge? What the Brits call a 'swot'?"

"A perfect one. She's very smart, and I'm going to have to spend some time showing her that she's stupid."

"Were you like that when you joined the Agency, Holly?"

"I was a babe in the woods."

Kate laughed. "I doubt that."

"Do you want this morning's report given to the NSC?"

"Not yet. First let's see what result a few days' work brings." There was a knock, and the door leading to the Oval's waiting room opened. "The secretary of labor designate is here, Madam President," an assistant said.

"Send him in." She stood up to greet the man. "See you later," she said to Holly.

10

STONE, DINO, AND VIV got to Manassas well ahead of time; they stowed their luggage, and Stone did a thorough pre-flight inspection, then he got a weather forecast—severe clear and light winds—and filed a flight plan.

At noon, the gate to the ramp slid open and three black SUVs cruised through and came to a stop at the left wingtip of N123TF. Will Lee hopped out of the front seat of the first one, and an agent retrieved a single duffel from the trunk. Stone shook hands with Will, stowed his duffel in the front luggage compartment, and walked Will around the airplane, pointing out features. Finally everyone boarded, including a young woman in a business suit and a shoulder holster who represented the Secret Service, and Stone helped Will into the right cockpit seat.

"It's snug," Stone said, "but you'll get used to it."

"Do I have a choice?" Will asked, struggling to get his left leg to follow his right leg into the footwell.

"Only the passenger cabin, and that's no fun." Stone climbed into the pilot seat and helped Will figure out the four-point seat belt, then secured his own. He started the engines, radioed for a clearance to Teterboro, and was surprised to be given a routing of direct to destination and an immediate climb to his cruising altitude.

"I made a call," Will said.

"I've never flown direct from Manassas to Teterboro," Stone said.

"It was the least I could do."

Stone asked for a taxi clearance, and to his further surprise, was immediately cleared for takeoff. That had never happened before, either.

As they taxied onto the runway, Stone said, "Watch the screen in front of you. You'll see the speeds come up and the flight director bars that show us we're climbing at the right rate." He pushed the throttles forward and began calling his own speeds, then rotated. "You just keep the bars together," he said to Will, then he switched on the autopilot and let it do the work. They got a spectacular view of Washington as they flew over.

"I talked them out of a fighter escort," Will said.

"Thanks so much. I don't know what they would think of that at Teterboro—I'd never live it down."

"My reasoning was that we'd attract less attention without it, and thus be more secure. We don't have to use an Air Force call sign, either, and you will have noticed that the 'football' no longer travels with me."

Stone had seen enough movies to know that the "football" was the briefcase containing the nuclear launch codes, carried by a military officer, who followed the president everywhere. Stone thought

Will seemed as delighted as a child on his first flight, and he was enchanted with the glass cockpit.

"Do you know this is the first time in nine years I've flown in any airplane smaller than Air Force One?"

"Welcome back to general aviation. Maybe you can start flying your own airplane again soon."

"Not going to happen," Will said. "Maybe after Kate's time is up I can get something like this, if I'm not too old to fly."

Stone showed Will how to set up the instrument approach to runway six at Teterboro, and they were cleared directly to the initial approach fix. He pointed to the little red airplane representing them that appeared on the screen, overlaid on the approach plate.

"Now that is fantastic!" Will said.

They touched down smoothly and taxied to Jet Aviation, where they were given the plum parking spot, next to the lounge. It wouldn't have mattered, though, because there was another three-car convoy waiting for them, and Stone's Bentley was right behind it. Five minutes later Will shook Stone's hand and thanked him again for the flight, then they were on their way back to the city. At the appropriate moment, Fred peeled away from the convoy for Turtle Bay, while the first gentleman continued uptown to the Carlyle. Fred left Stone at the house, then continued uptown to deliver Viv to her Strategic Services office, while Dino got into his waiting police SUV and headed downtown to One Police Plaza and his office. Stone went into his office via the street door.

"Welcome back," Joan said as he looked in on her. "How was it?"

"I've just had the best transportation experience of my life," Stone said. "I wish Will Lee could fly with me all the time." He gave her a blow-by-blow, then went into his office. There was a note from his younger law partner, Herbie Fisher, inviting him to lunch at the Four Seasons. Stone looked at his messages, found nothing very important, grabbed his coat, and left the office, telling Joan to call Herbie and tell him he was on his way.

The Four Seasons Grill had begun to empty, as it was nearly two o'clock, but Herbie was there, nibbling on a crust of bread. "I ordered you the Dover sole," he said as they shook hands.

"How've you been, Herb?" Stone asked. "I watched as much of your murder trial as I could. You did a great job."

"Yeah," Herbie replied, "and I feel a little guilty about that."

"You think you got a guilty client off?"

Herbie shrugged. He was not about to admit to that. "Let's just say that if she'd had any other attorney, she'd be upstate in the women's correctional facility."

"That's modest of you."

"It's the truth."

"What do you think of Greta Frank?"

"Greta Frank Lewin," Herbie corrected. "She is a piece of work: cold, calculating, always composed. She insisted on testifying, and the DA couldn't lay a glove on her. She had the jury with her the whole way. She'd make a great trial attorney."

"Her sister, Pat, flew back from Wichita with me. She's a very experienced pilot, and my insurance company wanted someone like her aboard the first time I flew the airplane. We've become, ah, friendly."

"Does she look anything like Greta?"

"Something like her, only younger and more beautiful."

"And a pilot, too? You should marry her."

"My experience with marriage has been less than satisfactory," Stone said.

Herbie laughed. Lunch came and they caught up as they ate.

"Did I mention that I'm single again?" Herbie asked when they were on coffee.

"I thought that was permanent," Stone said.

"She took a hike. It's probably just as well—what with our two schedules, we hardly saw each other."

"It happens," Stone said.

"Yeah, I guess it does. Her absence sort of opens things up, though. I've had a couple of dates."

"Take my advice and stay single for a while, then find somebody who doesn't have a schedule as busy as yours, and you'll have more fun."

"We'll see how it goes," Herbie said.

"It always goes," Stone replied.

11

STONE WENT BACK to his office and called Pat Frank.

"Pat Frank," she said.

"Is that the business or the woman?" Stone asked.

"Both," she replied. "Are you back?"

"Yep."

"Come over tonight and I'll cook dinner for you."

"Who'll be cooking? The business or the woman?"

"The cook."

"What time?"

"Seven?"

"I'll bring the wine—red or white?"

"Red."

"See you at seven."

Stone passed the remainder of the day with mundane chores. Then, at a quarter to seven he went down to the wine cellar and chose a bottle of Romanée-Conti Richebourg, from 1978. He lit a candle and decanted it, then rinsed the bottle of the lees, poured the wine back into it, and recorked it. He blew out the candle, locked the cellar, and left the house to find a cab.

At ten minutes past the hour he walked into a town house on East Sixty-third Street and rang the bell marked "Frank." The buzzer opened the door, and down the hall Pat stood in her open doorway.

She gave him a wet kiss and brought him inside. He had been expecting a single-girl walk-up, and what he found himself in was a large duplex garden apartment that was beautifully furnished, except that there were no pictures on the walls. Something from the kitchen smelled good. "Whatever I'm smelling, it will go well with this," he said, handing her the bottle of Richebourg.

She looked at it and smiled. "Where on earth did you come by this?" she asked.

"A French friend gave me some cases of wines, and that was in one of them. I decanted and rebottled it, so it wouldn't get shaken up in the cab."

"You have good friends," she said.

"One of them lives across the street from you," he said.

"Dino?"

"Yep." He looked around. "This is a beautiful place. Why no pictures?"

"Greta took those with her. Her first husband bought it as a pied-à-terre. They lived on the North Shore of Long Island, at Oyster Bay, but they spent a couple of nights a week in town. Her second husband has an even nicer pied-à-terre, so she rented this place until I could collect myself and get to New York."

"And you're going to buy it from her?"

"After I've saved some money." The doorbell rang.

"That's Greta now," she said. "She and her husband are stopping by for a drink on the way to the theater."

Ah, Stone thought, I get to meet the socialite murderess.

Greta Frank turned out to be totally disarming. She was cheerful, witty, and seemed delighted to meet Stone. "The first customer," she said. "I'm pleased to meet any customer of Pat's." She introduced her husband, who was handsome, ten years older than she, and very well-tailored. His name was Greg Lewin. They shook hands.

"I hear you're with Woodman & Weld," he said to Stone.

"I am."

"I do some business with Bill Eggers from time to time."

"I'm glad to hear it, we need all the business we can get."

"And you're on the board of Strategic Services." The man had done his homework. "I worked on their initial public offering, a while back."

"I have that honor. I'm afraid I don't know as much about you as you do about me."

"Hedge fund," Lewin said, as if that were all anybody needed to know about him.

"Ah," Stone said, "a money factory."

"That's a very good way to look at it," Lewin said, smiling broadly.

Greta rummaged in her handbag and came up with an envelope. "I have a present for you," she said to Pat, handing her the envelope.

"What's this?" Pat asked, handling it as if it were an explosive. "An eviction notice?"

"It's something I would have given you sooner, but I didn't really believe you'd resettle in New York, until you moved in."

Pat opened the envelope and peered at the sheet of paper that emerged. "What is it?"

Stone looked at the document over her shoulder. "It's a deed," Stone said.

"A deed to what?"

Greta laughed. "A deed to this apartment. It's all yours."

Pat was flabbergasted. She recovered enough to hug her sister. "Then I'll never be homeless."

"Never. My attorney is mailing you a package of stuff you need to know about the property."

Stone took the deed from Pat and examined it. "This is not a deed to this apartment," he said.

Pat looked worried. "What did you say?"

"It's the deed to the building."

Pat was speechless.

"There are three other apartments upstairs," Greta said. "And a professional suite next door. All rented, but the doctor's lease will be up soon. You might want to use that for your new business. The rents will give you some income while you get it up and running."

Pat collapsed into a chair. "I think I need a drink."

Stone went to a well-stocked wet bar, poured her a Knob Creek, and handed it to her. "There you go. Can I get you folks something?"

"We'd better get going," Greg said, looking at his watch. "The traffic is always very slow near curtain time in the theater district."

Pat set down her drink, struggled to her feet, and hugged her sister again. “You are incredibly generous, and I can’t thank you enough.”

She showed them out, and by the time she got back, Stone had his own drink. “You’re lucky to have a sister like that,” Stone said.

“She’s taken care of me since we were little girls,” Pat said. “She bought me a new wardrobe the last time I was in the city, and she gave me my last car. Now I’m rich!”

“Don’t start living that way just yet. The house is a nice asset, but this is an expensive city.”

“Don’t I know it.”

“What smells so good?”

“Beef bourguignonne. It’ll be ready in half an hour. We can drink until then. That should settle my nerves.”

12

STONE WOKE in the wee hours, still a little drunk from the bottle of wine. Pat slept silently beside him, and he didn't wake her. He quietly got dressed and tiptoed downstairs, got his overcoat from the front hall closet, and let himself out of the building. He turned to walk toward Park Avenue to look for a cab, but as he did he became aware that the engine of a car was running somewhere nearby.

He looked over his shoulder and saw the mist from a vehicle's exhaust coming from a car parked half a dozen spaces away. He could see the outline of a driver, a large man, behind the wheel. The car appeared to be some sort of Japanese sedan, but he couldn't tell which one. It wasn't big enough to be doing town car duty, and the driver had been sitting there long enough to keep the engine running for the heater. Why would anyone sit in a dark street in the middle of the night? If he had still been a foot patrolman, as he had been so many years ago, he would have rapped sharply with his nightstick on the driver's window and demanded ID and to know what he was doing there.

He stopped at the corner and looked back, then, on a whim, he turned and started walking purposefully back toward where the car was parked. Apparently the driver saw him coming because he abruptly put the car in gear and pulled out of the parking spot, switching on the bright headlights and momentarily blinding Stone, keeping him from getting a good look at the driver as he blew past.

The car drove straight across Park Avenue, running a red light, and raced toward Lexington Avenue, running another light as it turned right and was gone. Stone's impulse was to go back to Pat's apartment and stay the night, just in case the driver's interest was in her, but he didn't have a key, and he didn't want to wake her up. A cab showed up, sealing his decision, and he got in and went home.

STONE WAS at his desk at midmorning when Pat called.

"You sneaked out last night," she said.

"You were dead to the world and useless to me," he said.

She laughed. "I wasn't useless when I woke up this morning," she replied. "I would have been very useful if you had still been here."

"A nice thought—hang on to it for next time."

"I'll do that."

"You should write a letter to your doctor tenant whose lease is running out and tell him you won't be renewing and that you want the space back. Send it by registered mail."

"If I'm going to be a landlord I'll need a lawyer," she said. "Will you write it for me?"

"Sure—e-mail me his name, and I'll take care of it. Being a landlord's attorney is out of my line, though, so I'll find somebody with the correct expertise to represent you. You'll also need one for your business."

"Good idea. Did I mention that I have three more clients?"

"No, and congratulations!"

"I think somebody at Cessna is recommending me to owners taking delivery of new airplanes."

"That's a good source of clients—cultivate it."

"Don't worry, I will."

"Listen, I don't want to intrude on your privacy, but is there somebody in your life who might be a threat to you?"

She waited for a long beat before replying. "Why do you ask?"

"Because when I left your building around two AM, there was a man sitting in a car with the motor running a few yards down the street, and when I approached to try to get a look at the driver, he took off, ran a red light to get away from there."

She was still silent.

"Hello, hello, anybody there?"

"Nothing to worry about," she said.

"I'd be worried if somebody was parked all night outside my house," he said.

"He's harmless."

"Those could turn into famous last words."

"I lived with a guy in Wichita for two years. We were supposed to go into the business together, but I ended the relationship when I left."

"What's his name?"

"Kevin Keyes. We worked for the same airline, the one that went out of business."

"Would he know where you live?"

"He and I stayed with Greta once when we were visiting the city."

"Does he have a key to the apartment?"

"I . . . I don't think so."

"You don't sound certain."

"I had a key—Greta may have given him one, too."

"Do you have a security system in the house?"

"No. I asked Greta, and she said she never got around to installing one."

"Get a pencil. I'm going to give you a name."

"Ready to copy."

He gave her Bob Cantor's number. "He's a friend of mine, an ex-cop who's in the security business. Call him right now and get him over there. Have him change the front door lock to the building and the lock to your apartment, also the lock for the French doors leading to your garden. You want high-end locks—expensive, but necessary. And don't forget to give your upstairs tenants the new keys to the front door."

"I'm not sure if I'm ready to meet them, yet."

"Then put their keys in envelopes with a note telling them who you are and slide the envelopes under their doors."

"If you say so."

"This won't wait until tomorrow—get it done today. In fact, I'll call Bob for you, so if you want a shower before he gets there, do it now."

"Yes, boss!"

"I tell my friends that their lives would be so much richer, fuller, and happier if they would just take my advice."

"I'll take it, I'll take it!"

"See you later. Bob will be there in less than an hour."

He hung up and called Bob Cantor.

"Hey, Stone."

"Hey there. I've got work for you."

"Shoot."

Stone gave him the name and address and told him what was needed, and fast. "Use good equipment, especially the locks."

"I never use any other kind. Any particular reason for the rush?"

"She may have a stalker on her hands."

"Does she have a gun?"

"I don't know, and I don't want to know, but I wouldn't be surprised. The possible stalker's name is Kevin with a K Keyes. Former airline pilot. Run the name, will you?"

"Okay, I'm on it."

"I told her you'd be there within the hour."

"All right already!" Bob hung up.

Stone didn't feel relieved just yet.

13

STONE CALLED Herbie Fisher. "Hey there," Herbie said.

"Thanks for lunch yesterday."

"Anytime."

"I've got a small piece of business that would be good for an associate. It's nothing much now, but it could grow."

"What sort of business?"

"Her name is Pat Frank. She's just started a flight department business that would manage the maintenance and paperwork for owner/pilots of jets. Also, she owns a small apartment building on the East Side, and she'll need legal work for that."

"There's a smart kid down the hall named Richard Searle who would be good for it. He owns a small airplane, too, but I'm not sure what kind."

"Great. Have him call Pat this morning and make a date to meet with her." Stone gave Herbie the address and phone number. "Thanks, kiddo." He hung up and dictated the letter to Pat's doctor tenant, signed it, and told Joan to mail it.

There, he thought, I've got that one off my plate. He didn't know how wrong he was.

Dino called and asked him to lunch at that place on the East Side. Stone took a cab and entered by the front door; he was ushered in by one of the staff wearing the ubiquitous black suit and green tie.

"Good day, Mr. Barrington," the man said. "Welcome back. Commissioner Bacchetti is waiting for you in the bar, second floor." Stone took the elevator and found Dino in the cave-like, paneled room that sported a richly stocked bar and a few tables.

Stone joined Dino at a table. "You think they have Knob Creek in this joint?"

"If they don't, I'll shoot the bartender," Dino said. "You drinking at lunch these days?"

"Not really, just thought I'd ask."

"Phillip," Dino called to the bartender.

"Yes, Commissioner?"

"Do you stock a weird bourbon called Knob Creek?"

"Yes, sir, ever since Mr. Barrington joined us. Your Laphroaig is in stock, too."

"Thank you, Phillip."

"How did they know?" Stone asked.

"Word gets around."

"You've moved up to a single malt?"

"I think it's more in line with my station in life."

"I think you're right," Stone said.

"You're agreeing with my tastes?"

"Once in a great while."

"That about describes the frequency."

Others began to arrive in the bar, and the dining room filled quickly.

"Let's see," Stone said. "From here I can see a former secretary of state, a Supreme Court justice, and a producer of Broadway plays and Hollywood movies. There's also a great actress over there in the corner, having lunch with a very good actress, and that guy with a political show on MSNBC. Are there any nobodies in this club?"

"Probably, but none that you haven't heard of."

"Who proposed you?"

"Salton, just like you. Bill Eggers was my seconder."

"It annoys me that Eggers could have proposed me, but didn't."

"Relax, it's considered bad form to propose people you're in business with. The founders didn't want this to be a club of businessmen, and there are very few of them on the membership list."

"Where is the membership list?"

"Downstairs there's a board on the wall with all the names. When a member comes into the building a peg is put next to his name. When he leaves, the peg is removed. You can tell at a glance who's here and who isn't."

"It's a very quiet dining room, isn't it?"

"These are very quiet people, who are accustomed to being heard without raising their voices."

A well-known literary personage in the center of the dining room raised an index finger without looking away from his companion, and a waiter instantly appeared at his side.

"That's how you summon a waiter here," Dino said. "A finger is all it takes."

The mayor of New York City, formerly the commissioner of police and Dino's mentor, entered the dining room with the senior senator from New York, Stanley Bauer. He waved at Stone and Dino, then came over to their table in the bar.

"Welcome aboard, Stone," Tom Donnelly said.

"Thank you, Mayor," Stone replied, shaking his hand.

"Dino, you seem to be keeping a lid on things."

"That's because I sit on the lid," Dino said. "Something you told me to do a long time ago."

"It's always a pleasure to hear my words reverberate from those I instructed," the mayor said, then returned to his own table.

"He hasn't changed," Stone said.

"He's more relaxed, I think. It's a little scary to think he finds the mayor's job less stressful than mine."

Stone laughed. "Are you finding it stressful, Dino?"

"All the time—you just have to learn to live with it."

Stone looked up and saw a handsome man in a pin-striped suit and a dark, clipped beard enter the room. He wore a diamond earring in one ear. "Did you see that guy at the Saltons' house in D.C.?"

"Yeah, I did."

"Holly said something about him, I can't remember exactly what, but it wasn't favorable."

"He's a Saudi. He's something either at the embassy in Washington or the UN embassy here, I'm not sure which."

"What's his name?"

"I don't know. I've seen it in the papers—always on the party pages—but I can't remember."

"Who's he with?"

"I don't know the guy. Why are you interested in them?"

"I just feel as though I ought to be interested—something Holly said, I guess. I wish I could remember what it was. Maybe I should call her."

"Cell phones are a no-no here," Dino said. "Texting is okay, or e-mails, but not speaking into them."

They placed their orders but kept the table in the bar.

"So, Dino, what's keeping you awake nights?"

"Nothing keeps me awake, I sleep like a stone, you should pardon the expression."

"Not even terrorism?"

"What's the point of losing sleep?" Dino asked. "It wouldn't solve any problems. I do better if I sleep when I'm in bed and worry when I'm awake."

Their lunch arrived. "The food is excellent here," Stone said.

"There's a saying here," Dino said, "if the food were any better, you couldn't get a table."

14

HOLLY GOT to her desk on Monday morning at 6:40 AM. Ten minutes later a young woman she didn't know appeared in the doorway to her office.

"Yes?" Holly said, then looked again. "My God," she said. "Millie."

"Is this what you had in mind?" Millicent Martindale asked.

"It's actually better than what I had in mind. Sit down."

Ms. Martindale arranged herself artfully in a chair.

"Do you have any idea why I made you do the do-over?" Holly asked.

"I suppose you're adopting the sexism of the men around here."

"The men around here aren't sexist," Holly said.

"Then they're unlike the men anywhere else."

"The difference is, they're all working for a woman, and if you walk up and down the halls of the West Wing, you'll see that a small majority of the people at the desks are women. Men work for them."

"Okay, so why'd you put me through this?"

"Because I want you to be effective while you're working here. If you look like somebody who doesn't give a damn about how she looks to other people, you will put yourself at a distinct disadvantage."

"You mean, I only get to make a first impression once?"

"If you want to reduce it to a cliché, yes. You might recall I demanded something else from you besides clothes and a hairdo."

"Oh, yes, the attitude adjustment."

"You don't seem to be quite there yet."

"I'm working on it."

"I know, it's hard to present yourself well when you don't give a shit what people think of you. The trick is to start giving a shit. If you do, they'll look upon your advice more favorably, and they'll remember it, instead of trying to forget it." Holly sighed. "I don't know why I have to explain this to you."

"My parents have been explaining it to me my whole life."

"Try and remember that your parents don't work in the White House, so there's no point in continuing to rebel against them here."

"I get your point, I really do," she said, looking at her nails. "I despise nail polish," she said as an afterthought.

"Better keep a bottle in your desk so you can repair chips."

"You're not wearing nail polish."

"It's clear—you might try that, if color offends you."

"I'll do that."

"How's your memory?" Holly asked.

"Excellent."

Holly picked up a thick file on her desk and tossed it to her. "That's the latest on Al Qaeda. Memorize it. There'll be more tomorrow, if not sooner. It's classified Top Secret and Need to Know, but your security clearance came through on Friday, and you need to know, because I say you do."

"Yes, ma'am," Millie said, then got up and went to her desk alongside that of Marge in Holly's anteroom.

Holly was alone at a table in the White House Mess, having lunch, when another woman pulled up a chair and set down her tray. "Mind if I join you, Holly?"

"Not at all."

"I'm Ann Keaton, the president's chief of staff." She extended a hand.

Holly shook it. "It's a pleasure to meet you," she said. "I've heard a lot."

"I understand we have a mutual acquaintance in Stone Barrington."

"We do?"

"It's more in the past tense for me—I'm seeing somebody else now."

"Good for you."

"I just wanted to clear the air, because you and I are going to be seeing a lot of each other."

"The air is clear," Holly said. "I look forward to working with you."

Ann had some soup. "I hear you've been working practically underground for a while."

Holly laughed. "Practically. Now I get to see the sun sometimes."

"I know how you feel—working in the campaign was like that for me. I hear you found an apartment already. Where?"

"Down Pennsylvania Avenue a good ways, over an antique shop."

"Have the security people vetted it yet?"

"They spent most of the weekend with me, stomping around the place in their work boots."

"And you gave them a key?"

"Yes, and they were kind enough to give me my entry code, after they installed the new security system. They put in a direct line to the White House switchboard, too."

"Did they explain that any intrusions will alert our security police, instead of the old alarm system operators?"

"Yes, though I'm not sure yet that that is an improvement."

"You'll find that it is. Did they repair the plaster and clean up after themselves?"

"They did, amazingly enough. Then I had to explain to my landlord why his key doesn't work anymore and how he can't come into the apartment unless I'm there."

"How are you feeling about the security cameras?"

"I'm okay with that, now, after taping over the ones in my bedroom and bathroom."

Ann laughed. "I did the same thing. I expected to get flak for it, but I didn't."

"I'm glad to hear it. I'll look forward to no flak."

"Kate . . . I'm sorry, the president . . . thinks not just highly, but warmly of you—more so than just about anybody on the staff."

"That's very kind of her, but she has always been very kind to me, since I worked for Lance and, later, for her, at the Agency."

"Do you stay in touch with Lance?"

"He called on my first day to welcome me to Washington. That's it, so far."

"You need to be careful with Lance."

"I've been careful with Lance since the first time I clapped eyes on him," Holly said, "and I've never seen any reason to change that."

"Holly, I think you're going to do very well in the White House."

"I hope you're right, Ann."

The two finished their lunch talking about whatever came up, then they walked back to their offices, together most of the way.

15

THE FOLLOWING DAY Stone got a call from Bob Cantor.

"Hey, Bob."

"Stone, we're done at Pat Frank's place. We wired her apartment, the front door, and the doctor's office, after hours, and we changed the relevant locks. She's about as secure as she's going to get. Oh, and she does have a gun. When she was an airline pilot she qualified to be armed aboard her flights, and when the airline went belly-up, she kept the gun. She's licensed to carry in Kansas, but unlicensed anywhere else, except on a dead airline."

"Did you take it away from her?"

"I tried."

"Okay, I'll have that conversation with her."

"Somebody should. She strikes me as the sort who would use it if she felt the need."

"She strikes me the same way."

"And she may have the need," Cantor said.

"You ran Kevin Keyes's name?"

"Yep, and I came up with three arrests for incidents of domestic abuse, in one of which a gun got waved around. That was the last one, when he was living with Pat Frank."

"Who did the waving?"

"He did."

"Convictions?"

"None. He agreed to take an anger management course after the third one and did a few hours of community service."

"Did they revoke his carry license?"

"Nope."

"Figures."

"It's Kansas, what can I tell you?"

"Any other concerns, Bob?"

"I talked her into letting me put a really good camera covering the front door. She can check it on a screen in the entryway coat closet before she buzzes anybody in. Trouble is, an intruder could ring any of the rental apartment bells and get buzzed in, if the renter doesn't take the time to communicate with the one buzzing, or if they're expecting someone and assume that the one buzzing is their guest, and just buzz 'em in."

"Maybe Pat should have screens installed in the three apartments."

"Pat doesn't know her renters yet, and she's uncomfortable with asking them to have a screen installed in their apartments. She doesn't want to frighten them. I offered to frighten them for her, but she wouldn't let me."

"Maybe I'll write them a letter saying that someone has been troubling the landlord and not to admit anyone unless they know for sure who's at the door."

"Good idea, if you can talk her into it."

"She's coming over to dinner tonight. I'll see what I can do."

"Good luck, buddy."

Stone's bell rang at the stroke of seven. He tapped a code into his computer, and the screen showed Pat, in color and high definition, waiting at the door. He pressed a button to start a video, then he pressed another button. "Yes? Who is it?"

"How many people could it be?" she asked.

"There are eight million stories in the naked city," he replied. "You could be any one of them."

"Would you rather I go home and sulk?"

"I'm in the study." He pressed the buzzer, and she came in. A minute later, she appeared in the doorway, and he motioned her over to his desk and played the video, with sound.

"Wow," she breathed. "Can I do that with my system?"

"If you take the trouble to read the manual. I can do that with any outside door and inside the garage, as well. And the three people who live in the house next door—my secretary, my housekeeper, and Fred—can do the same thing. You should give your renters the same equipment, or one night they'll inadvertently buzz in somebody who's not delivering Chinese food or pizza."

"You've been talking to Bob Cantor."

"I certainly have." He got up from his desk and poured them both a Knob Creek.

"I just don't want to spend the money to put the equipment in the rental apartments."

"You've been given a free building, but you don't want to spend a few grand to secure it? If you don't, then one fine night one of your tenants will buzz in the wrong person, and all the money you've spent on Bob Cantor's services will be for naught. And worse, you'll probably end up shooting the guy, and you will not believe how much trouble you'd be in and how much it would cost you to get out of it."

"Are you going to give me the lecture about my gun?"

"You're not in Kansas anymore, Dorothy, you're in the Emerald City, where the local powers frown on the possession of firearms."

"And I can't get a carry license here?"

"Nope, not unless you can demonstrate that you regularly walk around in possession of large sums of cash or a briefcase full of diamonds. I can help you get a license to take your weapon to a firing range in the city, which is also a license to have it in your apartment, but you can't carry it anywhere, except to the range. How about that?"

"Okay."

"I'll have Joan get the application sent to you, but remember this: the first thing you have to learn about possessing a firearm is to never, *never* shoot anybody."

"What if he's shooting at me?"

"Maybe if he's already hit you."

"Oh, great!"

"All right, let's say you shoot the guy under perfectly legal circumstances: you then call nine-one-one, ask for the police, tell them there's been a shooting and to send two ambulances."

"Why two?"

"One for him and one for you. You must remember that you're

going to be in terrible, terrible shape, knowing that you've shot another human being. Spend at least one night in the hospital getting over it. That will impress the assistant DA, who will be assigned to decide whether to prosecute you."

"Okay, I'll remember that."

"And your second call will be to me. I'll get there before the ambulance takes you away. And, in the unlikely event that the cops arrive before I do, I want you sitting down with the gun unloaded and the slide locked back and at the other end of the coffee table from you. Cops don't really want to shoot people—not many of them, anyway—but they know that if they enter a room and see a person dead on the floor and another person holding a firearm, they can pretty much shoot first and ask questions later, and you don't want to put armed cops in that position."

Pat took a swig of her bourbon. "And why are you going on and on about this?"

"Because I've had a look at Kevin Keyes's arrest record."

"You mean that incident when I threw him out of the house and he objected?"

"That incident and the two before it with other women."

She set down her glass. "What other women?"

"Does it matter? You were his third strike, and he's still not out."

"Good God."

"And now, it's time you told me all about him."

16

STONE CLEARED AWAY the dinner plates and poured them both a glass of old Armagnac. She had been telling him the sorry details of her relationship with Kevin Keyes—his drinking, womanizing, and tendency to get physical when angry.

"Okay," Pat said, "now you get to ask the question."

"You mean the one about how a smart woman can get so involved with such a sorry shit?"

"That's the one. Only he wasn't a sorry shit all the time. We had fun together: he was smart and witty and had great charm, on his good days."

"And I've already heard about the bad days. My concern is that you haven't seen his worst days yet—those are yet to come."

"Why do you think that?"

Stone's cell phone rang, and he checked the caller ID before answering. "Excuse me, this is about you. Evening, Bob."

"Sorry to call at dinnertime," Cantor said, "but I thought you'd want to know."

"Tell me."

"I did a little under-the-table computer searching this evening, and Kevin Keyes is registered at a hotel in Times Square. He's been here for three days, and he booked in for a week. He's also got a rented Nissan Altima in the hotel's garage."

"Anything else?"

"That's it for the moment. How did she take the lecture?"

"Better than I had hoped. You can go ahead and install the video equipment in the tenants' apartments. You'd better drop them a note to let them know when you're coming."

"Will do. See ya." Bob hung up.

"I'm sorry, you asked me a question," Stone said.

"Why do you think Kevin's worst days are yet to come?"

"Ah, yes, that question. Here's your answer: old Kevin has checked into a Times Square hotel, booking in for a week, and he has a rental car at his disposal."

"Oh, shit."

"Exactly. Was he in the same armed pilots program as you?"

"Yes."

"And he still has the gun."

"He has several guns."

"Swell."

"Maybe he has some perfectly good reason for being in New York," Pat suggested.

"Is that why he spent yesterday evening parked a couple of doors from your house? For some perfectly good reason?"

"Why must you put the worst possible slant on every little thing Kevin does? You don't know him."

"I know him better than you do," Stone said.

"Oh? How's that?"

"I've known half a dozen women with exes who didn't like getting dumped, no matter how badly they had behaved. These men tended to think of themselves as being in the right, and the women, always, in the wrong. They thought of themselves not as husbands or boyfriends, but as owners of their women. Does that have a familiar ring?"

She said nothing.

"Do you think Kevin won't harm you because he loves you?"

"I think that, yes."

"Men like this, when they're caught after harming a woman, nearly always give love as their motive. They seem to think that love is an exculpatory emotion for a serious felony, even for murder."

"He's completed an anger management course since I last saw him," she said. "The judge made him. Maybe it took."

"And you think he traveled all the way from Wichita to New York to tell you he's not angry anymore?"

"He's not going to tell me anything—I'm not going to see him."

"He's not going to give you a choice," Stone said. "Tell me, does he have any money?"

"A tiny pension from the airline. He picks up an occasional charter flight."

"So he's just bought himself a week at an expensive hotel, when, more than likely, he can't even afford the garage for his rented car. He's probably maxed out his credit cards getting here, and I'm willing to bet he bought a one-way ticket."

"He can't carry a gun on an airplane," she said.

"Yes he can, if he registers it and keeps it in his checked luggage. Or maybe he got a deadhead charter job to Teterboro. Nobody searches luggage at a general aviation airport."

"You're scaring me," she said.

"Good, I've been trying hard to do just that. If I'm right, then he's a man with nothing more to lose. And that makes him dangerous."

"All right," she said resignedly. "What do you want me to do?"

"Move in with me for a few days. I'll have Fred, who has a carry license, take you home in the morning so you can pack a couple of bags."

"I've got a new business to run," she said.

"Have the phone company refer your calls here. We'll dedicate a line to Pat Frank's Flight Department. There's even an office downstairs you can use."

"All right, I surrender. I'll take this seriously."

"Hearing that is a great relief," Stone said.

17

HOLLY FILED into the Cabinet room for her second president's intelligence briefing. Kate Lee joined them. "Do we have anything on yesterday's item about a terrorist infiltration?"

Lance Cabot stood. "Yes, Madam President. As you recall, we sent out requests to locate the top twenty Al Qaeda subjects. We have reports back that place seventeen of them in various broadly defined areas—south Yemen, eastern Afghanistan, northern Pakistan, and the like."

"And the other three?"

Lance wielded a remote control and three photographs appeared on a large screen. "We apologize for the quality of these pictures, but they're the best we have." The names appeared under the photographs. "All of these men are active in contriving plots against us around the world. All three speak fluent English—two of them from having attended Eton College, in England, one having attended the University of California at Berkeley. As you can see, they all have full beards and are wearing the native dress of Mideast regions, so a clean shave and a change of clothing would make them substantially unidentifiable at points of entry into the United States."

"Won't the latest facial recognition program work?" Kate asked.

"Our software requires a distinct photograph for comparison, and as you can see, these photos are too indistinct to be useful."

"What about photographs from their time in English and American schools?"

"We have been unable to locate any photographs of them from that or any other period," Lance replied.

"But you believe that one of these men is our infiltrator?"

"All three certainly qualify for that distinction. Of course, that does not exclude many other male Middle Easterners, but their placement in the Al Qaeda hierarchy, their language skills, their past behavior, and the lack of any distinct photographs of them make them our three most likely suspects. Of course, all the agencies are combing their records for any other helpful information, but this is what we have now."

"I want this to be the first matter presented at all future intelligence briefings until we have resolution," Kate said.

AS THE MEETING broke up, Holly fell into step with Lance. "Will you e-mail me those three photographs and the files on these men?" she asked.

"Of course. You'll have them by lunchtime. How are you enjoying the West Wing, Holly?"

"It's too soon to tell," Holly replied. She waved goodbye and left him to return to her office.

Later that morning the photos and files arrived on her computer. She called in Millie. "I have an assignment for you," she said.

Millie turned over a leaf of her steno pad and waited to be told. Holly called up the three photographs. "One of these men may have entered the United States with the intention of carrying out a terrorist plot, probably in Washington."

"Very bad photographs," Millie replied.

"They're the only ones available." She brought Millie up to date on what they knew. "I want you to make it your first priority to track the investigation of these three until we have evidence that will help us locate them. We will be getting daily updates from all the intelligence agencies that should add to our knowledge. I can't devote myself to this full-time, that's why I'm devoting you to it. Their files are attached to their photographs. Get to know them as you would a new boyfriend that you suspect of being a complete shit, and keep me posted as often as you get usable intelligence." Holly typed a few keystrokes. "Everything is now on your computer."

"How long ago were these men at their respective schools?" Millie asked.

"I don't know—you find out."

"Yes, ma'am," Millie replied, and left the room.

18

FRED FLICKER TUCKED Pat Frank into the rear seat of the Bentley and used his remote control to open the garage door. "How are you today, Ms. Frank?" he asked.

"Very well, thank you, Fred."

"I understand you've had a bit of bovver wif a gentleman," Fred said, lapsing into his native Cockney for a moment.

"Well, your boss seems to think so. Nothing's happened yet."

"I understand," Fred said. "Prevention is the best cure."

"He believes that to be so."

"Could you describe the gentleman for me?"

"Six-one, two-twenty, heavily muscled, thick, dark hair going gray."

"May I ask, how did the gentleman come to be heavily muscled?"

"He was always a gym rat," she replied, "but a couple of years ago he really got into the bodybuilding thing."

"I see. Tell me, do you think he might have been using steroids?"

"It crossed my mind," she said. "It all seemed to happen pretty fast. He spent an inordinate amount of time at the gym."

"Does he use drugs?" Fred asked.

"He has, from time to time. I insisted that he stop it, if he wanted to be with me."

"Did he use cocaine?"

"That was his drug of choice."

"Oh, dear," Fred muttered to himself.

"How's that?"

"Sorry, just thinking aloud." He stopped the car. "Please wait until I've had a look around before you get out," he said. He opened the car door, stood on the sill, to make up for his short stature, and had a look down the block and at the cars parked nearby, then he opened the rear door. "Let's get you inside," he said.

Fred followed her to the door and waited until she had unlocked it. "Mr. Barrington has asked me to deliver security alert letters to your tenants, so with your permission, I'll find meself a parking spot, then I'll slip them under their doors and come back here," he said. "Please lock yourself in." He gave her a card with his cell phone number. "Ring, if you need me for anything at all. I'll come back in an hour or so and help you with your luggage."

"Have a good time, Fred," she said, then closed the door behind her.

Fred got back into the Bentley and circled the block, taking a look at every car, but watching for a Nissan Altima, as his boss had instructed. He didn't see one, but he found a good parking spot with a view of Ms. Frank's door, then returned to the building to deliver the letters.

He rang the bell, and she buzzed him in, then opened her door. "Fred, can you come here for a moment, please?"

"Yes, ma'am," Fred replied, and went to her. "How may I help you?"

She partly closed her front door and pointed to some marks around the lock. "What do you make of that?" she asked.

Fred held a finger to his lips and stepped inside the door. He examined the lock and the plate that received the bolt. "Someone has attempted to get into your apartment," he said softly, "but I don't think he made it. Please wait here and be very quiet." Fred drew his pistol and began walking silently from room to room. He checked her apartment's upstairs, too, then came back.

"No one is here but us," he said. "I'll go deliver the letters now. Please lock the door behind me, and don't open it for anyone but me."

"All right," Pat said. "Anything you say, Fred."

Fred went to the bottom of the staircase, slipped off his shoes, and walked slowly up the stairs, walking on the outside of each step to avoid squeaks, and with his pistol at the ready. He stopped on the third floor and examined the lock, finding no marks. He slipped a letter under the door and continued to the fourth floor, where he found the door closed and unmarked.

One more floor to go. He was feeling better about things now. His feeling changed when his head rose enough to have a view of the fifth-floor apartment. The door was ajar. Fred stopped and listened for about a minute, waiting for any sound at all—a footstep, a drawer closing, anything. He heard nothing. He continued up the stairs as quietly as possible and paused at the door and listened again. Still nothing. With a single finger, he pushed the door open slowly, hoping it wouldn't squeak. When the door was fully open he looked around the doorjamb and peered into the apartment. All he saw was a single foot, wearing a brown loafer and an argyle sock. It was entirely immobile. As he continued into the apartment a second foot came into view. The leg to which it was attached was drawn up, and another step revealed a man lying facedown on the floor, inert, with a bloody hole in the back of his head. His face rested in a pool of dark blood. He looked up and saw another man seated on a white sofa, his head flung back and the top of the sofa and the wall behind it covered in gore and blood.

Fred had seen such sights before on battlefields, and he knew that the color of the blood made the killings some hours old. Nevertheless, he carefully searched the rest of the apartment and found no one else there. He paused to look into a bedroom that had been converted to an art studio. There were two drawing tables in the room, and the cork-covered walls had various graphic designs, in various stages of completion, pinned to them. Fred called 911.

"Nine-one-one, what is your emergency?" a female operator asked.

"A double shooting," Fred replied.

"Is an ambulance required?" she asked, skipping the obvious question in favor of brevity.

"Only one from the morgue," Fred answered.

She asked for the address and his name, and he gave them.

"Do you live at this address?"

"No, I'm visiting a friend who lives on the ground floor. I came upstairs to deliver a letter."

"Please hold." Thirty seconds later she came back. "A unit has been dispatched. Please don't touch anything in the apartment, and wait at the downstairs door for the police to arrive."

"Will do," Fred said, then hung up. He left the apartment and walked slowly down the stairs, still using his phone.

"Woodman & Weld," Joan said.

"It's Fred. Give me Mr. Barrington, please."

"Hi, Fred, he's on a call. Can he call you back?"

"Please interrupt him and tell him it's urgent."

Stone was on the line in seconds. "What is it, Fred?"

"A double homicide on the top floor of Ms. Frank's building. I've already called nine-one-one."

"Is Pat all right?"

"Yes. Her door had been tampered with, but the bloke didn't get inside. She's safe, and the police are on the way. They told me to wait at the front door."

"Then you do that. I'll call the commissioner and make sure a good detective team is sent. Tell Pat to stay in her apartment until the police arrive."

"Yes, sir." Fred hung up and hurried down the stairs. He stopped for a moment on the ground floor to recover his shoes, then he went to the Frank apartment and rapped on the door, standing directly in front of the eyehole.

She opened the door. "Come on in, Fred."

"I have to wait by the front door."

"Why?"

"Do two young men occupy your top floor?"

"Yes, they're commercial artists. I haven't met them yet. Have you?"

"In a manner of speaking. They've both been shot and are quite dead."

Pat put a hand to her mouth.

"Powder room, miss, if you're going to be sick."

She took her hand away. "I'm not. What about the others upstairs?"

"No one's answering. I'll let the police take care of that."

They heard a police car coming down Park Avenue and turning into East Sixty-third Street.

"That will be them," Fred said. "Excuse me, please." He holstered his weapon, turned, and walked to the front door, in time to open it for two uniforms.

"Top floor," he said to the men, pointing upstairs. "I don't know if anyone's home on the third and fourth floors."

"Did you call nine-one-one?"

"Yes."

"Wait here."

"I'll be in there," Fred said, pointing at the door. "Landlady's apartment."

19

STONE GOT to Pat's building five minutes after the uniforms and ten minutes before the detectives. Pat buzzed him in and met him at the door; Fred brought him up to date.

The doorbell rang, and Stone buzzed in two detectives; he knew the older of the two but didn't like him much. "Hello, Harry."

"Barrington. You mixed up in this?"

Stone shook his head. "I just got here. Fred Flicker, here, found the bodies."

Fred told his story.

"Okay," Harry said. "We're going upstairs and check this out."

"You might check the apartments on the third and fourth floors," Fred said. "Somebody might be home."

"What about the second floor?"

"This apartment is a duplex," Stone said.

"Everybody stay here," Harry said, and the two detectives left, leaving the door open behind them.

"May I make some coffee?" Stone asked Pat.

"You sit down, I need something to do. Fred?"

"Thank you, miss, no."

Stone sat down and was presently rewarded with a steaming mug of strong black stuff.

The detectives returned. "All right," Harry said, "we've got a crime-scene team on the way, and the medical examiner will be here shortly, too. Who are the two dead guys?"

Pat got a notebook from a kitchen drawer. "David Teal and Bruce Palmer."

"Gay guys?"

"I've no idea," she replied. "I just became the owner of the building a couple of days ago, and I haven't met my tenants yet."

"Harry," Stone said, "you have any interest in my take on this?"

"Not much," Harry said, "but go ahead."

"Your suspect is a man named Kevin Keyes, who resides in Wichita, Kansas. He's an ex–airline pilot who does occasional charter flights, and he's the ex-boyfriend of Ms. Frank, here. I believe he followed her here after she ended their relationship. Mr. Keyes, or whoever the killer is, probably got into the building by ringing all the doorbells. The guys upstairs buzzed him in. He tried to get past Ms. Frank's front door and failed. One of the guys upstairs probably wanted to know who he'd let into the building, and he may have come downstairs. Keyes then marched him back upstairs and shot both guys, so they couldn't identify him. Keyes is registered at the Court Plaza hotel in Times Square, and he's driving a dark, rented Nissan Altima.

"Pat, you want to give them Keyes's description?"

"Six-one, two-twenty, dark hair going gray. He's a bodybuilder and heavily muscled."

Fred spoke up. "Ms. Frank believes he may be on both steroids and cocaine."

"A bad mixture," Stone said. "Pat, would you say that Keyes has a quick temper and is subject to rages?"

"I would," Pat replied. "And he owns several guns."

"Who owns this building?" Harry asked.

"I told you, I do," Pat replied. "My sister made me a gift of it."

The doorbell rang, and Harry admitted two men with stretchers and another with a large case. He sent them upstairs and returned to Pat's apartment. "You know what bothers me about this?" he asked nobody in particular.

"The double homicide upstairs?" Stone inquired.

"Nah. It's too simple—that's what bothers me. I never walked into a homicide before where I got handed the scenario and the killer on a platter, complete with an address. Jesus, I'm surprised nobody got his Social Security number."

"I probably have that somewhere," Pat said, "if you want it."

"Y'see? It's all too simple."

"Feel free to make it more complicated," Stone said.

"Oh, I don't have to do that," Harry said. "It will make itself complicated pretty quick."

"While it's getting complicated," Stone said, "you might send a SWAT team over to the Court Plaza and invite Mr. Keyes up to the precinct for a chat."

"You telling me how to do my job?" Harry asked.

"*Somebody's* got to," Stone said.

"And why do you think I need a SWAT team?"

"Oh, I don't know: the suspect is a big, strong, angry man who is known to own several guns and who is probably crazed by a combination of steroids and cocaine. If you'd rather just go over there and ask him a few polite questions, go right ahead."

"You were always a smart-ass, Barrington."

"And you were always a stupid ass, Harry."

The doorbell rang again.

"You get it," Harry said to his young partner.

He left and came back with two middle-aged men in suits.

"I'm Detective Robert Miller," one of them said. "This is my partner, Dominic Legano."

"What the fuck are you two doing here?" Harry asked.

"This is our case—the commissioner sent us," Miller said. "You can leave now."

"The fuck we're leaving," Harry said.

Miller produced a cell phone. "Let's see: you're out of the Nineteenth precinct, right? And your captain is Don Haley?" He started to dial a number.

"Awright, awright," Harry said. "Take the fucking case and stick it up your ass. Come on," he said to his partner, and they both walked out of the apartment. At the door, the younger man looked back and shrugged.

"Good day, gentlemen," Miller called after them. He turned to the group. "All right," he said, "will somebody fill us in?"

Stone and Fred went through the whole thing again while Legano took notes. When he had finished, Miller got out his cell phone again and pressed a speed-dial button. "This is Bob Miller. I need a SWAT team at the Court Plaza in Times Square to pick up a suspect in a double homicide. Name is Kevin Keyes, registered guest, six-one, two-twenty, dark hair going gray. Consider him armed and dangerous. Possibly high on something." He chatted for another minute with whoever was on the other end of the line, then hung up. "Okay, Dom, let's go upstairs and view the carnage, see what the boys have to say about the corpses and the scene. Please excuse us for a few minutes," he said to Stone, "and I'd be grateful if you'd all remain until we're done here."

"Glad to," Stone said.

"You bet," Pat said.

"Righto," Fred echoed.

ANOTHER HOUR PASSED, during which men with stretchers brought two body bags down in the elevator. The detectives returned.

"Anybody think of anything else?" Miller asked.

Everybody shook their heads.

"Ms. Frank," Miller said, "you should give some thought to getting out of the house for a few days. Do you have anywhere you can go?"

"She does," Stone said.

Legano took down their information, and the detectives shook their hands and left.

"I think it's time we got you to my house, Pat," Stone said. "Any objections?"

"Not even one," Pat said, "but I may have a better idea."

20

HOLLY ARRIVED at her White House office to find Millie Martindale already at her desk, and she was wearing the dress she had worn yesterday. "Good morning, Millie," she said.

"Morning, ma'am," Millie said.

"Tell me, did you get lucky last night, or did you spend the night at your desk?"

"Both," Millie replied. "Give me a few minutes, and I'll bring you some stuff."

Holly went to the adjacent utility room and made coffee. She came back with two mugs and found Millie sitting across from her desk, shuffling papers in her lap. Holly handed her a mug.

"Any cream and sugar?" Millie asked.

"If you drink it black for twenty-one days, you'll never have it any other way again, and you'll save yourself a lot of time, too."

Millie tasted the coffee and made a face.

"Tough it out," Holly said. "What have you got?"

"Identities for two of our fuzzy photographs."

"Shoot."

"I sort of took a shortcut," Millie said. "I spent my junior year at Oxford, and I have a friend from those days who's now teaching there. He's a couple of years older than me, and I knew he went to Eton, so I had a talk with him. His first year there he knew two boys, identical twins, who had unusual accents. Their names were John and James Whittleworth, and he made them as Arabs, though they didn't look it."

"And Whittleworth isn't a very Arabic name," Holly pointed out.

"They were a little darker of skin but had blond hair."

"Go on."

"I got the registrar's office at Eton at four o'clock this morning—it's five hours later there—and they dug up the boys' records. Their father's name was Martindale, like my last name, and their mother's Fatima, which might explain their appearance and accents."

"Makes sense."

"Not for long. I researched the father, and I'm pretty sure he doesn't exist. Not the mother, either. There was a record of only one visit to the school by the parents, early in the boys' three-year stay at the school. They never went home for the holidays, even at Christmas, and their school fees were paid by an official of a private bank in London, Devin's, which turns out to have Middle Eastern owners."

"How about graduation? Did the parents turn up for that?"

"Neither of them. A chauffeured car picked them up after the ceremony, which was twelve years ago, and they were never heard from again. Mail to them—invitations to alumni events, pleas for money, et cetera—was sent to the bank and never replied to."

"Did they go to university after Eton? Most of their graduates do."

"There is no record of the boys applying for any university."

"Are there any photographs of them—maybe in yearbooks?"

"None. They didn't play any sports or participate in other extracurricular activities, except shooting classes and chess. Otherwise they kept to themselves. One other thing, they were tutored in elocution by a young instructor there, and by the time they left school, their accents were indistinguishable from the upper-class English spoken by all the boys, except the Scots, the Irish, and some foreigners."

"Is there any indication of where they might be now?"

"None whatever—they simply evanesced. No British passport has been issued for either of them, so if they left the country, they had other papers."

"Well, wherever they are, they have been very carefully groomed," Holly observed. "What about the third man in the photos?"

"So far, a total blank. Can you ask your friends at the Agency why they believe he spent time at Berkeley? If we can find out when he was there, maybe we have a chance of running him down."

"I'll make a call," Holly said. "Good work on the twins."

Millie actually blushed. "Thank you."

"Go home, take a nap, and get a change of clothes."

"Thank you," Millie said gratefully, then evanesced.

Holly called Lance Cabot and was immediately put through.

"Good morning, Holly."

"Good morning, Lance. I have some information for you, and then I'd like you to get some for me."

"Do you mind if I record our conversation? It's easier than taking notes."

"Go ahead. Ready?"

"Ready."

Holly related what Millie had turned up on the twins.

"That's extremely good work," Lance said.

"I thought so. I have hopes for her."

"Just shows how one personal relationship can cut through the fog and turn up useful information."

"I wouldn't say it's useful in this case," Holly said.

"Au contraire," Lance said, in his best accent. "We now know the two are identical twins—that could be most helpful. We know Devin's Bank—we might even have an asset there."

"That would be very helpful indeed," Holly said.

"Now, what do you need from me?"

"Millie drew a blank on the third photograph, the one who was said to have spent some time at Berkeley. I'd like to know where that information came from and if there's any more of it."

"I don't believe it came from our people. I'll have some calls made and see if it can be tracked down. Talk to you later."

Lance hung up.

So did Holly.

LANCE MADE a call to the Agency officer who had helped prepare the file for the president's intelligence briefing. Her name was Charlotte Weir, and she was a fairly new officer, having joined three years before.

"Good morning, Charlotte."

"Good morning, Director."

"You are part of the collaborative effort, are you not, to prepare the president's daily intelligence briefings?"

"I am, sir."

"Do you recall that, in the discussion of our three persons of interest—those of the poor photographs—there was made mention that one of them might have spent some time at the University of California at Berkeley?"

"I recall that was said of one of the men."

"It was said of two that they were at a British private school. They have since been accounted for." He brought her up to date on the twins. "I now wish you to speak to whoever contributed the Berkeley information, to place a time frame on when he might have attended, and to thoroughly rake all of Berkeley's records that might tell us more about him."

"I'll get right on it, Director."

"That would please me greatly. Work as quickly as you can." Lance hung up.

21

STONE AND PAT got into the rear seat of the Bentley, and Fred drove them to Stone's house. He asked Fred to take her luggage upstairs.

"Which room?" Fred whispered to Stone.

"Mine," Stone whispered back. "Come on down to my office and tell me about your idea," he said to Pat.

Joan got them some coffee.

"Have you ever flown your airplane across the Atlantic?" Pat asked.

"Nope, but I've always wanted to. There's an awful lot of prep to do, I understand—a lot of paperwork."

"A client of mine who owns a string of Jaguar dealerships in Britain, Europe, and the States has bought himself a CitationJet4, and he wants it flown to Wichita, where he's going to do his training. Why don't you and I fly your airplane over there? Paperwork is what I do, and I can do it fast. I've already had a dozen crossings on the northern route, doing ferry flights, so I can show you the ropes. We'll land in Coventry, which is where both Jaguar and my client live. He's offered me the loan of a car, if I want to do some touring, and I've never had any time to myself in England—I was always in and out."

"That sounds very inviting," Stone said. "But what about your business?"

"The business is nascent. I can handle what I've got on the phone, and your airplane has a satphone. Also, I can't work out of my new office until this thing with Kevin is settled."

"Well, you know the northern route, and I know England. I hitchhiked around the island when I was a student, and I saw a lot of very nice country hotels that I couldn't afford to stay in. When do we go?"

"I can get the paperwork in hand by next Monday. How's that?"

Stone turned to his computer and checked the next couple of weeks. "Nothing here that can't be handled by phone or just later. You're on, but why do we have to do the northern route?"

"Your airplane has a thirteen-hundred-mile range, and that's not enough to go nonstop. We'll fly up to Goose Bay, in Labrador, then to Greenland, where we'll refuel, then to Reykjavik, Iceland. If we luck into a big tailwind, we might do Goose Bay–Reykjavik nonstop. We can do an overnight there, or we can press on to England. It'll be about ten hours overall, but we can take turns flying and napping."

"You've already got an office right down the hall," Stone said. "All my manuals and paperwork are in my flight bag right over there." He pointed. "So get to work."

She finished her coffee and did just that.

STONE WAS WORKING on his mail when Dino called. "Word has reached me that yet another of your friends is in trouble," he said. "Is Pat all right?"

"She is. I got her out of the house, and first of the week, I'm getting her out of the country."

"Where are you headed?"

"To England, and in my airplane."

"Your airplane would get halfway there, then *splash*!"

"We're going the northern route: Canada, Greenland, Iceland."

"Haven't you heard it's winter?"

"The airplane has a heater. You want to come along?"

"Is Pat doing the flying?"

"We're sharing. She's flying a delivery back from England, I'll make the trip back alone."

"I've got some business in London—maybe I'll fly back with you."

"I could use the company."

"How long will it take us, and where do we leave from?"

"A day or two, weather permitting. We'll leave from Coventry."

"I'm speaking in Birmingham next Wednesday, so that works for me."

"Can Viv come?"

"I'll ask and get back to you." Dino hung up.

LATE IN THE AFTERNOON, Stone had a call from Detective Robert Miller.

"Just an update," Miller said. "Kevin Keyes checked out of his hotel early this morning and turned in his rental car. He's in the wind."

"That's bad news," Stone said. "Did you check the airlines?"

"Yes—no reservation. We've alerted the Wichita police, in case he goes home, but it's a long bus ride."

"He's a pilot who does charters, remember? He could have flown out of Teterboro or White Plains, flying a charter or doing a delivery of an airplane. Check the FAA for any flight plans he might have filed."

"That's a good tip. Thanks." Miller hung up.

Stone thought it just as well that he and Pat were getting out of town.

Pat came into his office, and he told her about the call.

"God," she said, "Kevin could be anywhere."

"I told Miller to check for any filed flight plans."

"Good idea."

"Don't worry, they'll get him."

"I hope you're right," she said.

22

MILLIE MARTINDALE LAY in a tub of very hot water and tried not to fall asleep and drown. As the weariness soaked out of her body her mind began to race. What did she have on the third man? He may have been at Berkeley fifteen years ago; at least, that was when the twins were at Eton. Who did she know who went to Berkeley? There was someone in the back of her mind, but she couldn't put a name to that person.

She got out of the tub, dried her hair, and lay down on her bed, her hair swept out of the way. After a moment, she had an idea: she had heard that a guy a couple of years ahead of her at Harvard was in federal law enforcement, but she couldn't remember with what agency. She started with the FBI and got lucky, and she asked for Quentin Phillips. He answered on the fourth ring. "Phillips."

"Quentin, it's Millicent Martindale. How are you?"

"Millie? I'm great. How about you?"

"Just fine, thanks."

"Are you in D.C.?"

"Yep. I'm working at the White House for the national security adviser, Holly Barker."

"No kidding! Plum job!"

"If I don't eat, sleep, or drink, it is. What are you doing over there?"

"I'm low man on the totem pole in counterintelligence."

"Does that include terrorist threats?"

"In a manner of speaking. Mostly it includes whatever shit they throw at me."

"Well, I'm going to throw some shit at you, and I can't tell you why, and you can't tell anybody I asked."

"Sounds fascinating. Are you out to get some old boyfriend who done you wrong?"

"Nope, this is official business—it's just on a need-to-know basis, and I can't make a case for your needing to know."

"Okay, your rules, but it's going to cost you a very fine dinner."

"I'm up for that, if they ever let me have dinner again."

"Good enough for me. Tell me what you need."

"I'm going to make some assumptions, and you can correct me if I'm wrong."

"What assumptions?"

"I'm assuming that the Bureau has an ear to the ground on various college campi around the country for terrorist activity."

"A reasonable assumption."

"I'm assuming that one of those campi is Berkeley."

"A more than reasonable assumption."

"And I'm assuming that the listening post was operating at least as far back as nine-eleven, maybe even before."

"That's a possibility."

"I'm also assuming that you have or can get access to the files going back that far."

"Post nine-eleven, for sure. Before that, we're probably talking paper, and paper that's God-knows-where."

"Then let's assume post nine-eleven for the moment."

"Okay. What do you need?"

"I have reason to believe that a student at Berkeley during that period had connections to Al Qaeda or some other such organization."

"Name? Description?"

"I don't have either, that's what makes this hard."

"What have you got?"

"My best guess is he was studying under a non-Arab name, maybe even, but not necessarily, his own, and that he may have a family connection to the Middle East, or that he might have been part of some pro-Arab campus group, something like Students for Palestinian Justice, to coin a name. You get the picture."

"I believe I do."

"Get me a name and a background check, and I'll give you more than dinner."

"Now, that's an inviting thought. What does it mean?"

"Whatever you want it to mean."

"It would help if I could tell somebody else just a little bit about this. I've got to cover my ass."

"You can speak in generalities, but you can't mention me, my boss, or the White House—not under any circumstances. Are we clear on that?"

"Okay, while I'm covering my ass I'll cover yours, too. When do you need this?"

"Oh, last month would be good."

"I had a feeling it would be like that."

She gave him her cell number. "I'll wait impatiently for your call."

"One more thing: On a scale of one to ten, how important do you think this guy could be?"

"Twenty-five," she said.

He was silent for a moment. "No shit?"

"Absolutely no shit." She hung up.

QUENTIN HUNG UP, too, and he found himself sweating lightly. He had known Millicent Martindale to be a serious person at Harvard, and she was in a serious job now, but he had an annual performance review coming up, and he had to be careful not to get hung out to dry just because he wanted to fuck her, which he did, very badly. In fact, he had always wanted to fuck her, but she had been beyond him—more beautiful, more sophisticated, more desirable. "What the hell," he said to himself, and he left his cubicle and went down the hall toward his supervisor's office. This was Lev Epstein, who was assistant director for counterintelligence and, he figured, maybe the smartest person at the Bureau, an assessment with which Epstein would not disagree.

He walked past Epstein's office, and his secretary was refreshing her makeup—about to go to lunch, he figured. Epstein, however, didn't eat lunch, except at his desk. He made another pass and saw the woman look at her watch, pick up her bag, then pick up her phone, no doubt telling her boss she was going to lunch. As soon as she was gone, he walked past her desk and rapped purposefully on Epstein's door, which was open a couple of feet.

"Come!" the man shouted. "But it better be good!"

Quentin opened the door and entered. Epstein had a Mickey Mouse lunchbox on his desk, and he was eating a sandwich. He glared at Quentin.

"What?" he said, his voice muffled by the sandwich.

"I've got something important," Quentin said.

"You don't know enough to know whether it's important," Epstein replied. "You've got sixty seconds."

Quentin began talking; he chose his words carefully, but he didn't rush. "A well-placed person of my acquaintance has a lead on what might be a very important terrorist plot. This person has asked me to research who the Bureau might have been interested in at Berkeley just prior to or after nine-eleven. He would be American or American-educated with a non-Arabic name, a student at that time."

"Your time is up," Epstein said.

"That was only forty seconds."

"All right, you've got twenty more."

"I can't tell you the name of my contact or where this person works, but based on my prior knowledge, this is a serious request."

"Tell me who she is and where she works or get out," Epstein said.

"Sorry to trouble you, sir," Quentin said. He turned and walked out of the office.

"Come back here!" Epstein growled.

Quentin came back as far as the door. "Yes, sir?"

"You think I'm going to trouble myself just so you can get laid?"

"I happen to know you were stationed in San Francisco about the time of nine-eleven, and my guess is, you were probably running the operation there, so you won't have to trouble yourself in the least, just remember." Quentin took a deep breath. "I also know you're the smartest guy around this place, and you're not going to blow me off just because I'm low man here."

Epstein laughed, spitting pieces of sandwich on his desk. "I would call that hopeful flattery. Okay, I'll give you a B for balls," he said. "Now, tell me what you think this is all about."

"I think there may have been a deep-cover operative at Berkeley, and that his file, if he had one, might have crossed your desk."

"You have a name?"

"Nope, but it's probably not Arab. He might have been peripherally involved with some pro-Palestinian or other group, and it wouldn't surprise me if you remember somebody like that."

"Suppose I do?" Epstein said. "Why would I give it to your girlfriend?"

"Because this person is well-enough connected to make life hell for the Bureau, if we should know something but fail to share it. That's the sort of thing that could haunt the Bureau after a terrorist attack. On the other hand, if we do share and something comes of it, it will reflect well on counterintelligence." By which he meant, on Epstein.

"All right," Epstein said, "let me sift through my memories." He swiveled his chair around and stared out the window, his back to Quentin, still eating his sandwich.

Quentin, though uninvited, took a seat.

23

ALL WAS QUIET for the first day, as Pat worked away in her borrowed office. On the second day, packages began to arrive, and Joan stacked them in Stone's office, because, she said, they would end up there anyway, and there was no point in her humping them into the garage, then back again.

On the third day, Pat appeared in Stone's office with a stack of papers nearly a foot high. "Okay," she said, "you've got some signing to do."

"What is all this stuff?"

"Your paperwork for RSVM, MNFS, and a few other things. You have to satisfy both American and European regs if you want to fly above flight level 280, and you do want to fly higher because if you stay low, you'll burn so much fuel you'll end up in the drink well before your destination."

Stone began signing, while she double-checked that he had not missed any lines. "Fine," she said when he had finished. "Now we start opening boxes."

The first box yielded a six-man life raft, packed tightly into a bag that would explode when a cord was yanked. "Whatever you do," Pat said, "don't pull that cord until the raft is outside the airplane."

"I can imagine what that would be like."

Other boxes yielded a handheld aviation radio, a marine radio, a GPS locator, two super-duper life jackets, and see-through plastic bags.

"What are the bags for?" Stone asked.

"The small one is for the radios that we take into the life raft with us. The large one is for several thousand calories of trail mix and granola bars."

"I hate trail mix and granola bars."

"Don't worry, they'll taste great once you're afloat in the raft." She cut open a large box. "Now for the pièce de résistance," she said, producing two emergency-orange duffel bags. She tossed him one. "Put this on, and don't take your shoes off."

Stone shook the duffel out and unfolded what looked like the deflated corpse of a science-fiction creature.

"Go ahead, put it on," she said. "It will save your life, but only if you know how to wear it."

Stone took off his jacket, sat in his chair, and shoved his feet into the legs of the thing.

"Now stand up and put your arms into it," Pat said.

Stone wriggled his arms into the sleeves, which ended in integral neoprene gloves. "I could never play the piano in this thing," he said.

"Not to worry, there won't be a piano in the life raft. Now put the top onto your head and zip it up," Pat commanded.

With some difficulty Stone managed to get the thing closed.

"Great! Now you're ready to float on your back in the North Atlantic Ocean, as icebergs drift by."

"If we have the raft, why do we need these things?"

"To preserve your body heat, which the raft will only partly do. Besides, you'll want to look your best when the helicopter shows up."

"How do we know one will show up?" Stone asked.

"One will, if we ditch within helicopter range—maybe a couple of hundred miles."

"And if we're out of helicopter range?"

"Then a very large airplane, a C-130, will come and find our raft, using the GPS location sent out by our emergency transmitter, then circle overhead, tossing out food, water, blankets, and whatever we'll need until the ship shows up."

"What ship?"

"One that's passing not too far away from us that the C-130 has contacted."

"What if the ship's captain doesn't want to come for us?"

"He has to—law of the sea, and all that."

"How long will it take for him to come?"

"Oh, two, three days, depending on how far away he is when he gets the call."

"We'd have to spend two or three days in that raft?"

"Unless we're within helicopter range, then it would be only a few hours."

"How are we going to, ah, *entertain* ourselves while wearing these suits?" Stone asked.

Pat laughed. "Ingenuity."

"Nobody is *that* ingenious."

"Now, here's the drill," Pat said, ignoring that. "We've lost both engines. We start gliding in the direction of the nearest helicopter, say, in Reykjavik. At twenty thousand feet we attempt a restart of both engines. If neither restarts, we prepare to ditch in the sea. You leave your seat and buckle yourself into the nearest rear-facing seat. I'll take care of the rest."

"Oh, no you don't. My airplane, my ditching. *You* will strap yourself into a passenger seat."

"Oh, all right, exercise your ego, but have you ever ditched an airplane in the water?"

"Yes, I have," Stone replied firmly. "I took off from LaGuardia in a Citation Mustang, and at three thousand feet I encountered a flock of geese and they destroyed both engines. I tried to return to the airport but didn't have enough altitude, so I headed for the Hudson and ditched at about Forty-second Street. Nobody got hurt."

"In your dreams," she said. "If you had pulled that off, you'd be the new Sully Sullenberger."

"Fortunately, I was in the Mustang simulator at Flight Safety, in Orlando," Stone conceded.

"They let you do that?"

"I insisted, so I am not without experience in matters of ditching. How about you?"

"Oh, all right," she said, "I've never ditched, either, but I've got a lot more hours than you."

"Buy your own airplane, and you can do the ditching."

A voice came from the doorway. "Are you out of your fucking mind?"

Stone turned to find Dino standing there. He'd forgotten they had a lunch date. "Nope, we're just rehearsing our ditching in the

North Atlantic after a double engine failure." Stone picked up the other duffel and tossed it to Dino. "Your turn."

"I'm not getting into that thing," Dino said.

"Tell him, Pat."

"It will save your life if Stone has to ditch the airplane. You have to try it on now, so you'll know what to do."

"It's just a precaution," Stone said, unzipping his survival suit and wriggling out of it with Pat's help.

Dino shook the suit out of the bag and regarded it dolefully. "I *have* to?"

"You have to," Pat said.

Dino took off his jacket and struggled into the suit; it took him the better part of ten minutes. Pat zipped it up for him.

"Okay," Stone said, "everybody ready for some lunch? Pat, you're joining us."

Dino began struggling with the suit. "How the hell do I get out of this thing?"

"The same way you got into it," Stone said, "only backwards." He got into his jacket. "Come on, Pat, we can have a glass of wine while we wait for Dino to join us."

"You miserable son of a bitch!" Dino hollered.

Pat dissolved in laughter, then went to help Dino extract himself from the thing. Then they went off together to the Four Seasons.

24

MILLIE WAS GETTING dressed to go back to work when her cell rang. "Hello?"

"It's Quentin."

"That was fast. Have you solved my problem?"

"In a manner of speaking."

"In what manner of speaking?"

"I took your problem to my ultimate boss, the assistant director of counterintelligence."

"Did you tell him my name?"

"Not only did I not tell him your name, I told him you were a guy."

"Well, that was insulting."

"He knows nothing but the vague outline of what you want. The thing is, he was stationed in the San Francisco office at the time you're interested in, and after some thought, he thinks he might have something for you."

"Okay, shoot. What is it?"

"Hang on, he won't tell me, then let me tell you. He wants to meet you face-to-face."

"If I do that, then I'm working outside the boundaries of my assignment, and there will be hell to pay."

"It's the only way he'll tell you what he knows."

"I'll call you back in an hour," Millicent said, and hung up. She finished dressing and drove to the White House; five minutes later she was seated in Holly Barker's office. "I've got something on the third man, but I don't know what it is."

"Millie," Holly said, feigning patience, "that puts us at yesterday."

"I'm sorry, what I meant to say is . . . Oh, shit, here's what's happened." She told Holly of her two conversations with Quentin Phillips while Holly nodded along with her.

"I've done business with Lev Epstein before," Holly said when Millie had finished. "He's very smart—so much so that you can't let him outsmart you."

"How do you want me to handle him?" Millie asked.

Holly pressed a button on her phone. "Please get me Lev Epstein at the Bureau." A minute later, Epstein came on.

"Aha, it's you, Holly!" he said.

"I know," Holly said. "I've always known."

"But now *I* know," he said triumphantly.

"How are you, Lev?"

"Just great, thanks."

"And the wife and kids?"

"Just great."

"Are you still eating your noon meals out of your six-year-old's Mickey Mouse lunchbox?"

"Only every day. So it's *your* minion that's got my young agent's knickers in a twist?"

"I haven't explored their relationship to that point," Holly said.

"So why do you need to know what I know?"

"So that I can see that some very bad people don't harm our nation."

"Okay, you show me yours, and I'll show you mine."

"In your dreams. I know it's been a long time since anyone told you this, Lev, but what I know is above your pay grade."

"Oh, come on, Holly, I'm the assistant director for counter-intelligence—nothing is above my pay grade."

"If you like, I can have the president call your director, then he can explain it to you."

"Oh, come now, Holly."

"This is what we're going to do: you and Mr. Phillips are going to have a nice lunch with my assistant, Millicent Martindale—not at our mess nor at yours, but at a cozy McDonald's somewhere, and you're buying."

"Why should I buy?"

"I can arrange for your director to explain that to you, as well, if you like. Now I'm going to put Millie on the phone with you, and the two of you will arrange a lunch date."

"Oh, all right."

"And, Lev, don't show up with the Mickey Mouse lunchbox." She handed the phone to Millie. "He's all yours."

MILLIE FOUND the McDonald's in Arlington and sat in the parking lot until she saw Quentin Phillips get out of a car with a companion. The companion was short, thickly built, and looked more like how she thought an agent of the Mossad would look, rather than an FBI executive. She followed them into the restaurant and gave Quentin her order, then commandeered a booth and waited for them to join her.

"Millie, this is Lev Epstein, assistant director of counterintelligence. Lev, this is Millicent Martindale."

"Hi," Epstein said, digging into a Quarter Pounder with cheese.

"Hi, yourself," Millie said, following Holly's advice not to try to charm him. "I'm all ears."

Quentin flinched.

"Tell me what you know, first," Epstein said.

"Agent Phillips has already told you what I know."

"Oh, come on, you know more than that."

"I'm here for no other reason than to find out what you know, Lev. I believe Holly Barker already explained that to you."

"Okay. About a year before nine-eleven I got assigned to the San Francisco office," he said, "and then I got assigned to mingle with students—I was pretty young at the time. My orders were to detect dissident students who might become a problem for us. I did not hang out at Hillel House."

"So where did you hang out?"

"I adopted the pseudonym of Ali—I had spent two years in the Israeli army, and I'm very good with languages—so I spoke Arabic, which gave me some street cred with the Middle Eastern students, of which there were several dozen. I started going to discussion group meetings, which were informally organized and held at a different place every week or so. There were three people whose obvious assignment was to winkle out people like me, but I took them on and won their trust." He paused.

"Did someone in that group resemble the parameters I outlined to Quentin yesterday?"

"No. There was no one in the group who could pass as a non-Arab. They were too angry, mostly. However, after a dozen meetings or so, an observer appeared. He was young—not much older than I—handsome, and wore expensive clothes. He came to only one meeting, and he never spoke, but he made an impression on everybody. When the meeting showed signs of breaking up, he left immediately, without speaking to anyone. I made a point of not asking anyone about him, but I overheard two other students talking about him, and one of them said that he was an assistant professor in the economics department who had specialized knowledge of the Middle Eastern oil industry, and that he taught some sort of course that dealt with the subject."

"And you never learned his name?"

"No. And there was no point in asking about him, because nobody in the group seemed to know anything else about him, either, except that he was thought to be important."

"Did you pursue identifying him?"

"I wanted to, but about that time we lost an agent to a firefight with a bank robber, and I was promoted into his position. I wrote a one-page memo for my files before starting the new job, saying what I just told you. No one was appointed to fill my slot, so I suppose my memo went the way of all paper. It's probably in a file box in a salt mine somewhere out West."

"Describe him thoroughly, please."

Epstein closed his eyes and furrowed his brow. "Six feet, one-seventy, dark hair, fashionably cut, a permanent five-o'clock shadow, excellent teeth, skin on the pale side. If he's your boy, then he probably had a European parent." Epstein took another chomp of his Quarter Pounder. "Now tell me what you know."

"I know what you just told me," Millie replied. "That's all."

Epstein sighed. "All right, then this is what I want from you: if you're able to put what I told you with information from somewhere else and you start a hunt for this guy, I want dibs on the search. Got it?"

"I'll pass that on to Holly Barker," Millie said. She wiped the fry grease off her fingers with a couple of paper napkins and offered him a hand. "Neither you nor Quentin is to speak about this with anyone anywhere. Thank you so much for a marvelous lunch. I'll tell all my friends about this place."

He shook her hand, she leaned over and whispered to Quentin, "Call me. I owe you dinner."

Then she left the two of them to their sumptuous lunch.

25

STONE TAXIED onto runway 01 at Teterboro and smoothly shoved the throttles of the Citation M2 forward. The airplane accelerated as Pat Frank called the speeds: "Airspeed is alive . . . seventy knots . . . V1 and rotate."

Stone pulled back on the yoke and concentrated on keeping two angled bars nestled together, which gave him the proper climb rate.

"Positive rate," Pat said. "Gear and flaps coming up." She dealt with both levers.

Stone changed frequencies. "New York departure, Citation 123TF, off Teterboro."

"November One Two Three Tango Foxtrot, climb and maintain six thousand, direct BREZY," Air Traffic Control replied.

Stone dialed in six thousand feet and selected the intersection BREZY on the flight plan, and the button Direct. "Citation 123TF, out of twelve hundred for six thousand." They were off on the first leg, to Goose Bay, Labrador, in eastern Canada, the most popular airport en route to Greenland and Reykjavik.

ATC handed him off to Boston Center, which gave him an immediate climb to forty-one thousand feet, or flight level 410. Twenty minutes later he leveled off at that altitude.

"Free at last," Pat said. "Thank God Almighty."

"Have you been feeling unfree?" Stone asked, pressing buttons on the iPad-like controller and tuning in satellite radio and some jazz.

"Not until Kevin Keyes murdered two of my tenants," she said. "Ever since then, though. I'm so happy to be back in the air at the start of a long flight."

The satellite phone rang, and Stone pressed the appropriate icons to connect. "Hello?"

"Stone? It's Bob Miller."

"Hi, Bob, what's up?"

"Just an update: we've checked the FAA computer for flight plans with Kevin Keyes's name on them and came up with zilch."

"He'll turn up sometime, somewhere," Stone said.

"Right, he will. What was the number I dialed?"

"The satphone on my airplane. I'm getting Pat Frank out of town."

"Good idea. I was going to mention that."

"You can reach me at this number or on my cell while we're gone."

"I'll keep you updated. Bye."

"Bye." Stone broke the connection. "Did you get that?" he asked Pat.

"Most of it. I was fiddling with my headset. No luck with the FAA, huh?"

"Suppose he was flying as copilot?"

"Then his name wouldn't be on the flight plan."

"Oh, well."

They flew for nearly three hours with a light tailwind and landed at Goose Bay, a large airport without a lot of traffic at the end of a fjord. They taxied to the Fixed Base Operator, Irving Aviation, and found a cozy operation with coffee and cookies on offer. Stone ordered fuel while Pat checked the weather and filed their next flight plan, to one of two Greenland airports. She returned shortly. "It's Narsarsuaq," she said.

Stone groaned inwardly. He had heard a lot about the former U.S. air base, dating to World War II, from other pilots. The field was up a Greenland fjord, rimmed with mountains, and no one wanted to go in there except in excellent weather. "Not Sondrestrom?" he asked. This was also an ex–U.S. air base, now operated by the Danish Air Force, but it had a very long runway and a localizer approach, easier than the non-directional-beacon approach at Narsarsuaq, and it often had better weather.

"It's Narsarsuaq. The forecast is for six thousand overcast and light winds. That's good for us."

Stone shrugged. It would be a learning experience. They got back into the airplane, started the engines, worked through the checklist, and got a clearance from the tower. Their assigned altitude was 290 and their Mach speed, .67. "What the hell?" Stone said, outraged. "We filed for 410 and .70. Why are they giving us lower and slower?"

"The Canadians seem to think that the skies between here and Greenland are thick with airplanes, and since there's no radar en route, they space them out to avoid conflicts." She argued with the tower and got an increase in altitude to 310. "That's the best we're going to do," she said.

Shortly, they were over the North Atlantic Ocean at 310, and Stone throttled back to Mach .67. The multi-function display in the center of the instrument panel displayed two rings around their current position, the first a dotted one that showed their range with a forty-five-minute fuel reserve, and a solid one that indicated where they would have dry tanks. "We've got fuel for Narsarsuaq," he said, "even at the lower-than-best altitude."

"It's only a two-hour flight," she said. She pointed at a mark on the Greenland shore, labeled SI. "That's the first of two NDB beacons," she said. "We'll cross that at five thousand feet, then proceed to the next NDB, NA, which is on the field. If the forecast holds, we'll be able to see the airport and make a visual approach. If it gets lower, we'll have to fly the NDB approach."

Stone had not flown an NDB approach since he was a student; they were hardly ever used in the States, and his airplane was not even equipped with the relevant radio. He knew he could fly it using GPS, though.

They were out of radio contact with ATC for an hour or so, then at the assigned point, they contacted Narsarsuaq Radio and told the operator their plan.

"That's fine," he said, "as long as you can see the mountains. We have no radar here, so we can't advise you."

Stone set up the vertical navigation feature to cross SI at five thousand feet, and at the appropriate point, the autopilot started them down. They were in solid instrument meteorological conditions, or IMC, until they passed six thousand feet, when the landscape below them emerged. Stone took a deep breath. All he could see was a snow-covered landscape with mountains. The fjord was filled with ice floes. "I'd hate to ditch here with all that ice in the water," he said to Pat. "It would destroy the airplane. We'd never get into the raft."

"That's why we have two engines," Pat said.

At SI, the autopilot switched to the next NDB, NA.

"We can see to descend now," Pat said. "Let's get down to three thousand."

"Where the hell is the airport?"

"Be patient, it will reveal itself to you."

Stone was anxious, but he descended. A few minutes later he looked out the windscreen and saw what looked like an elongated postage stamp in a valley ahead of them. "Is that it? That tiny thing?"

"It will get bigger," Pat said. "Now just aim for the runway. Slow down and let's get some flaps in."

Now it was just an ordinary visual approach, Stone told himself. Try to relax. He slowed enough to get the landing gear down, which slowed them even more, but according to the approach lights, he was still too high. He steepened his descent. And then the runway—all six thousand feet of it—was under them and he was touching down. No sweat.

He taxied to the nearly empty ramp, where a lineman and a fuel truck awaited them. As he taxied to a stop and waited for the nosewheel to be chocked, he saw a tiny Inuit girl in the cab of the fuel truck. She smiled at him, and he waved.

They left the airplane with the refuelers and went into the terminal building and upstairs to where a young man and a beautiful

Inuit woman manned the flight department. They got a new weather forecast and a clearance, then used the toilets and walked back to the airplane, which was now replete with fuel.

Pat got out the departure chart and went over it with Stone. "What we're going to do is take off in the opposite direction of our landing, because there are mountains in the departure direction. After takeoff, we turn right forty-five degrees for a minute or so, then make a standard-rate turn to the left, three hundred and sixty degrees, climbing all the time. We may need a second three-sixty to get to an altitude above the mountains. I'll be comfortable at twelve thousand feet."

"Whatever you say," Stone said. They had a slight tailwind, but the runway was slightly downhill, so they got off the ground easily. Stone made the first 360-degree turn, then, suddenly, they were in the clouds and could see nothing except the moving map in front of them.

"Let's do another three-sixty," Pat said.

Stone did so, and then they were above twelve thousand feet, heading for 310. Stone looked at the synthetic vision display in the panel and found a spectacular view of mountains and valleys in front of them. They broke out of the clouds at 180, headed for their first waypoint to Reykjavik. The winds had changed, and now they had a headwind. Their assigned Mach number was down to .64, and they seemed to be making poor progress.

"Something's wrong with the range ring," Pat said, pointing to the multi-function display. Stone looked: it showed them with a dry-fuel range of about halfway to Reykjavik.

"Oh, shit," he said. "What's wrong?"

"The range ring is wrong," she said. "Look at your fuel gauges."

Stone did, and they showed nearly full fuel. "Well, I believe the gauges, not the range ring."

"Let me try something," she said. She brought up the fuel display and pressed a button labeled "sync fuel." When Stone checked the display, the range ring was back where it should be—well past their destination. He breathed a sigh of relief.

ICELAND APPEARED before them in due course, and they flew the ILS 10 at BIRK, Reykjavik Airport. As they taxied to the ramp, Stone saw a Citation Mustang, like his old airplane, parked there.

"I know that airplane," Pat said. "I did the acceptance for the owner last year. He must be making his first transatlantic, too. Maybe we'll bump into him."

They cleared customs and took a taxi to the Hotel Borg, an old hotel that had been redone in a stylish fashion set on a green square in the center of the city. They had dinner at an Indian restaurant around the corner, then got to bed.

They didn't run into the Mustang's owner, and when they arrived at the airport the following morning, the airplane was gone.

26

MILLIE GOT BACK to the White House after lunch and found Holly in the mess.

"How'd your fabulous lunch go?" Holly asked.

Millie sat down and told her about what Lev Epstein had said.

"So we have a suspect. Lev Epstein identified a likely man who was an assistant professor in the economics department and knows a lot about the Middle East oil industry. He never knew the man's name, but I tracked it down through the department office: Jacob Riis. That's almost certainly made up. It's the name of a famous journalist, social activist, and photographer from the late nineteenth and early twentieth century. That's a good start. How do you want to proceed?"

"I think we should kick it right back to Lev Epstein," Millie said. "He's got the manpower on the coast to run this down, and we don't want to appear ungrateful for his help."

"All right, call him and tell him that, before the day is out, the president will call the director and request his counterintelligence unit to identify and locate Mr. Jacob Riis."

"Perfect," Millie said.

"And tell him to copy us on all his reports."

"Will do." Millie ran back to her desk and called Quentin Phillips.

"Special Agent Phillips."

"It's Millie."

"Hi there."

"The president will call your director today and ask for your unit to be put on finding Jacob Riis. By the way, you know that's not his name, don't you?"

"If it were, he'd be a very old man. How about dinner tonight?"

"Not a bad idea, but I'll have to call you back when I see what the rest of the day is like. Where?"

"Your place?"

"Nah."

"My place?"

"All right, my place, but you have to bring food or have it delivered."

"What time?"

"Seven-thirty, subject to later confirmation."

"Great!"

"Now go tell Lev he's on the case. It'll make you look good if he hears it from you before he hears it from the director."

"Done. See you at seven-thirty, subject to confirmation."

Quentin walked quickly down to Epstein's office. "Please tell him I need to see him," he said to the secretary, Betty.

She buzzed her boss and got him admitted. "Why is he seeing you, instead of your supervisor?" she asked Quentin.

"It looks like I may be reporting directly on this one."

"I'm impressed," she said.

Quentin found Epstein tapping away at his computer. He took a seat and waited.

"Okay," Epstein said, "what now?"

"The president is calling the director requesting counterintelligence to handle Mr. Riis."

"I figured," Epstein replied. "You know that's not his name, don't you?"

"I know who Jacob Riis was."

Epstein's secretary buzzed. "The director, on line one."

He picked up the phone. "Good afternoon, Director."

He listened, nodding to himself. "Yes, sir, I understand. Special Agent Quentin Phillips, a Harvard man." He listened some more. "Right away, Director. Good day, sir." He hung up. And turned to Quentin.

"Betty has a ticket to San Francisco and a travel voucher for you. You're on an early plane tomorrow. Take the night off and collect your reward from Ms. Martindale. The AIC out there will assign a couple of rookies to you. I want to know who and where Jacob Riis is. Get out."

"Yes, sir!" Quentin replied, bolting for the door. "How did you know—"

"I said get out."

As he passed out the door, Betty held out an envelope for him. "Good luck," she said, then went back to her computer.

Quentin glanced at his watch as he ran back to his desk. He had time to pack and get to Millie's place; he could leave for the airport from there. The phone was ringing as he reached his cubicle. Millie confirmed.

MILLIE GOT HOME at six, an unheard-of hour for her. She vacuumed, dusted, and changed the sheets and washed three days of dirty dishes, then she showered, washed her hair, and put on a short dress, not bothering with underwear. She filled the ice bucket with cubes and sat down to wait. Her doorbell buzzed. He was not late. She opened the door to find him holding a suitcase and a briefcase.

"Going somewhere?"

"To dinner," he said, brushing past her and setting down his load. "The food will be here in half an hour. Can I have a drink, please?"

"Sure, what'll it be?"

He took her face in his hands and kissed her. "That, first," he said, "then scotch, rocks." He kissed her again.

"So what's the luggage for? I hope you don't think you're moving in."

"Just for the night," he said. "I've got a seven AM flight for San Francisco, car coming at five." He tried to kiss her again, but she fended him off with his drink.

"Take a slug of that and sit down," she said, pointing at the sofa, then poured herself a scotch and sat down beside him. "So you're on the case, then?"

"I'm in charge of it. They've assigned two agents to me out there.

This is one hell of a break for me, Millie, and I have you to thank for it."

"You certainly do," she said, "and don't you forget it."

They were halfway through their drinks when the doorbell rang. Quentin answered it and traded some cash for two large paper bags of food. "I hope you like Chinese," he said, kicking the door shut behind him.

"Love it," she said. "Have a seat at the table, and I'll make it look like I cooked it."

WHEN THEY HAD FINISHED, Quentin made short work of her dress, which she had counted on, and they flailed about in the throes of first-time sex for the better part of an hour.

When they had caught their breath and her head was on his shoulder, she said, "I hope you don't think we're going to make a regular thing of this."

"Not unless you can get loose to come to San Francisco," he said. "If not, then you'll have to wait until I'm back for it to become a regular thing."

"I don't think I'll be able to manage San Francisco," she said. "I'm too new to the job."

"Then I guess it'll have to be phone sex," he said, kissing her and rolling over on top of her.

27

THREE THOUSAND MILES and a big time change away, Stone and Pat were using their time well, at least until room service interrupted them by turning up with breakfast. They managed to climax everything just in time for the knock on the door.

"The front desk has booked you a cab in ninety minutes," the waiter said, putting the tray and a paper bag with their sandwiches on the bed, then retreating.

They breakfasted greedily, showered, packed, and were downstairs with the bill already paid when the cab turned up. Half an hour later Stone sat in the cockpit, running through the checklist while the fuel truck did its work and Pat filed their flight plan. By the time she got in and closed and locked the cabin door, Stone had his clearance from the tower and had one engine running. Now he started the other. He listened to the latest recorded weather, then asked for a taxi clearance. Five minutes later they were climbing to flight level 410 and headed toward an invisible intersection half-way to Scotland.

At noon, local time, they ate their sandwiches and settled down for the last hour of the flight. Scotland was under its permanent national cloud cover, but Stone sighted land on the synthetic vision display. "Land, ho!" he said.

"I knew you were going to say that," Pat replied.

"It's what you're supposed to say, isn't it?"

"Only if you're on a boat."

"I don't see the difference."

They passed over the northern coast of Scotland a few miles from the closest airport, Stornoway, and they were handed over to Scottish ATC. The controller, for reasons Stone could not fathom, seemed to have an Italian accent. With ten minutes left on their three-hour flight plan they passed Birmingham and were given vectors to the Instrument Landing System at Coventry, but they popped out of a cloud with the airport in sight and made a visual approach.

Stone set down on the six-thousand-foot runway and came to a stop, but he couldn't see a taxiway.

"There's no taxiway," Pat said.

He spoke to the tower and was told to reverse-taxi to the first exit, and when he did so, he found a small group of people waiting on the ramp, among them a large man leaning against a Jaguar XJ sedan. The Mustang they had been seeing along the way was parked on the ramp with nobody aboard.

"That's my client Johnny MacDee," Pat said, nodding toward the man with the car. "You'll like him."

Stone liked him immediately; he was warm, bluff, and welcoming. Pat made the introductions. "Where's your airplane?" Pat asked.

"My CJ4 arrived this morning at the Citation Service Center at Doncaster, north of here, for the pre-buy inspection," he said. "It's going to be there for a week or so. I'm sorry for the delay," Johnny said, "so by way of apology, I've arranged for you to stay in the Jaguar suite at the Taj Hotel, in Buckingham Gate, London. You've already cleared customs." The driver of the car got out. "This is Tony Ridgeway, who will be your driver while you're here. If you want to get out of town, you can ditch him and take the car. I'll keep you posted on the progress of the inspection, and, Stone, the folks here will hangar your airplane while you're here, if you like."

"I certainly like," Stone said. He unloaded their luggage, Tony put it into the Jaguar, and after turning off the airplane's battery and installing the engine covers, they were on their way to London, with Tony driving swiftly and smoothly through the English countryside.

IN LONDON they drove past Buckingham Palace and down a street into a central courtyard, surrounded by the hotel. Stone didn't know the Taj; he usually stayed at the Connaught, but when they were shown into the Jaguar suite, he didn't mind the change. They had two bedrooms, a living room, dining room, kitchen, and study, all of it filled with Jaguar mementos. Their butler, Sergio, explained that Jaguar owned the hotel, and that the company's design department had decorated the suite.

Stone's cell phone rang. "Hello?"

"It's Dino. You alive?"

"Don't I sound alive?"

"How was the transatlantic?"

"A piece of cake. I had a good copilot."

"We're leaving tomorrow night," he said. "We'll be at the Connaught."

"I've got a better idea," Stone said. "Cancel the Connaught, and when you arrive, tell your driver to take you to the Taj Hotel, in Buckingham Gate. We've got a large suite. Trust me, you'll love it."

"Whatever you say, pal. I always unquestioningly accept your recommendations of hotels and restaurants."

"Is Viv going to fly back with us?"

"No, she's staying in London for ten days, doing some work for Strategic Services." Dino's wife, Viv, was a retired police detective, now an executive of the second-largest security company in the world. "I'm going to be here for the better part of a week, too, meeting with various security people in the government. If you have to be back soon, you'll have to fly home alone."

"I don't need that. I'm good for a week here, anyway."

"See you the day after tomorrow, then," Dino said, and hung up.

THAT EVENING, Tony drove Stone and Pat to Langan's Brasserie, an old favorite of his. The place was as crowded as ever, and Stone insisted that Pat order the spinach soufflé as a first course, which came with hollandaise sauce flavored with anchovy.

"I've never tasted anything quite like it," Pat said. "Good choice." They both had the Dover sole and a good bottle of white burgundy. The only distraction was from a drunk at the other end of the restaurant who was singing, dancing, trying to disrobe, and, in general, making an ass of himself. Finally, the management came to his table and, apparently, requested his immediate absence; he was shepherded out of the restaurant by two men from his table, followed by the rest of his party.

"That's a relief," Stone said. "I feel sorry for the people at the adjacent tables."

"I know the guy," Pat said. "His name is Paul Reeves, and he's the owner of the Mustang we've been seeing in our travels. I'm just glad he didn't see me."

"I'm glad, too."

"I have another reason for being glad," Pat said. "One of the two men who got him out of the restaurant was Kevin Keyes."

"Oh, shit," Stone said.

"Who do we call about that?"

"Hang on a minute." Stone got up and walked quickly from the restaurant. As he came out the front door a large, old Daimler limousine drove away from the curb, down the block, and turned a corner.

Stone went back inside and called Robert Miller.

"Miller."

"It's Stone Barrington, Bob. I've just seen Kevin Keyes."

"Great! Where?"

"In Stratton Street, London."

"London, Ontario?"

"London, England. He just drove away with a man named Paul Reeves, an American, who was roaring drunk and got thrown out of a restaurant."

"This I hadn't expected," Miller said. "I haven't issued any international bulletins."

"Keyes may have arrived in England in Reeves's Citation Mustang. They were flying the same route we were, but a little ahead of us. I'm afraid I don't remember the tail number."

"I'll get on it right away. Thanks, Stone." He hung up.

"That's all we can do," Stone said to Pat.

"At least he doesn't know we're in London," she said.

"Maybe it's time to get out of London," Stone replied.

28

QUENTIN PHILLIPS ARRIVED at the San Francisco FBI office and was immediately admitted to the office of the agent in charge, who awaited him with two young agents.

"Welcome to San Francisco," the AOC said. "These are special agents Peter Egan and Annie Rogers, who will be helping you. You're booked into the Fairmont Hotel, a couple of blocks from here, and I've put a car at your disposal. Why don't you go get checked in and have some lunch, then you can drive out to Berkeley."

"Yes, sir," Quentin replied.

"Is there anything else we can do for you?"

"Yes, sir. You could have someone from the office telephone the head of the economics department over there and make an appointment for me to see him this afternoon."

"Certainly. I'll take care of that."

QUENTIN SHOWERED and had a club sandwich from room service, then went downstairs and got into the backseat of his loaned Crown Victoria. Peter Egan was driving, and Annie Rogers was riding shotgun.

"Okay," Quentin said, "anybody got any idea where the University of California at Berkeley is?"

"I got my law degree there," Annie said. "We'll be there in forty-five minutes or so, depending on traffic."

Forty minutes later they parked in a campus lot and walked to Evans Hall and the Department of Economics. After a trip up in the elevator and a short wait, they were ushered into the office of the head of the department, Dr. David Schmidt.

Quentin introduced his group, and they all displayed their credentials.

"Please have a seat over here," Schmidt said, waving them to a seating area, then joining them. "It's been a long time since this department has had a visit from the FBI," he said. "What can I do for you?"

"We're seeking information on and the whereabouts of a Jacob Riis—no relation to the journalist—who we believe taught in this department some years back."

"Ah, yes," Schmidt said. "That was the last time we had a visit from the FBI."

"Can you recall the circumstances?" Quentin asked.

"Only as a spectator," Schmidt replied. "I was too junior to be directly involved. I was an assistant professor at the time, and I came back from my summer break and was introduced to Dr. Riis—or so he called himself. He had been hired as an adjunct professor to teach a class on the economics of Mideast crude oil production, I believe. No one had ever heard of him, but he looked good, especially on paper, and I assume his credentials had been checked, and he made friends easily. He was handsome, charming, well dressed, and seemed to know his subject. Our department head at the time, who is now deceased, was particularly taken with him, and it seemed that he had a future in this department, perhaps even in the university at large."

"How long was he here?" Quentin asked.

"Until the middle of the spring semester," Schmidt said. "Then one day he didn't show up for his class."

"Was he ill?"

"I don't know, he just wasn't here. Dr. Fineman, the department head, had his secretary make inquiries, and someone was sent to his home to see if he was all right. His apartment, in a seedy neighborhood, was uninhabited, and there was no sign that anyone had lived there recently. Dr. Fineman—I got all this from his secretary later—called the police, concerned that he might have come to harm. After a few days they reported back that Dr. Jacob Riis did not exist, at least under that name. The information on his employment application, his academic record and degrees, and his references were either fiction or just lies. Everyone was baffled."

"Had some incident that might have disturbed Riis occurred? Had anyone come looking for him?"

"No, nothing. In fact, he had had dinner with Dr. Fineman at the faculty club the evening before, and they had parted on cordial terms."

"To your knowledge, had anyone contacted Dr. Fineman concerning Riis, or had any information emerged about his background?"

"I don't know," Schmidt said. "His secretary still works here, though, as head of departmental personnel. She hires and supervises non-academic employees. Would you like to speak to her?"

"Very much so," Quentin said.

"Give me a moment." Schmidt went to his desk and made a phone call, then returned. "Her name is Margaret Shames. She's just down the hall—she'll be here momentarily."

A middle-aged woman in a business suit entered the office carrying a file folder, was introduced, and took a chair.

"I've been wondering for years if and when someone from your office would turn up."

"Didn't the FBI visit the department after Dr. Riis disappeared?" Schmidt asked.

"For about five minutes. They said to file a missing persons report with the local police, and we did that, but nothing came of it." She placed the file folder on the coffee table. "This is Dr. Riis's personnel file," she said. "I made a copy for you."

Quentin opened the file and glanced through it.

"I know," Shames said, "it seems perfectly straightforward, even mundane, but then, Dr. Riis didn't have long to establish a record of working here."

"Ms. Shames," Quentin said, "who was in charge of vetting Dr. Riis after he applied for employment here?"

"I was," she said. "I sent out requests for his academic records and letters to his references, and they all came back seeming authentic." She paused for a moment, seeming to remember something. "There was something odd, though," she said.

"What was that?"

"It is my recollection—I had completely forgotten this—that his records and his references came back to us in a single packet that was delivered about a week after my letters went out."

"Do you remember where the packet came from?"

"No, it was delivered by messenger, I think, in a plain file folder."

"Didn't you think that odd at the time?"

"I did, but I was overwhelmed with work at the time, and I never thought to tell anyone or investigate further. His academic record was excellent and his references glowing."

Quentin looked through the references. "Are these fictitious?"

"Not the names—they were all established educators at various institutions. With hindsight, though, their recommendations were fictitious."

"May I have the original of this file and leave the copy with you?" Quentin asked.

"I suppose so, if it's all right with Dr. Schmidt."

"Perfectly all right," he responded.

"Dr. Schmidt, did you have any sort of personal relationship with Dr. Riis?"

"Not really. I had lunch with him two or three times in our cafeteria, but that's it."

"Did he ever reveal anything of himself during those lunches?"

Dr. Schmidt closed his eyes and seemed to concentrate. "He liked cars," he said finally. "Fast cars. He always had an auto magazine with him, and he talked about Ferraris and Aston Martins. He also seemed to like wristwatches. He never seemed to wear the same one two days in a row, and they were all expensive—Cartiers, Rolexes, that sort of thing. That's about it."

"You said he wore expensive clothes. Did you ever chance to see a label in a jacket, or anything like that?"

"No, but with hindsight, I would say that they were tailor-made, not off the rack, as they say. They fit him perfectly, and the fabrics didn't look like those that anyone I knew wore. I didn't think much of it—lots of people have family money or independent means. Still, he had awfully good taste."

"You said he liked cars: Did you ever see what he drove?"

Schmidt thought about it. "No, I don't think I ever saw him drive or get into or out of a car."

"Any references to his background? Family?"

"I believe he said he was from Los Angeles. He didn't elaborate, and I didn't ask."

Margaret Shames left the room, came back with the original file, and exchanged it for the copy she had given Quentin.

On the way back in the car, Quentin looked through the file again, then handed it to Annie. "Send this to the lab and have it checked out—paper types, ink, watermarks—anything they can come up with."

"Sure thing," Annie said.

29

OVER BREAKFAST the following morning, Stone tried to make sense of Kevin Keyes's actions. "There are too many coincidences," Stone said.

"I'll grant you, there are coincidences, but they seem to be easily explained," Pat said.

"Then how come every time we land, Paul Reeves's airplane is just ahead of us?"

"That's because we flew the same route. Lots of owner-pilots want to do a transatlantic, and his Mustang wouldn't be equipped to do it any way but the Blue Spruce route."

"And why would Reeves choose Keyes to fly with him?"

"Paul knew Kevin through me. I think Kevin did a delivery of his previous airplane—a King Air 190. So Kevin would be a logical choice as a backup pilot. Would you have done the flight alone without me or someone like me along?"

"Good point. Then they end up in the same restaurant with us."

"It seemed to be a very popular restaurant," she said. "And I don't think Reeves or Kevin saw us. We wouldn't have seen them if Reeves hadn't been so drunk."

"Would you mind if we left London early?" Stone asked.

"It's not my first trip to London. When would you like to leave?"

"After breakfast?"

"Hang on, Dino's coming this morning and you promised him a room. Let's give it a couple of days. We can make a point of going to places Kevin wouldn't know about."

"You're right."

"Where are we going when we go?"

"To the country. Let me have a chat with the concierge about some reservations."

"Okay, I'm in your hands. I'd like to do some shopping today, if you don't need the car."

"That's all right, I thought I'd visit my tailor and shirtmaker, but I can take cabs for that."

PAT LEFT with Tony and the car, and Stone shaved, showered, and dressed, just in time for Dino and Viv to walk in.

"Hey, buddy," Dino said, slapping him on the shoulder.

"How was the flight?"

"Not bad. I actually got some sleep, but I think I need some more." He looked around. "This is some place," he said.

"A client of Pat's arranged for Jaguar to put us up. They own the hotel."

Viv gave him a hug. "You don't look jet-lagged. How do you do that?"

"I guess our overnight in Iceland helped." Stone showed them to their room and directed the bellman there when he arrived.

They disappeared into their room, and Stone didn't want to disturb them, so he left a note. He took a taxi to Mount Street, in Mayfair, to Hayward, his old tailor. Doug Hayward had passed on some years ago, and the shop had been bought by another, larger tailor. When he walked in, he didn't recognize the place. Doug's cozy shop had been gutted and replaced with a shopfitter's dream—lots of chrome and white walls. Les, Doug's old cutter, was still there, and Audie, who had run the front desk. She didn't seem to have a desk anymore.

He met the new head cutter and looked at some fabrics. He chose a couple of lightweight cashmeres for jackets and was measured, explaining that he'd have his next fitting when they made their regular visit to New York in the spring.

He went to his shirtmaker, Turnbull & Asser, in Jermyn Street and had a look around. They had a shop in New York now, but he liked to visit the old place. He was looking at ties when Paul Reeves, the Mustang owner, walked in, looking hungover.

Stone picked out some ties and pocket squares, and when he had finished, Reeves was gone, to his relief. He went next door to the bespoke department to order some shirts. As he walked in he heard an American accent.

"Barrington? Isn't your name Barrington?"

He turned to find Paul Reeves sitting at a table, poring over shirtings. "Yes. Have we met?"

"Not exactly. I was at Flight Safety at the same time as you, but I was in the Mustang class, and you were in the MC2 group." He offered his hand, and Stone shook it. "I'm Paul Reeves."

"I'm Stone. What brings you to London?"

"Business, ostensibly," Reeves replied. "But I really just wanted to fly my airplane over here."

"Same with me," Stone said. He thought it better not to mention Pat.

"You're in the MC2?"

"Right."

A salesman walked up to the table. "Good morning, Mr. Barrington. May I help you?"

"Yes, thanks." He turned to Reeves. "Have a good flight home." He joined the salesman on the other side of the room, and Reeves left after a few minutes, giving him a wave.

"You know Mr. Reeves?" the salesman asked.

"Not until just now."

"He was asking about you earlier."

"Really? What did he want to know?"

"He said he thought he saw you in the shop next door, and that the two of you had been in flight school at the same time."

"Yes, he mentioned that. We were in different classes, and I didn't meet him at the time."

"Ah."

Stone picked some fabrics and ordered his shirts, for delivery at their New York shop. He went back to the shop next door to retrieve his purchases, and as he arrived there it began to rain, so he added an umbrella to his purchases. He managed to get a taxi in Jermyn Street and went back to the hotel.

Dino and Viv were up and looking refreshed and were ordering lunch. Stone picked something from the room-service menu. "How are you spending your afternoon?"

"I was going shopping," Viv said, "but it's pouring out there."

"It certainly is. It's a shame you missed Pat—she's got our car and driver."

As if on cue, Pat bustled in and greeted everyone. Their butler arrived with her packages.

"I saw Paul Reeves this morning," Stone said.

"Where on earth did you see him?"

"At my shirtmaker's. Turns out we were at Flight Safety at the same time, he for his Mustang, so he knew me."

"Did you meet him there?"

"No, I have no memory of him."

"Very odd," she said.

"Just another coincidence," Stone replied. "They're piling up, aren't they?"

30

MILLIE HAD JUST arrived home from work when Quentin called.

"Hey," he said.

"Hey, yourself. What happened today?"

Quentin related the details of his interview with Dr. Schmidt.

"So our Riis likes fast cars, good clothes, and expensive watches? I guess that's a start."

"Our lab is going through his file from Berkeley. We'll see what they can come up with."

"You think we have any hope of finding this guy?"

"There's always hope. The Bureau is pretty good at finding people who don't want to be found."

"Yeah, even if it takes years—I read about that."

"We're more nimble than we used to be," Quentin said defensively.

"Don't tell me, show me."

"I miss you," he said.

"I know what you miss," she replied with a laugh.

"I miss that, too. In fact, I miss the whole package. I'm still stunned with how great a Chinese cook you are."

"When are you coming back?"

"Not until I've wrung California dry for Dr. Riis. His made-up background says he did his undergraduate work at UCLA. It made me think he might have spent some time there, though there's no trace of a Jacob Riis there, of course."

Millie's cell phone rang, and caller ID said NSC. "I've got a call coming in from Holly. Talk to you later."

"You sure will." He hung up.

"Hello?"

"It's Holly."

"Hi."

"Pack for a week. You're going to London tomorrow morning."

"No kidding?"

"I kid you not. The president is making a European tour to rub noses with the various leaders. She starts in London, and she wants me with her. A car will pick you up at six AM and take you to the airplane."

"Am I going to need anything special in the way of clothes?"

"Sure, bring a riding habit for the foxhunting and a ball gown and a tiara, just in case."

Millie laughed. "No kidding, what?"

"A business suit or two, a nice dress or two, and one knockout dress, in case we get asked out."

"I just heard from the FBI." She brought Holly up to date.

"Well, you've done such a good job of motivating the Bureau, we'll see how you can do with MI6. See you on Air Force One." Holly hung up.

Millie hung up; she jumped up and down for half a minute, making teenaged-girl noises, then she went to pack.

MILLIE'S FIRST IMPRESSION of the airplane was of its enormous size. She had flown aboard Boeing 747s—who hadn't? But she had always entered the airplane through the boarding tunnel and had seen only that part of the interior in which she was seated. Now, after she was deposited at the bottom of the rear boarding steps, the giant airplane loomed over her. After someone took her luggage, someone else checked her name off a list, and someone else passed a security wand over her body, she was surprised at how long the climb up the stairs was. One engine was already running. She was directed past the press and security and guest areas forward to the senior staff area, which was over the wing root. Holly was already there, seated in a large chair, her briefcase open on the floor beside her, reading papers.

"Good morning," Holly said. "What do you think?" She waved an arm around.

"'Spectacular' is the only word I can come up with."

"Good word. The president will be aboard in ten minutes, and shortly after takeoff we'll brief her in her office, up front."

Millie nodded.

"I want her to know every step we've taken in the search for the Three Stooges, which is how I've come to think of our carefully cultivated moles. The twins are Larry and Curly, Dr. Riis is Moe."

Holly looked at her quizzically. "It's just occurred to me that you are probably not old enough to know who the Three Stooges were."

"I saw the movie about them on TV, and I watched a couple of shorts on the Internet, so I've got the general idea."

"I'm always impressed by the depth and breadth of your knowledge," Holly said.

"It's the Harvard education. I have a question."

"Spit it out."

"You mentioned MI6, which is the foreign intelligence service. I would have thought we would be dealing with MI5, which covers the domestic side, like our FBI."

"I suppose we could do it that way," Holly replied, "but the people we're looking for are foreign agents, and anyway, the president already has an established relationship with Dame Felicity Devonshire, the head of MI6, dating back to her time as director of Central Intelligence and before. They're quite good friends."

"I see."

"It's possible a name will come up in conversation: Stone Barrington."

"I think I read something about him in *Vanity Fair*: New York lawyer, murdered wife?"

"That's the one. As it happens, he is a friend of the president, of Dame Felicity, and of mine."

"That's an intriguing set of acquaintances," Millie said. "I don't suppose I should inquire as to the nature of those relationships?"

"You should not. You may recall that his name came up during the presidential campaign, when some people hinted at something intimate between Stone and the candidate. That was entirely false—they are, as the cliché goes, just good friends."

"What about Dame Felicity and you?"

"As another cliché goes, none of your business."

Millie nodded. "Got it." She glanced out a window and was surprised to find that the big airplane was already moving. She had not even heard the second engine start. "I take it the president is aboard," she said.

"The airplane always goes the moment she arrives."

"No waiting around the airport lounge, huh?"

"Not even the VIP lounge. Fasten your seat belt."

AFTER A FEW minutes the seat belt sign went off and a woman appeared in the doorway. "The president will see you now."

They followed her past a large galley and a room that seemed filled with medical equipment, then through a door and into the president's airborne office, which would not have seemed large if it had not been on an airplane. Katharine Lee sat at her desk, tapping the keys of an Apple Air laptop. She looked up.

"Good morning, Holly, and good morning, Millie. Good to meet you. I've been hearing good things."

"Good morning, Madam President," Millie managed to say. She had not blushed since she was twelve, but she felt the warmth rising as she took a built-in seat next to Holly.

"Tell me about the Three Stooges," Kate said. "What's the latest?"

Holly gave her a summary and all the credit to Millie.

"That's a very good start," she said. "I'm having lunch with Dame Felicity Devonshire tomorrow, and I'd like you both there. She already knows about Larry and Curly. Millie, I'd like you to brief her on what we know about Moe."

"Yes, ma'am," Millie said. She and Holly rose and returned to their cabin. To Millie's surprise, one of the three chairs was occupied by the secretary of state, former senator Sam Meriwether, who greeted them cordially.

Pretty good company you're traveling in, Millie, she thought.

31

DINO GOT a phone call in the middle of lunch. He listened, then covered the phone. "We're invited to have dinner with the commissioner of Metropolitan Police," he called to Stone. "You two up for that?"

"Sure," Stone called back.

Dino spoke into the phone again, then hung up. "The Garrick Club at eight o'clock," he said.

"Sounds great." Stone had been to the Garrick Club a couple of times, and he loved the place.

TONY DEPOSITED them in front of the Garrick Club. "I'll be nearby," he said, handing Stone his card.

They walked into the club and up a few stairs. They were met in the entrance hall by a couple.

"Sir Martin," Dino said, shaking his hand. "This is my wife,

Vivian, and my friends Stone Barrington and Pat Frank. This is Sir Martin Beveridge and his wife, Elizabeth."

Everyone shook hands and they went into the main dining room, where the walls were hung with portraits of famous actors and paintings of scenes from various dramas. They were seated at a round corner table and champagne was brought. Sir Martin raised his glass. "To Anglo-American friendship," he said, and they drank. "Now," Sir Martin continued, "we are Martin and Liz—I hope we may all be informal."

Everyone murmured assent, and they drank their champagne.

Stone looked up to see two couples entering the dining room and being seated a few tables away. "Look who's here," he whispered to Pat. One of the men was Paul Reeves.

"Ignore him," Pat whispered back.

The conversation over dinner was about everything but police matters, until, as dessert arrived, their host turned toward Dino. "Dino, I want you to know that I am grateful to your people for alerting us to the presence of a fugitive American, this Keyes fellow, a double murderer, I believe."

"You're very welcome, Martin, but you should know that it was Stone who alerted *my* people to his presence here."

"Then I extend our thanks to you, too, Stone."

"You're welcome, Martin, and you should also know that the man who transported Keyes to Britain in his private jet, however unknowing he may have been, is sitting three tables from us to your right, with his back against the wall. His name is Paul Reeves."

"In *my* club? Good God!" There was irony in his voice. "One can't go anywhere these days without encountering the criminal classes."

Pat spoke up. "I should tell you, Martin, that Mr. Reeves is a respected businessman in his hometown of Dallas, Texas. I've known him for some years, and I'm sure he has no idea that Kevin Keyes is a wanted man."

"However," Stone said, "Mr. Reeves might be helpful in locating Keyes."

"Would you excuse me for a moment, please?" Martin said. He rose and left the room, then returned a couple of minutes later. Nothing more was said of Reeves or Keyes.

THEY LINGERED over port and Stilton for a while, then made their way to the foyer and their coats. Reeves and his party had left five minutes ahead of them. As they said their goodbyes at the curb, where Tony and the commissioner's cars were waiting, Stone heard his name called. He looked across the street and saw Paul Reeves talking to two men, while the rest of his party stood by waiting.

"Stone!" Reeves called again.

"I'll be right back," Stone said to his group. He walked across the street. "What is it?" he asked.

"I'm being questioned by the police," Reeves said, "and I need a lawyer."

"I'm afraid I'm not licensed to practice in Britain," Stone said. "I suggest you be as helpful to the police as you possibly can, and if you are further detained, call the American embassy and ask for legal assistance."

"Thanks a lot," Reeves said acidly to Stone's departing back.

"What was that about?" Dino asked when they were in the car.

"Reeves wanted a lawyer. I told him I'm unlicensed here and to cooperate with the police, and if he needs further help, to call the embassy."

"How do you know this guy Reeves?"

"I met him for the first time at Turnbull & Asser this afternoon."

"And you, Pat?"

"On the recommendation of Cessna, I handled the acceptance of his new airplane from the factory," she said. "His insurance company had recommended me as a mentor pilot when he bought his last airplane a few years ago. That's it."

"Perhaps these coincidences will come to an end now," Stone said. "Dino, we're getting out of here to go to the country tomorrow morning. Pat checked, and you're okay to remain in the suite. We'll be back in a few days."

32

MILLIE WAITED with Holly in a closed road behind the American embassy for the president to come down.

Holly looked around her. "The last time I was here someone had driven a delivery truck into this alley and unloaded a large crate outside that door down there." She pointed. "When the bomb it contained went off, it blew a chunk out of the building and injured people in every direction. There were a couple of dozen dead, too."

Millie didn't know what to say, so she didn't respond.

Her phone rang, and she answered it. "Yes?"

"It's Quentin," he said.

"Pretty early in the morning in California, isn't it?"

"I'm back in D.C. I took the red-eye, and I haven't been to bed yet."

"Anything new?"

"We met with the head of the business school at UCLA yesterday afternoon."

"Did you get anywhere?"

"We didn't have a name or a photograph, but when I described Riis and his taste in fashion and cars, the president's executive assistant, who had been a student at the time, remembered him, and they even had a record of him. He was registered under the name of Harold Charles St. John Malvern, and his record showed him as having studied at Eton and Oxford. He was at UCLA for a little more than a semester, right before he turned up at Berkeley as Jacob Riis. He was British and something of a ladies' man, it seems. Our office out there is trying to run down some of his female acquaintances, and, overnight, his record at UCLA was scrutinized. He was highly recommended by the head of his college at Oxford, the headmaster at Eton, and two members of the House of Lords—all forged, of course, but beautiful forgeries that impressed our lab. The letterheads were real, and the signatures appeared to be genuine, until the gentlemen denied any knowledge of Harry, as he was called."

"Good work!"

"It's ongoing. I'm going to get some sleep now, and I'll call you when I have more. Bye."

A gate at the other end of the alley opened and, led by two Metropolitan Police vehicles and followed by as many black SUVs, the president's limousine pulled up by the door where the bomb had been placed. Holly and Millie waited by the car until the president emerged a minute later, talking on her cell phone, and they followed her into the car.

Millie sat back in her jump seat and was impressed by the foot-thick car doors and the two-inch-thick glass in the windows. She had never felt safer. The president continued her phone conversation until they had driven through an alley behind the anonymous building that housed MI6 and had been greeted at the door by Dame Felicity Devonshire. Only then did she hang up her phone and introduce Holly.

"Holly and I have met, of course," Dame Felicity said. "How are you, my dear?"

"Very well, Dame Felicity," Holly said. "May I introduce my colleague Millicent Martindale?"

Millie was greeted warmly and followed the group into an elevator that opened into an elegant foyer that opened into Dame Felicity's large office, which Millie thought looked more like an Oxford library than a workspace. A gleaming burled walnut table in the center of the room had been set for lunch with handsome silver and beautiful china, but they were first shown to sofas and chairs across the room.

Chitchat was kept to a minimum. "We're anxious to hear about any progress on your investigation of the Eton twins," the president said, "and, of course, we'll bring you up to date on our investigation."

"Madam President, immediately after I received your telephone call and your request, I assigned various groups to the task," Dame Felicity said. She opened a file folder and consulted her notes. "The twins led a sequestered existence at Eton," she said. "They showed no interest in athletics at the school and devoted themselves to language studies and reading. They were cared for by a well-tailored gentleman, not British, but a reasonable facsimile, who took rooms at a local inn, where he received the boys on a weekly basis. They always returned with fresh haircuts and, we suspect, their blond hair retouched at the roots.

"On the pretense of an audit of the Devin Bank by the Bank of England, records were unearthed of the money that flowed through the bank to pay the boys' expenses, which were considerable. The funds were transferred from the Bank of Dahai, in the small sultanate of the same name, which is sandwiched between Yemen and Oman, on the southern border of Saudi Arabia. The funds originated from the account of one Sheik Hari Mahmoud, a shadowy figure who hovered around the edges of the sultan's court, and who was said to own more camels and goats than any man in the kingdom save the sultan himself. The source of this display of wealth was, of course, not livestock but oil, with which the kingdom is richly endowed.

"On the day the boys left Eton, we believe them to have been taken directly to Heathrow Airport, from whence a large private aircraft belonging to the sultan departed for Dahai. There is no record with customs and immigration of the boys having been seen at Heathrow, but they have not been seen anywhere since. An inquiry at the London embassy of Dahai met with blank stares and a denial of any knowledge of the twins. That is where we are at the moment, but we have assets in Dahai, and the investigation is being pursued there."

"Thank you, Dame Felicity," the president said. "Holly, what have you to report?"

Holly recounted the investigation to the point where the head of the economics department at Berkeley was interviewed. "I believe my colleague Millicent has later information to report." She turned to Millie and waited.

"Madam President, Dame Felicity," Millie began, "I have had the most recent report from our FBI agents in California only a few minutes ago. The agent in charge of the investigation, Special Agent Quentin Phillips, informs us that a man using the alias of Jacob Riis was hired by the economics department of the University of California at Berkeley to teach a class on the economics of oil production in the Mideast. He subsequently left without giving notice, and an investigation into his background and references conducted by the university yielded only that his name and credentials were false.

"Armed with only a physical description of the man, Special Agent Phillips called on the head of the business school at the University of California at Los Angeles, a member of whose staff recognized the description of the man in question and identified him as one Harold Charles St. John Malvern, a British subject and a student at UCLA fifteen years ago, who arrived with references from Eton, Oxford, and two members of the House of Lords, and who spent less than a full academic year at the university before disappearing. The FBI has since confirmed that all of these references were forgeries, albeit very good ones. And that is where we stand at the moment. I regret that this information is so fresh that we have not yet compiled a written report, but you will have one before the day is out."

"Thank you, Miss Martindale," Dame Felicity said. "It appears that we all have an intriguing mystery to solve. Now, may we have lunch?" She moved to the table, and her guests followed.

The conversation at lunch was fairly inconsequential, but Millie found it fascinating. She did not speak unless spoken to.

33

STONE AND PAT were downstairs at nine AM sharp, and Tony met them with the Jaguar and turned over the keys. "It's keyless entry, Mr. Barrington, and there's a start button, but your foot must be on the brake. The knob on the center console is the gearshift, foot on the brake again. The engine is a diesel, and the tank is full. There's a GPS navigator built in. Would you like instructions?"

"I can handle that, Tony," Pat said.

Tony handed her some maps. "These might come in handy at times," he said.

The bellman arrived with their luggage and stowed it in the boot. Stone tipped him, thanked Tony for his help, tipped him, and they drove the car out through a short tunnel into Buckingham Gate. Stone followed the road to Buckingham Palace, around the roundabout, and thence to Hyde Park Corner, from where they headed west.

"If you don't mind, I'd like to make a stop," Pat said.

"Where?"

"Stonehenge."

"Put it into the GPS." She did, and a voice began to speak in BBC English.

"Pat," Stone said, "I have to ask you something."

"Anything you like."

"Is there anything you haven't told me about Kevin Keyes?"

"A great deal. I've told you only the basics."

"Is there anything else I should know about him that might be relevant in the circumstances?"

"You're going to have to be more specific."

"It troubles me that he got out of New York and to England so easily."

"Well, as you said, his name wasn't on a flight plan. You told the police about eAPIS, didn't you?"

"What is that?"

"I thought you knew about it. I took care of it before our departure."

"Took care of what?"

"It's a sort of registry. You have to notify the government before you leave the country, and you have to list the crew and passengers, their dates of birth and passport numbers."

"Where did you get my date of birth and passport number?"

"From Joan, where else?"

"And Paul Reeves would have had to file that report?"

"I suspect that Kevin filed it for him, as I did for you. He would have omitted his own name and information, of course, and nobody would know, unless they had a ramp check for documents, et cetera."

"I've never been ramp checked," Stone said. "How would that go?"

"Officials in the relevant country would ask to see your aircraft registration, airworthiness certificate, radio station license, proof of international insurance, weight and balance calculations, plus your RVSM and MSNP authorizations—those were the papers you signed. They'd also check to see that the airplane's flight manual and avionics manual were aboard and that you had the required safety equipment—life raft, life jackets, et cetera, and they would check our licenses and medical certificates, in addition to our passports."

"The only place where anyone showed the slightest interest in any of that was in Iceland, where they asked for our passports, but didn't look inside the airplane."

"That is correct. It's also quite common for general aviation aircraft and crews on the Blue Spruce route not to be checked too closely."

"So if Keyes wanted to bring a gun into Britain, he wouldn't have had any problem?"

"Only if they found it during a ramp check. I mean, the authorities at every stop have the right to make you empty the airplane and unpack your luggage, if they want to."

"Then I'll just assume that Keyes, wherever he is, is armed."

"Look, we've only set eyes on Kevin once, at the restaurant. You've no reason to believe that he's looking for us, so don't let it bother you."

"That's true, but we've seen Paul Reeves *everywhere*, and that bothers me a lot. I can't help having a bad feeling about this."

"Stone, I don't know what to tell you. Do you want to just pack this in and go home? If you want to fly commercial, I'll arrange for a good pilot to fly your airplane home."

"No, of course not. Anyway, where we're going today *nobody* could find us."

"Oh? Where is that? All I can see on the GPS map is a checkered flag in the middle of nowhere."

"That's a pretty good description of where we're going. You'll see, later in the day."

THEY SPENT an hour being amazed at Stonehenge, then continued their trip west on surface roads, which were alternately choked and lightly traveled, things improving as they left the tourist attraction behind. They stopped at a country pub and had a lunch of sausages and mash, then continued. The GPS predicted they would arrive at their destination at five-thirty PM. Half an hour before that, the roads had dwindled in size until they were down to a single track between high hedgerows.

"What *is* this place we're going to?" Pat asked, laughing. "Has anyone ever been here before, except farm animals?"

Now and then they had to deal with a car or farm vehicle going in the opposite direction, which involved one of them reversing into a slightly wide indentation in the hedgerows and allowing the other to pass, or wait for a cow to make up her mind about where she was going. Encouragingly, they saw a sign or two for Gidleigh Park.

"What is Gidleigh Park?" Pat asked. "Some sort of tourist attraction?"

"Sort of, if the tourist is very discerning."

Then they saw an occasional farmhouse and suddenly, they were at a side door of a very large house, in the Tudor style, and their luggage was being taken inside.

Pat peeked into various rooms as they followed their bags down the main hallway, then they were in a comfortable suite. "I think," she said, "that as hideaways go, this one is top-notch. I smelled something good cooking, too."

"Oh, they've won all sorts of awards over the years, including Best Restaurant in Britain, I think."

"Did you find this when you were hitchhiking?"

"No, much later. I met the original owners, Paul and Kay Henderson, in London during their first summer in operation, and I've been back a couple of times since then."

"Will we meet them?"

"No, they retired a few years ago. They live nearby but are, apparently, away for a few days."

They unpacked, and without any discussion, got naked and fell into bed. Soon they were ready for a nap.

34

THEY WERE BACK in the motorcade, headed for the embassy, when the president put away her cell phone. "You did very nicely in there, Millie," she said. "Mainly, you didn't overdo it. It would have been a big mistake to try and make Felicity think you had more than you did, and to your credit, you stuck to the facts."

"I didn't think there was another choice, ma'am," Millie said.

"Quite right."

"You managed to keep your mouth shut at lunch, too," Holly added.

"I had a father who didn't much like chitchat at lunch. He wanted something substantive from me or nothing."

"Sometimes nothing is the best choice," Holly said.

"That was my father's belief."

"Is your father still alive?" the president asked.

"Yes, ma'am, and kicking."

"Retired?"

"Yes, ma'am."

"What did he do?"

"He was an attorney and a Republican, pretty much in that order. He clerked for Chief Justice Burger, and during the Reagan years he worked at Defense."

"During what period?"

"If you're referring to Iran-Contra, right about then. He knew nothing about it, until it hit the news, and when it did, he resigned and went to a Washington law firm."

"Which one?"

"Miller, Chevalier, Peeler & Wilson, as it was in those days—Miller and Chevalier, by the time he retired."

"My grandfather knew Stuart Chevalier," she said. "They were both friends of Franklin Roosevelt when they were all young lawyers. Chevalier had polio as a child and spent his life on crutches or in a wheelchair. I suppose that helped create a bond between him and FDR."

"I'll tell my father about that. He would find it very interesting, if he doesn't already know."

"When will we have more on the Three Stooges?" she asked.

"Daily, I hope. Quentin Phillips is working on it flat-out."

"He works for Lev Epstein?"

"Yes, ma'am."

"He'll learn a lot from Lev. He was considered a candidate for attorney general. He turned down an offer to head the criminal division of the Justice Department—said it was less interesting than what he's doing now. It was a smart move, and Lev is noted for smart moves. I might call on him again before I'm done."

"I've met him only once, but he impressed me," Millie said.

The president was about to speak again when something struck the window on Millie's side. She turned to look at it and saw a thick liquid streaming down the glass, then there was a faint *whoomp*, and the limousine was suddenly enveloped in flames.

"Nobody move," Kate said firmly. "Just sit tight, and they'll deal with it."

Millie sat tight, willing herself not to open the door and run. Only the thought of what else might be out there stopped her.

There were gunshots now, muffled by the thick body and windows of the car, and then a white cloud surrounded the car and the flames went away. Police sirens and whoopers sounded, both near and far away, but approaching.

The car began to move again. They were in Grosvenor Square, no more than a block from the embassy, and the car bumped over the curb and into the park, swerving to avoid pedestrians. The motorcade left the park at North Audley Street and whipped around the embassy to the rear, where someone opened the door and the three passengers were hustled inside and, followed by four Secret Service agents, into an elevator operated by a marine sergeant. They got off on the top floor, and the president led the way down the hall with long strides into the apartment she was occupying. She walked over to the Grosvenor Square side and looked out the big windows.

"Please, Madam President," an agent said, "step away from the windows. We still don't know what else might be down there."

"I'm sorry, Ted," she replied, stepping back, "that was foolish of me. The rubberneck instinct, I suppose."

The building was not as soundproof as the limousine, and the noise from outside continued, minus the gunshots.

"Sounds like the firefight is over," the president said.

The agent stood behind a column and peeked around it at the square. "That's correct, ma'am, the fire trucks are making the most noise now, but the fire is out."

"Did you see anything when we were on the ground, Ted?"

"No, ma'am. I was operating a fire extinguisher while others were shooting. I think the car suffered only damage to the paint."

"It was napalm," Holly said. "Homemade. They must have dissolved Styrofoam in gasoline."

"Yes," Millie said, "I saw it oozing down the window—it was thick."

The phone rang, and an agent picked it up and listened. "One moment, please. Madam President, it's Pres . . . it's the first gentleman for you."

Kate took the phone. "Hi. I'm fine. Everybody did his job, and Holly, her assistant, and I are safe in the embassy. I don't know much, except somebody threw a thick liquid at the car, then set it afire. It was all over in a couple of minutes. I'll call you when I know more. I love you, too." She hung up.

There was a sharp knock on the door, and two more agents were admitted. "I have a first report for you, Madam President," one of them said.

The president sat on a sofa and motioned Holly and Millie to do so, as well, then nodded for the agent to continue.

"There were four young men involved," the man said, "of Middle Eastern appearance. One of them threw an accelerant on the car, then threw a cigarette lighter at it—a Zippo, I believe. The others began firing light machine guns—Uzis. Our people returned fire in kind, and all four of the attackers went down. Three are dead, one is on the way to a hospital."

"Casualties on our side?"

"Two with non-fatal gunshot wounds, both treated downstairs in the embassy clinic, both will recover quickly."

"I don't suppose we know who yet?"

"We may find a note on one of the bodies—otherwise we'll have to wait for someone to claim credit."

"Here are your instructions," she said to the agent. "We will not miss a beat in today's schedule. Everything will proceed as normal, including my speech tonight. Is that perfectly clear?"

"I'm waiting to hear from our commander on that, ma'am—he's surveying the damage downstairs."

"Tell him my order will not change," she said. "Now, let's go downstairs. I want to speak to the agents who were wounded." She stood up and started for the door.

Agents raced to open it for her.

35

AT SEVEN-THIRTY, Stone and Pat went down to the large, ground-floor drawing room for a drink before dinner. The establishment didn't offer Knob Creek, but they had Blanton's, which Stone found almost indistinguishable from his favorite, but without the 100-proof kick. They had taken their first sip when, in the company of a young woman, Paul Reeves entered the room. Reeves spotted them immediately, as Stone did him, and walked over to where he and Pat were sitting.

"What a surprise," Reeves said, not sounding surprised.

Stone didn't rise until the woman joined him. "And what a coincidence," he said, his words seasoned with sarcasm.

"May I introduce Ms. Smith," Reeves said, indicating the woman, who was much younger than he and very alluring.

"Ms. Smith, this is Ms. Frank," Stone said, and sat down.

"May we join you?" Reeves asked.

"Please excuse us," Stone said, "but I've seen quite enough of you for one week."

Reeves turned crimson. "If you're implying that—"

"I've never liked coincidences," Stone said, "and I like them even less now. I would be grateful if we could get through the remainder of our stay in this country without *accidentally* encountering you."

Reeves would not be dismissed. "That's the most outrageous thing I've ever heard," he hissed. "And after you refused to render me any assistance in my encounter with the police."

"Are you aware," Stone said, "that the pilot with whom you crossed the Atlantic is a fugitive from American justice, the only suspect in a double murder?"

"That's nonsense—Kevin Keyes wouldn't hurt a fly."

"So you knew about his fleeing the country and resisted telling the police?"

"I knew it was you who sicced them onto me!"

"You made the mistake, when following me around, of having dinner two tables away from the commissioner of Metropolitan Police and the commissioner of police of New York City," Stone said. "How's *that* for a coincidence? I'm surprised you're not in jail."

Reeves turned on his heel, jerked the arm of his girlfriend, and went to the farthest corner of the drawing room.

Stone was approached by the dining room manager. "Forgive me, Mr. Barrington," he said, "but were you disturbed by that other guest?"

"I was," Stone said. "I noticed that you have two dining rooms. Would you kindly see that that gentleman and I are not seated in the same one for dinner?"

"Of course, and I extend our apologies for the interruption of your evening."

Stone thanked the man, and he left.

"That's the first time I've ever seen you angry," Pat said.

"Stick around," Stone said, "you may see more."

"I don't know what it is with that man," Pat said.

Stone looked at her. "It has just occurred to me that Reeves may be following you, instead of me. Do you have some sort of history with him?"

"I told you, I took delivery of his airplane."

"Was there something else?"

She sighed. "All right, he made a pass at me once—no, twice."

"So, having been rebuffed, he's in hot pursuit of you?"

"I suppose that might have something to do with all these 'coincidences.'"

"The man is a stalker? And I flattered myself to think he was stalking me, when it was you all the time?"

"Stone, I don't know. Now please calm down."

Stone took a deep breath and let it out. "You're right, I'm letting him get to me."

"I should have told you about this earlier," she said, "but I was embarrassed. Paul has been pursuing me, in his ham-handed way, for a month or more. He's been calling my cell phone incessantly, and I had been in my new house for less than twenty-four hours when he was calling there."

"So you have *two* stalkers on your trail?" Stone held up a placating hand. "I'm sorry, I didn't mean to make it sound like it's your fault."

"Maybe it is my fault," Pat said, taking a swig from her drink.

"You know, I've dealt with some crazy ex-husbands and boyfriends before, but I don't think I've ever encountered anything quite like this."

"That makes two of us," Pat said. "I moved to New York to lose both of them, and they found me in no time. I took this delivery job and flew across the Atlantic to get rid of them, and they beat me here."

"I'm beginning to wish that I had brought a weapon," Stone said.

"I'm glad you didn't," Pat said, "or Paul Reeves would be dead by now."

36

WILL LEE GOT BACK from his trip north, where he had spoken to the Oxford Union, and found Kate dressing for bed. He took her in his arms and held her for a moment. "You must be exhausted, after your day."

"Oh, I am," she said, leaning into him. "I think the worst of it was seeing the two agents who were wounded defending me. That's the first time anybody has gone into harm's way on my account."

"There'll be more before you're done," he said. "You have to get used to it." He led her to the bed and tucked her in.

"How did your speech go?"

"Very well, though I started poorly. I was shaken by the attack this afternoon. I warmed up, though, and it got to be fun when they started asking questions." He sat on the edge of the bed and took her hand, but she was already asleep.

MILLIE SWITCHED OFF the TV in her room next to Holly's suite at the Connaught. CNN was wall-to-wall on the attack on the president, and she was sick of hearing about it. Holly's name was mentioned in the reports but she, herself, had been referred to only as a "staffer," and that was all right with her. Her cell phone came alive. "Hello?"

"It's Quentin."

"How are you?"

"I'm perfectly fine, thanks, but how about you? I assume you were the staffer the news keeps referring to."

"I'm just fine, thanks. It was over very quickly, so I didn't have time to get too scared."

"The news said the car was engulfed in flames."

"That's how it looked from the inside," she said. "Kate was marvelous, though, very cool and unaffected. The exciting part was when we drove through the middle of the park in Grosvenor Square, when the driver took evasive action."

"You're calling her Kate, now?"

"That's what Holly calls her in private, so I guess I do, too. Do you have anything new on Harold what's-his-name?"

"Harold Charles St. John Malvern," Quentin said. "The St. John is pronounced 'sinjin.'"

"Sounds almost Arabic, doesn't it?"

"The San Francisco office has located a woman who went out with him when he was at Berkeley, and she'll be going into the office tomorrow with her lawyer for an interview."

"Her *lawyer*?"

"Everybody lawyers up these days—it's TV. Pisses me off."

"Now, now, it's everyone's right to have an attorney present when questioned."

"Yeah, but it's a pain in the ass, especially when someone like this woman isn't suspected of anything."

"Oh, I managed to get a good word about you into a conversation with Kate."

"No kidding? That will be the first time she's ever heard my name."

"It won't be the last," she said. "You can tell your boss she had good things to say about him."

"What did she say?"

"She said he was considered for attorney general, and that he turned down head of criminal investigations at Justice."

"I didn't know either of those things."

"She also said turning it down was a smart move, though I'm not sure why."

"Because he can make more of a difference at the Bureau," Quentin said. "He can actually stop terrorist acts, instead of just prosecuting them after they've happened."

"She said she would think of him again another time. That sounds good."

"It sure does."

"Quentin, how many people at the Bureau are working on finding Harry Sinjin?"

"Fewer than a dozen, in three offices. We're holding this very tight, as you asked us to do. We don't need this to get into the papers or on TV, because he'll disappear into the Middle East somewhere."

"Speaking of the Middle East, I have something else that might help you. Have you ever heard of a country called Dahai?"

"Vaguely."

"It's a sultanate south of Saudi Arabia, between Yemen and Oman."

"Oh, right, the sultan is one of the world's richest men, on a par with the sultan of Brunei."

"Did I tell you about the twins? I can't remember."

"No."

"In addition to Sinjin, there were mysterious twin boys who were sent to Eton under false names. They were educated there, and when they left, they were whisked away to Dahai on the sultan's airplane."

"I'm sorry, but that sounds preposterous."

"Well, I heard a report from the head of MI6 about it today."

"*Directly* from the head of MI6?"

"From Dame Felicity Devonshire herself. Holly and the president and I had lunch with her today. She's got agents tracking the boys. Apparently, they kept to themselves at Eton—no participation in sports or clubs. Their bills were paid from an account at Devin's Bank, and the funds were traced to a Sheik Hari Mahmoud, who is close to the sultan. And this was around the time that Sinjin was in California."

"Verrrry interesting. Lev will be excited to learn about that. Anything else to report?"

"Not for the moment."

"Tell me, are you naked?"

"Near enough."

"One hand is holding the phone—where's your other hand?"

She laughed aloud. "Wherever I want it to be. Good night, Quen." She hung up, still laughing.

37

STONE WAS GETTING out of the shower when Pat walked into the room, her arms full of coats and rubber boots. She dumped them onto the bed. "I think the gum boots are the right size. I compared them to your shoes."

"I'm sorry," Stone said, "but you're way ahead of me. What's going on?"

"We're going for a walk on Dartmoor—that's the moor where we are."

"I know that. I didn't know you did."

"I've been reading about it in the brochure. There are walking trails marked on their map, and we're going to take a walk."

"Okay, I'm up for a walk. Are we going to do it underwater?"

"I don't know if you've heard about this," she said, "but it sometimes rains in this country."

Stone went to the windows and swept back the curtains, letting in a gray light. It was drizzling outside. "I believe you may be right," he said.

"Get dressed, then."

He looked at his watch. "Half past ten. What about lunch?"

"They're packing one for us as we speak."

THEY LEFT the hotel, their lunch in a waterproof backpack worn by Stone, crossed a bridge over a fast-running river, and headed, according to their map, toward the heart of Dartmoor. Shortly, they had left behind the trees in the vicinity of Gidleigh Park and were on a rocky, green, treeless expanse of moor, a place where trees could not thrive because there was too little depth of soil to support them. Gorse grew, though: a hardy shrub sporting yellow flowers, and there was plenty of that about.

The ceiling was low—Stone reckoned a couple of hundred feet—and the mist cut the visibility down to half a mile or so. He was glad he wasn't landing an airplane in the circumstances.

They walked until they began to get hungry, and they looked around for a place where their food would stay dry while they consumed it. They came upon a shed with a bench, which might have been placed there for hungry hikers on a damp day, and took possession of it.

There were smoked salmon sandwiches and potato salad in their pack, and a slightly chilled bottle of white wine, which had had the cork pulled far enough to remove by hand. Pat dug out two plastic glasses and some utensils, and they ate everything and drank most of the wine. There were a couple of slices of moist cake, too, and those went down well.

Then, when they had packed their trash and started to walk again, the moisture in the air turned from mist to drizzle to steady rain in a matter of about two minutes, and they reversed course. Stone found a tweed hat in the pocket of his Barbour jacket, and that kept most of the rain off his head. Pat found a plastic scarf that did much the same for her.

They were proceeding back up the path that had brought them there, which now sported a great many puddles, when one of the puddles exploded a few feet ahead of them. Stone stopped for a count of about one, then grabbed Pat's arm and hustled her behind a large boulder.

"What are you doing?" she asked. "I'm sitting in a puddle."

"Something just happened," Stone said.

"I saw that puddle ahead. Is somebody throwing rocks at us?"

"I hate to put the worst possible slant on events," Stone said, "but I think somebody is shooting at us."

"Shooting what?"

"Bullets. Or, so far, a bullet."

"I didn't hear a gunshot."

"Neither did I, and that especially worries me." Stone got to one knee, took off his tweed hat, put it on a stick, and handed it to her. "I want you to slowly raise this hat on your side of the boulder to a point where it will look as if it's on my head."

Pat took the stick and slowly hoisted the hat, while Stone moved to the other side of the boulder. Something ricocheted off her side of the boulder and Stone stuck his head up on the other side and had a good look around. Then, at the extremity of his vision in the rain, perhaps a hundred yards away, he saw a dark figure running with something in his hands. "Man with rifle," he muttered to himself.

"What did you say?"

"I said 'man with rifle.' I should have said 'silenced rifle.'" He stood up.

"Are you crazy? Get down!"

"He's not trying to kill us," Stone said, "he's trying to scare us. We were a good target on the trail the first time he fired, but he aimed three or four feet ahead of us, and he didn't even shoot the hat off the stick. Anyway, the visibility is no more than a hundred yards or so, and if I can't see him, he can't see me. Let's go." He took his hat off the stick, wrung it out, put it on his head, and started walking.

"I'm staying behind you," she said, following him.

"Good idea."

They were a couple of hundred yards up the trail when he heard a vehicle start, maybe a Land Rover, then drive away until the engine noise faded into the downpour.

After another hour of walking the hotel hove into view, and they shed their coats and boots in the mudroom. Twenty minutes after that they were sharing a soak in a hot tub that was just large enough for two friendly people. Two brandy snifters floated near at hand.

"In a minute, we, the brandy, and the water will all be the same temperature," Stone said, "and the brandy will go down easily."

"And then we'll drown," she said.

"I'm not getting what's going on here," he said.

"Drowning?"

"No, getting shot at, being pursued but not caught. What do they want?"

"They?"

"I'm assuming that Reeves and Keyes are in this together. Is this just an elaborate practical joke, or do they want something? And if so, what? Do you have any idea at all?"

There was a long pause before she said, "No."

38

MILLIE WALKED OUT of the Connaught with Holly, and they turned up Mount Street, with its elegant shops.

"Pity there's no time for shopping," she said.

"Maybe later," Holly replied.

"Are we going on with the president to Paris, Berlin, and Rome?" Millie asked.

"Would you like that?"

"I wouldn't mind, but I think I might be of more use here, working with MI6."

"You have a point," Holly said. "I have to stick with her, since I came along to consult as we traveled, but you're running out of things to do for her."

"I've felt that."

They walked up South Audley Street to the embassy and entered through the rear door, showing ID, even though the guards knew them by now. Holly led the way to a different elevator at the north end of the building. She ran her White House ID through a scanner to summon the car, and to Millie's surprise, they went down a couple of floors before getting off.

When they did there was a door ahead of them marked "No Entry." Holly ran her ID through the scanner again; there was a clicking noise and the door opened half an inch. "Follow me," she said, pushing the door open.

Millie found herself in a suite of offices that did not resemble those on the upper floors of the building. They were smaller, dingier, and less decorated, and there were no windows. Holly led her down the hallway to a corner office and rapped on the door, looking up at a camera screwed to the wall. There was another click.

"Come in, Holly," a deep male voice said.

They went into the room and Millie was surprised to find that the big voice belonged to a pale, skinny man wearing black glasses. "Heard you were in town," he said, standing up to shake her hand.

"Bill, this is my colleague Millicent Martindale. Millie, this is Bill French."

Millie shook his hand and accepted the gesture offering them seats.

"What's up?" Bill asked.

"We've both been traveling with the president on this trip, but we're also working on something with MI6."

"And what would that be?"

"It's not passing through the station," Holly said.

Bill nodded sagely, as if that were neither unexpected nor a bad idea.

"I'm going on to the continent with the president, but Millie is going to stay in London to work with Felicity's crowd and liaise with the FBI—in D.C., not here."

Bill nodded again. "You need anything?"

"Do you have a vacant office where Millie could camp for a while?"

"I've got an officer on maternity leave—she gave birth last night. Millie could sit there, after we've swept it clean."

"Thanks, Bill, that's very good of you."

Bill picked up the phone and pressed a button. "It's Bill," he said. "Please thoroughly clean and secure Vanessa's office, ASAP," he said. "We're going to have a guest with us for a while." He listened for a reply. "Thanks." He hung up. "Half an hour," he said. "Would you two like some coffee while you wait?"

"Sure," Holly said. "Both black."

Bill got up, opened a cabinet door, and came back with two steaming mugs. "How's life at the White House, Holly?"

"Very interesting, but a little crazy."

"Do you miss the New York station?"

"Every time I request something and have to explain why."

"I know what you mean. How's the living in D.C.?"

"I got lucky with an apartment in Georgetown. It was easy to secure. The owner is ex-military and has an antique shop downstairs. The apartment was his, until he moved into a house."

"You wouldn't believe what the housing prices are like here. The city has been ruined for regular folks. Everything's a zillion dollars. I heard a big-time movie star wanted to buy a flat here—nothing terribly special—and the price was fourteen million pounds."

"That's pretty breathtaking," Holly replied. "Who has that much?"

"Arabs and Russians. The Arabs have been around forever, but who knew there would suddenly be Russian billionaires?"

"How about schools?"

"That's pretty easy for us, with the embassy doing the looking. As long as the kids can cut it, they're in. My boy is at Harrow, the girl is at Lady Eden's. They're going to have to learn to talk American again when they get home, or they'll be beaten up daily."

"I was an army brat," Holly said, "so it was pretty easy for me. Every time we moved, all I had to do was either talk southern or talk Yankee, depending."

Bill's phone rang, and he picked it up. "Yeah? Thanks."

He hung up again and got up. "Come on, I'll walk you down there." A few yards down the hall Bill stopped at a cubicle and spoke to a middle-aged woman. "Hey, Tip," he said. "This is Holly Barker and your sublet, Millie Martindale."

Tip shook both their hands. "The place is clean," she said, handing Millie a key card. "I'll help you with whatever you need—don't hesitate to ask. I've got time on my hands with Vanessa out."

"Thanks, Tip. What's the name short for?"

"Tatania—everybody here thinks it's too Russian."

Millie laughed.

"Millie's clearance is White House," Bill said to her.

"Got it."

"Right there," Bill said to Millie, pointing. "I'll leave you to it." He walked back toward his office.

Millie went to the door and unlocked it with her key card, then entered a room larger than what she had expected. She sat down at the desk. "No computer," she said.

"They've locked that up. Ask for a fresh one—better yet, use your laptop. Some things you should know: if you want to receive phone calls from outside, use your cell. Anybody who calls the embassy switchboard will be told they've never heard of you. Your White House ID will unlock secure doors and elevators. You can make outgoing calls on your desk phone. There's a decent cafeteria in the building—Tip will direct you. You never bring anybody down here, of course."

"What about FBI?"

"Is Quentin coming to London?"

"Who knows?"

"If you want to bring anybody down here—on business—give his name and affiliation to Tip, and she'll get him in the computer, just as I did for you. If you want to meet with somebody who's not cleared, ask Tip to get you a room upstairs. The key card she gave you will work there. By the way, don't lose that card—replacing it is a genuine pain in the ass, and you may be locked out of your office for a few hours."

"I can imagine."

"When you leave the station your office will automatically lock for everybody but you and Tip."

"Can I call on Bill for file searches and technical assistance?"

"You can call on Tip for everything. She'll get the necessary permissions. Try not to ask Bill for help, unless it's something Tip can't handle, then don't hesitate to ask."

Millie nodded.

"Do you have any experience with firearms?"

"I grew up hunting with my father. I've had a forty-hour handgun course at SigArms, in New Hampshire."

"Ask Tip to get you a weapon. There's a range downstairs."

"After yesterday, I think I'll do that."

"I took pains to see that your name wasn't mentioned in the press reports of yesterday's incident. That will help, but it's possible you've been seen with me, like during our stroll over here this morning. Tip can always get you a car and driver—don't be shy about asking, even when you leave the hotel in the evening. Request light armor—that means doors and glass, it won't protect you from a large bomb."

"I'll remember that."

"Felicity has assigned an MI6 officer who will be your contact with her and her organization, generally. Do everything through him." She handed Millie a card. "His name is Ian Rattle."

Millie nodded.

"When I leave tomorrow, you can move into my suite—it's leased by our government. If somebody more important than you—that's almost anybody—wants a room, you'll be moved, probably back to the room you're in now. The suite is secure—reinforced outer walls and armored glass. There will always be those who don't like us."

"I understand."

Holly looked at her watch. "I've got to see the president. If you want to do some shopping, now would be a good time. I'll see you around six for drinks in the suite, then dinner?"

"That's fine."

"Have a nice day," Holly said, then left.

Millie gave her five minutes to clear the building, then picked up the phone and pressed a button with Tip's name on it.

"Yes, Millie?"

"Could you find me a weapon? Something light and concealable, maybe a .380?"

"Ten minutes," Tip replied.

"And can you please get me a car and driver, light armor?"

"Twenty minutes, out back," Tip said, then hung up.

39

BEFORE DINNER Stone called Dino's cell.

"Hey there."

"How's your trip going, Dino?"

"Pretty well. I'm wrapped up, more or less, or will be by tomorrow afternoon."

"How about Viv?"

"She's got a meeting on Monday—nothing until then."

"Good. Why don't you meet us tomorrow night at Cliveden? It's a country house hotel near a village called Taplow, in Berkshire—an hour's drive from London."

"I guess we can do that. Are you and I flying from there?"

"From Coventry, an hour's drive north of the hotel. Book us a two-bedroom suite for two nights. The concierge will do it for you and get you a car and driver."

"Hang on." Dino covered the phone and conversed with his wife, then came back. "You're on," he said.

"Dino, did you come over here armed?"

"Nope, didn't figure I'd need it. Have you got some reason to believe I might? Or you might?"

"Forget it. I'll explain when I see you. No need to call back, unless the hotel is fully booked or there's some other problem."

"See you tomorrow." Dino hung up.

THEY WENT DOWN for drinks at seven-thirty and were greeted with a smile by the restaurant manager. "Good evening, Mr. Barrington. You'll be happy to know that Mr. Reeves and his companion checked out this afternoon."

"I'm delighted to hear it," Stone replied. "Was there a third person in his party?"

"Yes, a gentleman he described as his pilot. We were fully booked, so we put him in a B&B up the road and loaned him our Land Rover to get around."

"Ah, that explains a lot. Tell me, when did Mr. Reeves book in here?"

"The day before yesterday," the man replied. "He asked if we knew where you were headed next—said he wanted to avoid running into you again. I didn't know what to tell him."

"Telling him nothing was just fine."

"May I get you something to drink?"

Stone placed their order, and they found a seat by the fireplace.

"What were you and the manager talking about?" Pat asked.

"Paul Reeves. He booked into here the day before yesterday, same day I did, and Keyes came with him. They didn't have room for him in the house and put him in a nearby B&B."

"So it was Kevin that was shooting at us today?"

"Shooting near us."

"Near enough for me."

"Pat, tell me everything you know about Reeves, and please don't leave anything out."

She took a sip of her drink. "I've told you how I know him."

"And now I want to know what you know *about* him."

"When we met he described himself as an entrepreneur," she said. "I don't know about all his interests, but I do know he has some sort of electronics company and that it has to do with security equipment. He also mentioned cattle and oil. It's hard to pin down somebody like him."

"What did he mean, exactly, by 'security equipment'?"

"I'm not sure—that was his description."

"Would it include surveillance equipment?"

"Maybe, I'm not sure he mentioned alarm systems. When I was flying with him, he wanted to go to odd places."

"How do you mean?"

"Well, his airplane was based at Love Field, Dallas, but his trips took him mostly to small towns in the Midwest and the South. He said he chose them for cheap fuel, but that wasn't always the case. He had a briefcase with him, and he wouldn't leave it on the plane. Once I saw him exchange his briefcase for another, identical one, with a man at an FBO. I mean, I was sitting there and saw the guy come into the building. He just walked over to where Paul was sitting and handed him a briefcase, then picked up Paul's and walked away. They didn't even shake hands or say hello. I thought at the time it might have something to do with drugs."

"More likely with cash," Stone said. "If he were in the drug business, he'd have somebody else do the transfers, and they would probably be bigger than what he could get into a briefcase. On the other hand, he could pack a million, maybe two, into a briefcase."

"I see what you mean."

"You say you did the acceptance on his new Mustang. Did you attend the closing?"

"Yes."

"How long did it take?"

"Five, ten minutes. He handed them a check, and they all signed some documents."

"Was there any mention of a lender? Were any of the documents thick, with lots of signatures?"

"No."

"Closing an airplane sale with a lender involved is like closing a real estate transaction where the buyer is taking out a mortgage. There are lots and lots of documents and signatures required. Sounds like he just gave them a cashier's check."

"I think you're right. They didn't call his bank while I was there."

"How many individual flights did you make with Reeves in the new Mustang?"

"Half a dozen, eight. Kevin made some with him, too. His insurance company wanted him to have thirty hours with a mentor pilot, since it was his first jet. I guess I flew, maybe, twelve with him."

"Did he have the briefcase with him on all those flights?"

"Yes, and as I said, he always took it into the FBO with him. I offered to lock it in the airplane once, but he insisted on having it with him."

"How did he pay for his fuel?"

"Always in cash. I noticed that, because it's very unusual where a fill-up is fifteen hundred, two thousand dollars. Most people have dedicated fuel cards to get the best prices."

"As I do," Stone said. "I've never once paid for fuel in cash. Have you ever seen any other client do that?"

"Nope, not once."

"So we know that he's in several businesses and that he prefers landing at small-town airports, rather than large ones, where there might be a police presence, and he pays his personal expenses with cash."

"He paid me in cash. Kevin, too."

"It does sound like drugs," Stone said. "He has someone else deliver, he gets paid in cash. He's probably in some legitimate businesses, so that he can account for the sources of his income. I'll bet the IRS would like to know more about him."

"Are you going to turn him in to the IRS?"

"I don't have enough on him to do that, but if I can get more, then you should turn him in."

"Why me?"

"Because you'd get whistle-blower money—I think ten percent, maybe more, of what they recover from him. That could be useful in establishing your business."

"That's a thought," she said, "but not unless you're sure about what he's doing."

"Maybe I'll do some looking into Mr. Reeves," Stone said.

40

MILLIE GOT into her car, an anonymous-looking British Ford, and introduced herself to the driver.

"I'm Denny," the man said.

"Are you armed, Denny?"

"I have a Glock on my belt and an Uzi in the center console and five magazines for each." He had, maybe, a Cockney accent.

"Then I am reassured."

"And there's a turbocharged V8 under the bonnet and a racing suspension."

"Just what we need to get to Harrods."

Denny drove away in a sedate manner.

Her cell rang, and she looked at her watch. Quentin, maybe. She got a little tingle thinking about him. "Hello?"

"My name is Ian Rattle," a very British voice said. "Do you recall it being mentioned to you?"

"I do," Millie replied. "How do you do?"

"I do better after a good lunch. Will you join me?"

"Where and when?"

"Where are you now?"

"We've just left the embassy."

"Then meet me at the Grenadier, a pub in Wilton Row, behind Wilton Crescent. Your driver will probably know it. Fifteen minutes?"

"Sounds good."

"Right." He hung up.

"Denny, do you know a pub called the Grenadier?"

"In Wilton Row? Of course."

"There, then. Harrods later."

"Righto."

Ten minutes later they came to a barrier with a guardhouse. Denny had a word with the uniformed security guard there, and the barrier rose. They drove into a charming mews and stopped at the end, before the Grenadier.

"I'll be nearby," Denny said, handing her a card. "Ring me when you're ready."

She climbed the steps to the pub and entered a bar, where a dozen or so well-dressed people and a few men in working clothes were having a pint. She looked up to see a tall, slender man beckoning to her from the adjacent dining room, and she joined him.

He was well-tailored, well-barbered, and looked well-heeled. His suit fit, and his shirt and tie were a little offbeat. "I'm Ian," he said, "and you're Millie. Take a pew." He sat her down at a table with her back to the door, and he took the gunfighter's seat in the corner.

"Now," he said, "drink?"

"I'll have a glass with lunch." She picked up a menu. "The gammon steak, please, and chips."

A waitress appeared, and he ordered for both of them, including a bottle of wine. When she was gone he handed Millie a card. "Whenever you need anything from our shop, call me at this number. I can get through faster to anybody than you can going through the switchboard. Half the people who ring that number are crackpots with conspiracy theories." He had a very upper-class drawl, probably an Oxbridge man, she reckoned.

"I know little about you," he said. "Mind a few pointed questions?"

"Not at all. I expect I'll have a few for you, too."

"Fair enough. Give me a sixty-second bio, please."

"Born Washington, Connecticut, small village. Educated in the Montessori school there, followed by Harvard, undergrad and law, followed by White House staff."

"Pretty short."

"I'm pretty young. You?"

"I'm forty. Born Cowes, village on the Isle of Wight, off the south coast from Southampton. Educated Eton, Cambridge. Royal Marines intelligence, then MI6. How long have you been at the White House?"

"Not too long."

"Have you had any intelligence experience?"

"Not until recently."

"Do you *know* anybody in intelligence?"

"My boss was CIA station chief in New York before becoming national security adviser to the president. Her boss was the director of Central Intelligence."

"Do you know Lance Cabot?"

"Slightly."

"Have you ever heard of someone called Stone Barrington?"

That stopped her. "Yes, I have."

"Ever met him?"

"Not yet. How did that name pop into your head?"

"It popped into my computer this morning," Ian said. "He's on a kind of watch list—not the pejorative sort, it's a bit of a compliment, really. His name just pops up when he enters the country, and when it happens, I let my chief know."

"Mr. Barrington and your chief are acquainted, I believe, and he's close to my boss and our president, as well."

"I reckoned something like that."

"So he's in the country?"

"Apparently so, though he did not clear immigration at any port or airport. A friend of ours, retired officer, reported him at quite an elegant country hotel in Devon called Gidleigh Park. Heard of it?"

"No, I've not been to Devon."

"Quite posh, I believe. Can you fill me in on Mr. Barrington?"

"He's a New York attorney with a very prestigious firm, Woodman & Weld. A widower—wife murdered by a former lover a few years back. One son, now a Hollywood producer and director. The dead wife was previously married to the film star Vance Calder, and she left a good deal of Calder's money to Mr. Barrington when she died. That's about it. Oh, when Katharine Lee was preparing to run for president, a group of twenty-one people contributed a million dollars each to get her started. Mr. Barrington was one of them."

Ian winced slightly. "So he is important, then." It wasn't a question.

"Important to your boss and mine," she replied.

"Now I'm left with wondering how the hell he got into the country. Any ideas on that?"

"I'll see what I can find out," she said.

Their lunch arrived, and Ian tasted the wine. "We'll drink it," he said to the waitress.

They ate in silence for a little while. Finally Millie broke it. "Anything new on Larry and Curly?"

He looked at her askance. "Are we talking about the Three Stooges?"

"The twins," she replied. "Moe is the one we're tracking in the States."

"Ah, the twins."

"Did you know them at Eton?"

"I was at Oxford when they were at Eton."

"Does your service have any assets in Dahai who could be of help?"

"I can neither confirm nor deny that. Suffice it to say that they are scratching around the edges of the sultan's court for word of the boys. Optimism is high."

"It would seem that the boys were trained to be British, and that Moe, as we call him, was trained to be American."

"Yes, it would seem so. Worrying, isn't it? It's so much easier to spot them when they wear turbans and costumes and speak in tongues."

"Isn't it? Easier, too, when they have names and photographs and fingerprints in our databases."

"That would be convenient, yes. But someone has gone to a great deal of trouble and expense over a period of many years to hide those things from us, and I find it very annoying. Perhaps you and I and your FBI friend can do something about that."

"It's why I'm here," Millie said. Her cell phone rang. "Hello?"

"It's Quentin. We have a photograph of Moe."

41

THEY WERE at mid-morning before leaving Gidleigh Park, after a hot breakfast and hot sex. Pat's packing took longer than Stone thought it should.

They loaded the car, paid the bill, and made their way back up the single track between the hedgerows, not meeting any opposing traffic on the way, and were soon on the motorway, headed north, then east. They stopped at a restaurant recommended by their GPS, for lunch, and then they pulled up in front of Cliveden House, a huge residence going back to the eighteenth century, lately a hotel. They had barely gotten out of the car when Dino and Viv arrived in a chauffeured Mercedes.

"Holy shit," Dino said quietly, looking at the imposing house, "I hope the concierge didn't take the whole place for us."

They entered an enormous hall furnished with scattered furniture, and with a huge fireplace at one end. An assistant manager registered them and delivered them to their suite, and their luggage was not far behind. Stone poured them all a glass of sherry from a decanter on the coffee table, and they relaxed.

"This is wonderful, Stone," Viv said. "Can we live here, please?"

"Sure, if Dino can convince the mayor he can run the NYPD from here, and he can get a bill through the city council to pay for it."

"Shouldn't be a problem," Dino said.

"I saw something about Lord Astor in a brochure downstairs."

"This was his home, and his wife, Nancy, who was American, became a member of Parliament. This house was the center of an amazing group of characters called the Cliveden Set, which included people like George Bernard Shaw, Charlie Chaplin, and a few Mitford sisters, one of whom was married to Sir Oswald Mosley, the British fascist who was imprisoned during World War Two to keep him out of mischief. Also a part of the crowd was John Profumo, minister of Defence at the time, who met a young woman here called Christine Keeler, a sort of part-time prostitute, I think, who was also having an affair with the Soviet military attaché. Between the three of them, they nearly brought down the government. Profumo lied to a parliamentary committee about it and got sacked for his trouble."

"I'm not sure I can keep that pace," Viv said. "Dino will have to trade me in on a racier model."

"You'll do," Dino said.

"Now all that remains," Stone said, "is to wait for Paul Reeves to show up."

Viv and Pat excused themselves to unpack, and Dino poured himself and Stone another glass of sherry. "So," he said, "bring me up to date on Reeves."

Stone told him about the events of yesterday.

"I'd better call Sir Martin and give him the latest sighting of Kevin Keyes," Dino said.

"They may have already left the country by now. We last saw Reeves's airplane at Coventry when we landed. It might be a good idea to alert U.S. Customs that they're on their way home. They have to file a notice of when and where they'll cross the border and clear customs. Keyes won't put his name on it, but Reeves will, and that will be a good excuse to throw a net over both of them."

"I'll call everybody," Dino said.

"What bothers me is I think Pat is still holding out on telling me the whole story. I've gone at her three or four times, and on each occasion she's told me a little more, but I still don't think I have it all, and I'm worried that she won't confide in me."

"What do you think she's hiding?"

"If I knew that, I wouldn't be worried."

"When are you and I headed back?"

"The day after tomorrow. Pat will drop us at Coventry Airport, then we'll go on to Reykjavik from there, about a three-hour flight. Pat will drive on to the Cessna Service Center north of there, where her client is having the pre-purchase inspection done on his new airplane."

"Will she take the same route back as we do?"

"No, she's got a twenty-five-hundred-mile range with the CJ4, so she can refuel at Shannon, then go nonstop to Newfoundland."

"Alone?"

"No, her client is going along, because he has to train for his new airplane in Wichita. She'll deliver him there, then fly commercial back to New York."

"What about Reeves? What route will he take?"

"The Blue Spruce route, like us. His airplane has less range than mine."

"And where will he clear U.S. Customs?"

"Bangor, Maine, I guess."

"So that would be the place to interrupt his trip and bag Keyes?"

"I guess. He has to clear customs at the nearest airport of entry after crossing the Canadian border."

Dino got out his phone and started making calls.

They had dinner in the main dining room, and Stone kept expecting to see Paul Reeves stroll in.

"Relax, Stone," Dino said. "You're looking way too nervous for you."

Stone ordered another bottle of wine.

42

MILLIE GOT EXCITED. "That's great news. Can you e-mail it to me?"

"Already done," Quentin said. "Mind you, the photo is fifteen years old, and it's not perfect, but our lab can do some work on it to help bring it up to date."

"And when will we see that?"

"Later today, maybe tomorrow. I've put a rush on it."

"That's terrific. I'll pass it on to MI6. Talk to you later." She hung up and turned back to Ian. "That was my FBI guy. He's turned up a fifteen-year-old photograph of Moe." She went into her phone and found the e-mailed photo. "There," she said, holding it up for inspection. The photo showed a young couple sitting on a stone wall with some mountainous scenery in the background.

Ian examined it closely. "Not bad," he said. "Pity we can't judge his height, since he's sitting down."

"I'll e-mail it to you," she said, and did so, copying Holly.

"I'll send it on to our wizards and see what they can tell us from it."

"The FBI is doing the same."

Ian asked for the check, and Millie excused herself and went to the ladies' room. Once there, she called Holly.

"What's up?"

"Quentin just called. He's found a photo of Moe, and I've e-mailed it to you."

"Just a minute," Holly said. "Okay, got it."

"Both the FBI and MI6 are working on it. I'll copy you on any results."

"You do that."

"Something else: I've just had lunch with Ian Rattle, from MI6, and he's concerned about Stone Barrington."

"Why on earth would Stone concern him?"

"Stone is on some sort of watch list that alerts MI6 when he enters the country."

"That sounds like Felicity wanting to know when he's here, for her own purposes. Is he in the country?"

"They got word that he was reported at a country inn in Devon, but he's not shown as having entered at any port or airport of entry."

"Let me call you back," Holly said.

Millie used the toilet and was freshening her makeup when Holly called back. "I talked to Stone's secretary. Here's what happened: Stone flew his own airplane across the Atlantic and landed at Coventry Airport. They have customs there, but apparently didn't check him in. That sort of thing happens with general aviation."

"Okay, I'll pass that on."

"Anything new on the Stooges from Ian?"

"Not yet."

"Where did Rattle take you for lunch?"

"A pub called the Grenadier, in Belgravia."

"I know it well. Word has it, Rattle is something of a rake, so watch yourself."

"I'll watch *him*," Millie said. They said goodbye and hung up, and she returned to the table. "I have some news on Stone Barrington," she said.

"Fire away."

"He flew his own airplane across the Atlantic and landed at Coventry. Apparently, the officials there didn't bother checking him in."

"Ah, makes perfect sense. I'll pass that on."

"To Dame Felicity?"

"To a list of people who will want to know."

He walked her back to her car, which was waiting nearby. "I see you've got Denny for a driver," he said.

"You approve?"

"He's good. He'll get between you and any passing bullet, and he's a damned good shot."

"I'm delighted to hear it. Can I drop you anywhere?"

"Where are you headed?"

"To Harrods."

"I'm going the other way. I'll find a taxi."

She shook his hand, got into the car, and Denny drove her away.

"Interesting companion, your lunch mate," Denny said.

"He speaks highly of you, too."

"I saved his arse once. Don't be misled by the good suits and haircut. Ian is very good at what he does, and that includes killing, when he needs to. He's almost as good a shot as I am."

"I'll keep that in mind."

"He's honey for the honeybees, too, if you catch my drift."

Millie laughed. "I believe I do."

She spent two hours in Harrods, then Denny drove her back to the Connaught, where a fax from Quentin awaited her.

"The lab ran Moe through our facial recognition software and came up with zilch," he said. "Attached are two versions of how he might look today."

She looked at the photos: one with a receding hairline and a little more weight; one with a short beard. She studied them carefully, committing them to memory.

Holly arrived around six, and they ordered drinks.

"I just got this fax from Quentin," she said, handing her the report.

She read it carefully. "Let me see the photographs," she said.

Millie handed them to her. She studied both carefully. "Holy shit," she said.

"What?"

She handed Millie the photo with the beard. "This one. I saw him at a party in D.C. the night of the Inaugural Ball. I thought he looked familiar, but I couldn't place him. Someone told me he was some sort of official at the Saudi embassy."

"Could it have been the Dahai embassy?"

"Maybe." She got out her secure cell phone and called a number.

Millie waited to see who she was calling.

"Lance? It's Holly." She gave him a description of the man, while Millie photographed the image and e-mailed it to Lance Cabot.

"Do you know him?"

"No," Lance replied.

"I saw him at a big party in D.C. on inaugural night. I remember he had a good-sized diamond in one ear, I'm not sure which."

"I'll get somebody on it."

"We need a name and a location," Holly said. "This one is very important."

"We'll do our best," Lance said.

Holly hung up. "Progress at last," she said.

43

HOLLY WAS GONE when Millie woke up, and after breakfast she busied herself with moving into the suite. The maids had just left after changing the bed and cleaning when her cell rang. "Hello?"

"It's Ian. Sleep well?"

"It's one of the things I do best."

"Anything new from the FBI?"

"Yes. They were unable to match the photograph of Moe with any existing face in their database, but they came up with two drawings of how he might look now. I showed them to Holly Barker last night, and she believed she recognized one of them as someone she saw at a party in Washington on the night of the inauguration of the president. He may be an official at either the Saudi or the Dahai embassy in Washington. It's being checked out."

"I hope that's true—it would be very helpful."

"What did your people come up with?"

"Nothing on Moe. However, I've been chatting with some of our people who have served in Dahai in the past, and one of them provided an interesting rumor."

"I love a good rumor."

"Well, hang on to your hat. The rumor is that a favored woman in the sultan's harem gave birth to twin boys around thirty years ago."

"That works, doesn't it?"

"It does. Apparently, there was great excitement surrounding the births. Some adherents of Islam believe that twins are a special gift from God and that they have unusual powers."

"What sort of powers?"

"I don't know, and I haven't been able to find out."

"Does Dahai keep birth records?"

"Yes, but we don't know yet if members of the sultan's household would be registered. It's being checked. Another thing—the woman who was the mother was Egyptian and had very light skin. Most people took her for a European."

"This all fits with the boys from Eton," she said, "and with the special transportation provided for them when they left. Surely not even a sultan would send a large private jet for non-royals of no particular distinction. But if these boys are his sons . . ."

"Yes, it all ties in very neatly, and it's not the sort of thing one could make up, is it?"

"What we need now is an asset in the sultan's household. Does MI6 have one of those?"

"If we did I would deny it."

"Are you denying it?"

"Yes, but that doesn't tell you anything, does it?"

"I suppose not."

"I believe the next step is to find out if your people down at that place in Virginia have such an asset."

"If they did," Millie said, "I think their attitude would be much the same as yours."

"You said your boss was an old Agency hand—maybe they'll tell her."

"She left this morning to fly with the president to Paris, Berlin, and Rome."

"I believe they have telephone service on Air Force One, do they not?"

"I'll call her. You go and rattle the cage of your tech guys. I want to know if they were able do anything with that photograph."

"Roger, over and out." Ian hung up.

Millie called Holly and got her voice mail. "Call me, as soon as you can," she said.

Less than an hour later, Holly called. "We're in the motorcade to the Élysée Palace," she said. "What's up?"

Millie passed on the rumor regarding the twins. "Can you find out if the Agency has an asset in the sultan's household? We need to know a lot more."

"I'll call Lance," Holly said. "Gotta run, we're passing through the gates of the palace." She hung up.

Millie had nothing to do for the rest of the day, so she went shopping again.

Two hours later, while sharing the backseat of her car with half a dozen carrier bags, her cell phone rang.

"Hello?"

"I have Lance Cabot for you," a woman said. "Can you accept the call?"

"Yes."

"Is that Millicent Martindale?" a smooth voice asked.

"Yes, it is."

"Are you on a secure line in a secure location?"

"I'm on my White House cell phone in an embassy car, in London," she replied. "Is that secure enough?"

"That will do," Cabot said. "This is the first time we've spoken, is it not?"

"It is."

"I trust it won't be the last. Tell me about this rumor you've heard. It's from our friends at MI6, I believe?"

"It is." Millie explained about the twins.

"I don't believe our British friends have enough imagination to invent that," Lance said. "I'll see what assets we might have in place."

"You might check with former or retired assets," Millie said, "since the births would have been around thirty years ago."

"Very good. Now, about the stooge you call Moe: we have ascertained that the photograph—the one with the beard—may be of the chargé d'affaires at the Dahai embassy in Washington. His name is Ali Mahmoud, and he's quite the social animal around town."

"That's very interesting," Millie said, "because the twins, while they were at Eton, received regular funds from an account at the Devin Bank in London belonging to a Sheik Mahmoud, of Dahai."

"Very interesting, indeed," Lance said. "Perhaps you should ask your friend at the Bureau to begin surveilling him."

"I'll do that."

"You should ask him for maximum surveillance, which means by every available means."

"I'll ask for that."

"When do you return to Washington?"

"I don't know. That will depend on what I can get done here."

"It sounds as if you're getting quite a lot done. When you come back, perhaps you should come out to Langley for lunch and meet some people."

"Thank you, I'd like that."

Lance hung up.

"Denny," she said to her driver, "I'm starving. Where can I go for lunch?"

"Do you like Italian food?"

"Very much."

"Well, then, it's La Famiglia." He made a quick U-turn and aimed at Chelsea.

44

DENNY PULLED UP outside a modest-looking restaurant near World's End, in the King's Road. "La Famiglia," he said. "I booked you a table in the garden. Alvaro Macchione, the owner, died a few months ago, but it's still up and running, and the food has held up, too."

"Thank you, Denny." He opened the door for her, and she got out and went inside. She was wondering how chilly it might be in the garden, but she was led through the restaurant and into a space with a glass roof and heaters. It was quite comfortable. The menu was very large, but she was hungry and got through it in a hurry. She ordered the bruschetta and the roasted wild boar. She had never before had that.

The place was only half full, and she didn't feel crowded, so she called Quentin at home.

"Hello?" he said sleepily.

"Aren't you up and about yet?" she asked. "I've already consulted with MI6 and the CIA."

Quentin groaned. "You'd better have something good," he said.

"How about this: Moe—Harold Charles St. John Malvern—has been made."

"You're kidding me. How did you do that so fast?"

She explained the process she had been through. "His name is Ali Mahmoud, and he's the chargé d'affaires at Dahai's embassy in Washington."

"Jesus, that's troubling," Quentin said.

"You have a point—too close to home."

"Damn straight."

"All the more reason to start surveilling him pronto. I'd like maximum surveillance, please, of every sort. I'm told the FBI is good at that."

"We are indeed. I'll have to get Lev Epstein's approval, but he'll go for it."

"Will you get back to me the minute you've talked to him? I need to know that the work is under way."

"All right. He gets in early, so I'd better get to the office. I'll call you." He hung up.

She had barely hung up when some Americans were seated next to her—two men and a woman. They seemed to have had a couple of drinks before arriving, and it was now one-thirty PM. They immediately ordered a bottle of wine, and continued to talk loudly, especially a red-faced man who looked as if he'd done a lot of drinking in his day—maybe on this day.

She finished her lunch and asked for the check. Then she heard a familiar name.

"So," the younger and beefier of the two men said, "how are you going to handle Barrington?"

"I have already handled him," the other man said, and they laughed loudly again.

Millie paid her bill, then went back into the restaurant and found the headwaiter. "Could you please tell me the names of the people at that table?" She nodded toward the garden door. "I think I may know them."

The headwaiter consulted his reservations book. "The table was booked in the name of Reeves," he said. "I'm not sure which gentleman he is."

"Thank you. It was an excellent lunch." She went back to the car, where Denny was waiting with the door open.

"Where to?" he asked.

"Oh, I don't know."

"National Gallery? Tower of London? Anything touristy you haven't done?"

"Just back to the Connaught, I think." She dialed Holly's cell number. It was answered immediately.

"What have you to report?" Holly asked.

Millie told her about the conversations with the new men in her life. "Quentin has to get Lev's authorization to set up the surveillance—they'll get back to me. And Lance will call me back when he's looked into the sultan's household in Dahai."

"Good. We're making progress."

"Something odd just happened."

"Uh-oh."

"At lunch today I overheard some Americans talking at a table next to mine."

"What about?"

"Barrington. I suppose that could be Stone?"

"It's not a very common name. What did they have to say?"

"One of them asked the other, 'What are you going to do about Barrington?' And the other replied, 'It's already done.' Then they had a good laugh."

"Any idea who they were?"

"The table was booked in the name of Reeves."

"Doesn't ring a bell with me. Write down a number." She dictated. "That's Stone's cell number. Call him and tell him about it. I'm too busy right now."

"Where are you?"

"At the Hôtel de Marigny. It's sort of the guesthouse for the Élysée Palace."

"What's it like?"

"Palatial. Got to run." She hung up.

Stone, Dino, Viv, and Pat were finishing lunch at the Waterside Inn in Bray, a spectacular French restaurant in the village of Bray on the banks of the upper Thames River, not far from Cliveden, when his phone rang.

"Hello?"

"Stone Barrington?"

"Speaking."

"My name is Millicent Martindale. I work for Holly Barker."

"You're a lucky woman, then," he said. "How is Holly?"

"She's very well. She's with the president in Paris right now, and she asked me to call you."

"Oh?"

"Are you still in England?"

"At the moment I am in surroundings so French that I could doubt that."

"MI6 said you were in the country."

"How the hell would they know that?"

"Apparently, they know when you enter and leave Britain, but I understand that you flew yourself this time, so somehow you slipped past them. Someone at a country hotel spotted you—a retired MI6 officer."

"Well, that's fairly creepy," Stone said.

"It gets creepier. I was at lunch today at a restaurant called La Famiglia . . ."

"I know it well."

". . . and I was seated next to two men and a woman—all Americans—and I heard your name mentioned."

"In vain?"

"Maybe." She told him about the overheard conversation.

"Well, he's wrong, I haven't been taken care of. Any idea who they were?"

"The table was booked in the name of Reeves. That's all I know."

"Swell," Stone said with some feeling.

"I hope that's not too upsetting. Holly felt you should know."

"And I'm glad you called. Thank you very much. Can you describe the two men?"

"One was in his mid to late thirties, very beefy-looking. The other was, maybe fifty, florid complexion."

"I believe I know them," Stone said. "How long ago did you see them?"

"I left twenty minutes ago. They had just sat down for lunch."

"That's good to know," Stone said.

"I'm based at the American embassy for a few more days. Is there anything I can do for you in London?"

"I don't think so, but I'll be in touch if anything comes up."

He hung up. "Another coincidence," he said to his party.

"Reeves again?"

Stone nodded. "This time in a London restaurant, sitting next to one of Holly Barker's people." He told them about what she had overheard.

"You've already been taken care of?" Dino asked. "Is that what Reeves said?"

"Apparently. Do I look taken care of to you?"

"Nope."

"Then that must lie in my future," Stone said.

"I think you'd better be careful until we're out of the country," Dino said. "And right now, I'm going to have a look around this place."

"I think you should call Sir Martin and tell him that Reeves and Keyes are at La Famiglia, World's End, Chelsea."

"Right." Dino got up and left the table.

"Well," Stone said, having some more cheese, "I'm not going to let this ruin a good lunch."

45

QUENTIN PHILLIPS got into the office an hour before hardly any-body else did, and he found Lev Epstein at his desk.

"Good morning," Quentin said.

Lev looked up. "What the hell are you doing here at this hour, sucking up?"

"I suck up only when absolutely necessary. I've heard from Millie Martindale in London: Moe has been made and located."

"You're shitting me."

"I shit you not. Our lab couldn't match the snapshot to anybody in our database, but they did two drawings of how he might look now. Holly Barker made one of them as somebody she saw at an inaugural party. His name turns out to be Ali Mahmoud, and he's the chargé d'affaires at the embassy of Dahai."

"*I* know that son of a bitch! I've had dinner with him at a big party! *He* is Moe?"

"He is also Jacob Riis and Harold Charles St. John Malvern."

"Let this be a lesson to you on the importance of even tiny pieces of evidence. If that snapshot hadn't been taken fifteen years ago, we might never have found the bastard."

"The White House has requested maximum surveillance on Mahmoud around the clock. Shall I move on that?"

"What's your idea of maximum surveillance?"

"Eight four-man teams working around the clock, a dozen different vehicles and disguises for them, full electronic surveillance on office and home, fixed and mobile."

"And how much is that going to cost?"

"Half a million dollars for the first week, maybe three hundred thousand a week after that. Can you authorize it?"

"I can *get* it authorized."

"Today?"

"This morning!" He opened his laptop and started typing. "I'm calling an agency-wide emergency conference, everybody from assistant director up."

"Hang on a minute, Lev."

Lev stopped typing. "Don't slow me down."

"We promised the White House absolute secrecy, closely held. You're talking about at least three dozen people when you include deputies and secretaries."

"My boss is in South America," Lev said. "There's nobody between me and the director." He picked up his phone and dialed a number from memory. "Good morning, sir, it's Lev Epstein. I'm sorry to have to trouble you at home." He didn't apologize for the hour. "I need an immediate appointment with you. It's an emergency. Let me brief you when you come in. How long? Thank you, sir." He hung up. "You and I are seeing the director at eight-thirty. We've got less than an hour to put our briefing together."

"Right."

"You put together a list of agents and equipment you need, and a list of tech people, as well. We'll meet in my conference room at ten AM. Oh, request a fully teched-out conference room in the basement, in my name. You ever done a stakeout, Quentin?"

"No, sir."

"It's going to bore the ass off you."

MILLIE WAS STRETCHED out on the bed in her suite, trying to make sense of a cricket match, when her cell went off. She muted the TV. "Hello?"

"It's Quentin. Listen fast, I'm on the run."

"Go."

"Lev and I just met with the director, and it's a go. We're starting a meeting of the team in five minutes. They'll be on the job by noon. It's a maximum effort."

"Go, then!"

"Bye." He hung up.

Millie punched the air. "Yes!" she screamed. She called Holly.

"Yes?"

"Big news—the Bureau will be all over Moe by lunchtime in D.C. Maximum effort."

"That's great news, Millie. Congratulations on moving it so fast. Right now, I'm half dressed for a state dinner that started ten minutes ago. Gotta go." She hung up.

Millie called Ian Rattle.

"Hahlew," he drawled.

"The FBI has just uncorked a maximum-surveillance effort on Moe. I thought you and Dame Felicity would like to know."

"She will be very pleased to hear it," he said, "as am I. Will we get to watch any of this in progress?"

"Ian, it's surveillance, not a raid. What's to watch?"

"Oh, all right. When you do make a move, please remember that Dame Felicity becomes orgasmic when watching an operation in real time. It makes her feel omniscient, I think."

"Whatever turns her on," Millie said, then hung up.

AFTER DINO had cased the neighborhood to his satisfaction, checking out the rowers, the fishermen, and the swans on the Thames, they got into Pat's borrowed Jaguar and left the restaurant. Stone drove quickly, turning down country lanes, seemingly at random.

"You going anywhere in particular?" Dino asked from a comfortable rear seat.

"Looking for a tail," Stone said. "It bothers me that Reeves says I'm already taken care of—makes it sound like I missed it."

"I'm going to take a nap," Dino said. "I'm unaccustomed to port at lunch." He thought about that. "I could get used to it, though." He lay back on the cushioned headrest and closed his eyes.

Stone loved these country roads: they were beautifully engineered, perfectly drained, and always in good repair. He kept an eye on the GPS navigation display to be sure he was always headed in the general direction of Cliveden.

"You drive beautifully," Pat said. "Especially right now—and with the steering wheel on the wrong side!"

"Thank you," Stone said. "I hope we don't meet too many vehicles coming the other way. My instinct would be to go left."

"And the instinct of the oncoming driver would be to go right," she replied. "And that would not be a good thing."

Stone narrowly missed a baker's van going the other way.

"Stone," Pat said, "what do you think Paul Reeves meant when he said you had already been taken care of?"

"I don't know," Stone said. "And I don't want to know. But I have a feeling I'm going to find out."

He drove on.

Back at Cliveden Stone was given a hand-delivered note on very heavy paper. He read it and turned to the others. "I'm sorry," he said, "but I can't be with you for dinner, and I've been asked not to tell you why. I hope you will forgive me."

46

MILLIE HAD JUST given up on the cricket match when Ian Rattle called again. "Are you up for a last-minute invitation?" he asked.

"If it's a good enough invitation," she replied.

"Dinner at Dame Felicity's."

"Dame Felicity's what?"

"House."

"Sounds nice."

"I hope you brought a good dress. It's black-tie."

"I did, and I've bought two more since I've been here."

"Do I get a choice?"

"I'll do the choosing, thank you."

"I'll pick you up at six-forty-five. May we meet downstairs at that hour? Dame Felicity is a stickler for punctuality."

"I will be on time. See you then." She hung up, emptied two shopping bags, and hung up the three competing dresses for comparison. She awarded the prize to a simple black one that would show off just enough of her ample breasts, and with a slight flare just above the knee. It had not required alterations. She checked her watch, called downstairs and asked the concierge to send up a manicurist in an hour, then headed for a shower and shampoo.

MILLIE WAS STANDING under the outer canopy at the front door, all shiny and new, when a steel-gray Jaguar pulled up front. The doorman helped her into the rear seat next to Ian.

"You look perfectly marvelous," he said, as the car moved away and into Mount Street.

"Where does Dame Felicity live?" she asked.

"I'm afraid you may not know that," Ian replied, "and if you figure it out, you are sworn to secrecy. Or I can blindfold you."

"I swear," she said. They were there in twelve minutes, and she knew it immediately. It was a house in Wilton Crescent, one that backed up onto Wilton Mews, where the Grenadier was situated.

"You know it, don't you? I can tell by your look."

"Well, of course I know it, we had lunch right behind it."

They got out of the car and rang the bell. "I believe this was formerly the home of Edward Heath, a prime minister of his day," Ian said. There was no more time for history, because a uniformed butler admitted them, and as they entered the drawing room, announced them. "Mr. Ian Rattle and Ms. Millicent Martindale," he intoned just loud enough to be heard, but not loud enough to bring all conversation to a halt.

Dame Felicity separated herself from a knot of guests and came toward Millie with her hand out. "Good evening, Millie. I'm so glad you could come on such short notice. One of my guests died, figuratively speaking, and you are such a lovely replacement. What a perfect dress!"

"Thank you, Dame Felicity. I'm very pleased to be here."

Shortly she was conversing with the foreign secretary and his wife. The man leaned in and whispered, "I've been briefed on your, ah, project, and I am delighted with the results so far."

"Thank you, sir," she replied.

"You are awfully pretty for a spy," his wife said, giving her husband a sharp look.

"Thank you, ma'am, but I am only a White House staffer, with no cover story." Over the next few minutes she was introduced to the home secretary and a Sir Edward Antrim, who, Ian whispered, was the director of MI5, Dame Felicity's counterpart on the domestic side. At seven-fifteen, the prime minister and his wife arrived and took a glass of champagne, then Millie was introduced to them, she being the only guest with whom they were not acquainted. She thought of curtsying, but then thought better of it.

At precisely seven-thirty a silver bell tinkled, and the butler announced dinner. As they were filing into the dining room the doorbell rang, and another guest was admitted, and more introductions were made around the table.

"Millie, this is Stone Barrington, whom you may already know."

"Only on the phone," Millie replied, shaking his hand. His place card was on Dame Felicity's left, and Millie's was next to his. The prime minister was seated on her hostess's right.

A first course of sautéed foie gras was brought immediately, and champagne was poured. Millie tasted it and rolled her eyes.

"Do you like it?" Barrington asked her.

"It is the best champagne I have ever tasted," she replied.

He laughed. "That's because it is the best champagne ever made: a Krug 1978—I caught a glimpse of the label."

"I shall never drink anything else," she said, taking another sip.

"The best of luck with that," he replied, then turned to chat with his hostess.

Millie thought that the back of his head looked better than the face of most men.

"Now may I have your attention?" Ian asked in a low voice. "You're not going to just sit there and wait for him to speak to you again, are you?"

"Of course not," she replied with a smile, trying not to blush. "I will dance with who brung me." As it happened, Stone did not speak to her again during dinner—he was too occupied with Dame Felicity and the prime minister.

The foie gras melted in her mouth, and a second course of fried goujons of Dover sole did, too. The main course came: a perfectly cooked fat duckling, and with it a Chateau something-or-other; she couldn't see the label—but it was wonderful. A mille-feuille was served for dessert, and when everyone had finished, all the women at the table got up and left the room. Millie suddenly remembered the British custom of the men being left to their cigars and port, and she started to rise, but Dame Felicity stopped her.

"Millie, please remain," she said. "Stone, would you be kind enough to attend to the ladies? We have business."

"Of course," Barrington said. He got up and was let out of the dining room by a man with a bulge under his black jacket and a military haircut, whom Millie had not noticed before.

"Now, if everyone has enough port, two of my guests have information to impart. I thought it better to do this at my home rather than attract attention by a more noticeable meeting of you all. First, Millicent Martindale, who is assistant national security adviser to the president of the United States. Millie?"

Millie noted the inflation of her importance by the omission of "to" from her title.

"From the beginning, please."

"Dame Felicity, Prime Minister, gentlemen," she began, keeping her voice low and steady, "after reports from two intelligence sources that a major terrorist plot against the West was being put together, the president assigned my superior, National Security Adviser Holly Barker, and the directors of Central Intelligence and the FBI to locate and identify three deeply buried persons who may be crucial to the effort, who we now call Moe, Larry, and Curly, the Three Stooges." That got a short laugh. "After an extraordinarily cooperative effort among our services and MI6, we have managed to identify all three. One is located at the embassy of Dahai, in Washington. The other two, while associated with that country, are so far unaccounted for, though a spirited search is under way. In Washington, as of this hour, some three dozen FBI agents and as many technical supporters have undertaken a round-the-clock surveillance of Moe, whose name is Ali Mahmoud and who is the chargé d'affaires at the Dahai embassy. Ian Rattle will bring you up to date on Larry and Curly."

Ian took a sip of his port. "Dame Felicity, Prime Minister, gentlemen. Larry and Curly are believed to be the natural sons of the sultan of Dahai, mothered by an Egyptian member of his harem thirty years ago. They were sent to Britain to study at Eton, where they led an unusually sequestered existence, chaperoned by a member of the sultan's household and supported by funds sent through the Devin Bank from the account of Sheik Hari Mahmoud, who is very likely the father of Moe, Ali Mahmoud."

"Excuse me, Mr. Rattle," the prime minister said suddenly, "are we to understand that the whereabouts of these two men, now grown, are unknown to your service?"

"They are being actively sought, Prime Minister. This should be thought of as a preliminary report."

"Dame Felicity?" the prime minister said.

"Prime Minister," she replied, "there is a beginning, a middle, and an end to every operation. We are now in the middle of this one."

"I see," the prime minister said, though he obviously did not.

"Now," Dame Felicity said, "I think we've kept the ladies waiting long enough." They rose and went back to the drawing room.

LATER, AS THE GUESTS were leaving, Stone Barrington took Millie's hand. "I'm delighted to have met you face-to-face," he said. "I hope I'll see you again."

"Thank you," she replied, "I'll look forward to that." She watched Barrington kiss his hostess on the cheek, then get into a waiting car.

BACK IN THE CAR, Ian said, "You did very well."

"You did better than could have been wished, in the circumstances," Millie replied, "and Dame Felicity backed you."

"Thank God for that," Ian said.

47

STONE LET HIMSELF into the suite at Cliveden and found himself alone in the sitting room. He shucked off his jacket, pulled his bow tie loose, unbuttoned his collar, poured himself a glass of sherry, and collapsed into a chair.

Dino appeared from his bedroom, clad in pajamas and a silk dressing gown.

"I can see that Viv has visited Turnbull & Asser," Stone said.

"Yeah, she insists that I be well dressed, even in bed." He poured himself a sherry and occupied the sofa, putting his feet up. "So, what took you away from us this evening that you couldn't tell us about?"

"When we got back here this afternoon I found a note waiting for me from Felicity Devonshire, commanding my presence at dinner at her house, and it was top secret."

"Commanding?"

"She's like that on her home turf. It was a glittering party, if small: only the prime minister, the foreign secretary, the home secretary, and the director of MI5, and their wives. Also, Millie Martindale—Holly's assistant—and one of Felicity's minions."

"That's pretty rich cream. What was the occasion?"

"I never really found out. When the ladies excused themselves after dinner, Felicity invited me to join them. All I heard about was the appalling prices of ladies' designer clothing these days."

"I could have told you about that," Dino said ruefully.

Stone laughed. "I expect you could. Anyway, when I returned to the table for port and Stilton, the beans had already been spilled to those authorized, and nothing more was said about it."

"I'm fascinated by the makeup of the party," Dino said. "That would be like Viv and me having the president, the governor, the secretary of state, Lance Cabot, and the Bureau director at our table. That could never happen."

"I suspect that whatever was discussed is so hot that Felicity didn't want the meeting to take place in a public building, so as not to raise questions." Stone looked at his watch: "I guess it's a little late to call Holly and ask her what the hell is going on."

"Not that she'd tell you."

"You have a point."

"I had a stroll around the grounds before bedtime," Dino said. "I even circumnavigated this house, which took a while. Nothing going on."

"I'm glad to hear it," Stone said, "although I wish Reeves would get over with whatever he has planned for me. I mean, he could have easily had me shot on Dartmoor, if he wanted me dead."

"And why would he want that?"

"It's something to do with Pat, but I don't know what. She says he made a couple of passes at her a while back, but who's that jealous?"

"Her former boyfriend Kevin Keyes?"

"Then why didn't he shoot us both? He had a silenced rifle and it was foggy and pouring with rain. Nobody would have seen or heard anything, and we wouldn't have been found until the next day."

"Maybe more important, why would Keyes have a silenced rifle? Nobody has those, except military snipers and pro hit men."

"Maybe he has a sideline in contract killing," Stone ventured, "with Reeves as his employer. Certainly Reeves is dirty—probably drugs."

"What is Reeves's legal business?"

"Pat says electronics—surveillance equipment, or something like that. He may be in oil, too."

"If he's in oil, why would he bother with drugs?"

"Maybe he hit a dry well."

"He just bought a new jet airplane," Dino pointed out.

"Maybe, but one of the smallest on the market, so he's not a king-pin at whatever he's into."

"Maybe, like you, he wanted one he could fly himself. You could certainly afford a bigger airplane."

"I'm just working my way up the tree," Stone said. "Cessna is revamping their CitationJet 3, installing the identical avionics I have in my M2, so I could step into it with very little retraining. The cockpits are identical. I'd want High Definition Radio to go oce-anic, instead of the Blue Spruce route."

"Why would you want it?"

"Because it has range of a little over eighteen hundred miles. We could have flown nonstop from Newfoundland to Shannon, obviating Greenland and Iceland, and flown home via the Azores, where the weather is very nice most of the time. I'm already worried about what the weather will be like on our return trip."

"Gee, that's exactly what I wanted to hear—thanks a lot."

"Oh, I always worry about the weather, until I break out of the clouds and see the runway dead ahead. We'll be okay."

"Until we're not."

"The weather forecasts are very good these days."

"Until they're not."

"I'm just a worrier—you're an out-and-out pessimist."

"Life has taught me that if something bad can happen, it will."

"I take the view that if something bad can happen, I need to be ready to handle it." Stone tossed off his sherry and stood up. "I'm going to bed, before you get *me* worrying."

"Sweet dreams," Dino said sweetly.

"Yeah, sure." Stone went to bed.

48

ALI MAHMOUD stepped outside the door of the large house where Dahai's highest-ranked diplomats lived. It was an unusually warm and sunny morning, and he thought he might walk to the embassy. Then he saw the Comcast cable truck across the street, and a man wearing a tool belt up a utility pole, poking around inside a steel box at the top. Ali stretched, all the while eyeing the van from side to side, top to bottom. In the center of the O in Comcast, he saw a hole. Not a very big one, but a hole nevertheless. Something to think about.

He walked down the steps of his building to the sidewalk and turned toward Dupont Circle, near which lay his embassy. As he walked he heard a car stop behind him, and a mid-sized Japanese sedan drove slowly by, a woman at the wheel, a man in the front passenger seat, and a baby seat mounted in the rear. Neither of them looked at him, although he thought he saw the woman driving glance into her rearview mirror after she had passed him.

He walked on, and a man in a suit left an apartment building ahead of him carrying a briefcase, a newspaper tucked under his arm, also headed toward Dupont Circle. That's three opportunities, Ali said to himself. Then the Comcast truck passed him and there was a small hole in the O on the other side of the truck, too. That's four. He continued to the circle, crossed it, and walked the dozen yards to his embassy. Once inside, he went to an entrance hall window and watched the street for a moment. Down the street perhaps forty yards he saw the Comcast truck parked on the other side, its driver taking his tool belt from the rear and hooking it around his hips.

Ali took the elevator to his top-floor office and sat down at his desk. A year and a half he had been here, and all of a sudden he felt watched. Or maybe this feeling was a product of the hangover he had from last night's party. He tried to shake it off.

He got up and swung open a fake bookcase, revealing a large safe behind it. He tapped in the combination, spun the wheel, opened the door, and removed his laptop and brought it back to his desk. While it booted up he phoned the embassy's head of security. "In my office, now," he said.

The man rapped on his office door less than a minute later.

"Come!"

The man walked in, looking nervous. "Yes, sir?"

"Come and sit down," Ali said, indicating a chair across his desk. The man sat. "Did you make your usual rounds this morning?" he asked.

"Yes, sir, of course. I started at six AM and finished at around seven-thirty."

"Was there anything—*anything*—out of order in the slightest degree?"

"No, sir. Everything was perfect. I ran all the security system checks and tested the firewalls, as usual."

"Was there a broken window? A mark around the lock on a door? Anything at all that might appear insecure?"

"No, sir, not a thing. Everything was perfect."

"There's a cable repair truck down the street about thirty yards. Was that there when you arrived this morning?"

"No, sir, but there are cable trucks everywhere. They always seem to be repairing something—under the street, in a building, up a telephone pole."

"Have you noticed a couple—a man and a woman—in a blue Nissan sedan with a baby seat in the rear?"

"No, sir."

"I want you to sweep my office."

"When, sir?"

"Now. Get somebody up here and go through the room, and be thorough."

Shortly two men in coveralls arrived with ladders and began sweeping the bookcases, the bar, the concealed safe, his desk and chair, the draperies, and the carpet edges. They were at it for more than an hour.

Finally, their supervisor came back. "Your office is clean," he said to Ali.

"How clean?"

"Squeaky clean, not a sign of anything—no cameras, no bugs, no anything."

"Thank you," Ali said. "Now get these people out of here. Go down to the garage and sweep all the cars." They took their gear and left, and he felt a bit better.

He checked his e-mail. Only one message, in Arabic, interested him. *The birds have arrived from the south and are nesting*, it read. Finally, he thought. The attempt on the president's life in London by some Al Qaeda affiliate or other had queered everything for a week, brought things to a halt. Now that the papers were reporting that the fourth man had died in the hospital, maybe things would return to normal.

One of his two cell phones vibrated on his belt, and he retrieved it. "Yes?"

"Did you get my message this morning?"

"Yes," he said, irritated, "why would I not get it?"

"I'm simply being thorough," the man said placatingly.

"Are the birds happy in their nest?"

"Chirping, just as they should. They are anxious to be out and about."

"Not until you are absolutely certain that there is no interest of any kind in the house. They are not to go out, until then."

"I understand."

"And I want everything in the wine cellar inventoried and confirmed to be in perfect working order. I want no chance of a mistake, do you hear?"

"I understand perfectly. It will be done as you say."

"I have had an e-mail this morning confirming the receipt of funds by the bank. There will be no check written, except those cashed inside the bank. They may use their cash cards at machines for day-to-day expenses."

"I understand."

"Be certain that the birds do, too. And keep them out of Annabel's—it's a nest of Americans, half of them CIA."

"Perhaps that is too strict, Ali. They would not be out of place there, not attract attention the way they might at other places. I would see that they were accompanied."

"Well, all right, you have a point. They should pay cash, though, no credit cards."

"They are well-disciplined men, Ali, you should trust them more."

"They have been cooped up at home for too long," Ali said. "I don't want them to start feeling their oats. I want them to view every stranger as a threat. I want them anxious and on their toes at all times."

"They want to do some shopping, too."

"All right, they can do that. Again, cash only."

"A good decision. Is there anything else?"

"No, not for the present. Perhaps we will speak tomorrow."

IN A BASEMENT ROOM at FBI headquarters a man picked up a phone. "Special Agent Phillips?"

"Yes."

"Everything is working perfectly. His laptop must have been stored somewhere, but we've got their wi-fi now. You'll want to read the e-mails. There's an interesting phone conversation to listen to, as well, but, of course, we have only his end of it."

"I'll be right down," Quentin said.

49

MILLIE'S PHONE RANG as she was having breakfast in bed. "Yes?"

"Good morning," Ian said. "We have a teleconference to attend with milady at ten. A car will collect you at nine-thirty."

"All right. What's the subject?"

"We'll both find out together." He hung up.

Millie hung up, too, and she picked up her iPhone to check her e-mail. There was an unheard voice mail message waiting. She pressed the button.

"Hi," Quentin said. "We've got some new material, and it's being forwarded to your friends across town. I expect you'll be hearing from them about it. Miss you much."

She erased the message. He must have called in the dead of night, and she had been too out to hear it. She finished her breakfast, then got into the shower.

SHE WAS DELIVERED to the rear entrance of the building and a plainclothes guard escorted her up to Dame Felicity's aerie. She was the first to arrive, being ten minutes early, and she used the opportunity to have a good look around. An entire wall of the study was taken up with history and biography, mostly of a foreign policy nature. On a small shelf under a window, she was surprised to find a leather-bound collection of Ian Fleming's James Bond novels.

Then, from somewhere behind the paneling she heard the muffled flushing of a toilet, and Dame Felicity emerged, immaculate, from behind a bookcase that was also a door. It was exactly ten AM. "Good morning, Millie. I'm sorry to be tardy. I hope you amused yourself."

"I was admiring your James Bond collection," Millie replied.

"Oh, yes, I'm a fan. I knew Fleming when I was a girl. He worked for my father, during the war. I was besotted with him."

"I've read a lot about the war," Millie said. "It is endlessly fascinating."

"I'm rather surprised that you didn't plump for the Agency. Did you ever consider it?"

"A campus recruiter got in touch with me once, and I had a meeting with him. I didn't hear from him again. But then, I suppose the interview was more of an argument."

"Their loss," Dame Felicity said. "I would have recruited you after the first five minutes."

"That is high praise."

There was a rap on the door, and Ian Rattle stuck his head in. "They're ready for us in the conference room," he said.

It was just the three of them; she was clearly holding this operation close.

Ian picked up the phone. "Tell them to push the material," he said, "and be sure you record it."

A large screen descended from the ceiling, and a picture appeared. The voice over the action was that of Quentin Phillips. "This is Ali Mahmoud leaving his residence," he said. "The sultan bought the house a decade or so ago and converted it to apartments for his higher-ranking diplomats." At least three cameras followed the man down the street toward Dupont Circle and across to his embassy. He walked inside and closed the door behind him.

Then there was a cut to a shot high up in a large room. The door opened and Mahmoud entered and went to a desk. Millie was astonished that they had a camera in that room. As he sat down and picked up a phone, there was a cut to another angle, and a slow zoom to a medium close-up. "In my office, now," Ali said into the phone, and they could hear both ends of the conversation.

They watched, then, as Mahmoud addressed his security chief, followed by the entrance of two men in coveralls. "We cut ahead here to an hour later, after the men left. Note that his laptop was stored in a large safe behind a bookcase," Quentin's voice said. The screen split, and Mahmoud's computer screen filled half of it. There was a message in Arabic. "Translation: 'The birds have arrived from the south and are in nesting.'"

Then Mahmoud was on his cell phone, and they could hear only his end of the conversation. When he was done, the screen went dark, then Quentin appeared, sitting at a desk in a room full of monitors.

"There was nothing interesting after that, except that we have noted that Mahmoud does absolutely no work as chargé d'affaires. He is pure intelligence, or perhaps terrorist. We interpret this conversation as a confirmation of the arrival of two agents from Dahai. Please note his concerns about them. He could very well be talking about the twins. Over to you and yours, Dame Felicity."

"Special Agent Phillips, please allow me to say that what you have just shown us is nothing less than brilliant."

"Thank you, ma'am."

"Please tell Assistant Director Epstein that I would like to speak with him, at his first opportunity, about sending some of my people over there to learn about your techniques."

"I'll pass that on, ma'am."

"Tell me, do you know the location of the other man on the phone?"

"We believe the e-mail came from London," Quentin replied.

"Was there any other indication in anything you collected about a London location?"

"No, ma'am."

"Then I suppose it's over to us, is it not?"

"As you wish, ma'am. We'll continue to monitor the subject, and I'll report anything that might help on your end."

"Thank you, I would be very grateful for that. I look forward to speaking with Assistant Director Epstein." They said goodbye and hung up.

Millie felt a warm glow of pride at the quality and extent of what she had just seen.

"Absolutely astonishing," Dame Felicity said.

"I agree," Ian said. "I had no idea they could do that—and so quickly, too. Those two techs spent an hour in that room and found nothing."

"Now," Dame Felicity said, "Larry and Curly. What are the residential facilities for senior Dahai diplomats in London?"

"There are two," Ian replied. "A large house in Regent's Park, not far from the American ambassador's residence, and two adjoining houses off Belgrave Square, quite near their embassy. Rather large facilities for such a small country."

"Then start there. Also, learn if any individual senior people from the embassy have flats or houses either in London or in the Home Counties."

"Wilco," Ian replied. "Is there anything else, Dame Felicity?"

"No. Report back when you have something for me."

Ian got up and left.

"Well," Dame Felicity said, "you must be feeling very proud of your FBI."

"I am as astonished as you are, ma'am, and of course I am proud of them. I'm acquainted with the agent you spoke with, and he is very impressive."

"A Harvard man, I understand."

"Yes, ma'am. We knew each other there. I was very pleased when I learned that he was in counterintelligence at the Bureau."

"Something occurs to me," Dame Felicity said. "It appears that two agents in London are being run by another in Washington. I think there must be a very important reason for that, and I fear it does not augur well for either of us."

"The FBI has only just begun, Dame Felicity. We'll be hearing more from them."

50

AFTER BREAKFAST, Stone got a phone call on his cell from his tailor in London. "I'll be there around eleven," he said, and hung up. "Anybody want to go to London this morning?"

The women both declined. "We're spending the day in the spa," Pat said.

"Why are you going?" Dino asked.

"I've got a first fitting on some clothes I ordered, and getting a fitting today will shorten the time until they're delivered."

"I'll go with you," Dino said.

The drive to London took an hour, and Stone found a parking place in Mount Street, near Hayward. When they entered the shop the cutter was busy fitting a young man with a suit, and Stone took a seat and found a magazine, while Dino looked at fabrics for an overcoat.

"Anything else you'd like to order?" the cutter asked his customer. "We'll be in Dahai for our semiannual visit in about six weeks. We could have fittings ready for you then."

"Perhaps," the young man replied. "David?" he called.

Another young man emerged from a dressing room, clad in a half-finished jacket. "Yes?"

"They'll be in Dahai in six weeks. Anything else you want to order?"

Stone did a double take. The two were identical twins—blond, reedy, typically upper-class British.

"I'll think about it," David replied. Then he said something in a foreign language, and his brother laughed and replied in kind.

"I think we've bought enough," the first twin said to the cutter. "When may we have these things?"

"How long will you be in London?"

"Another week or so."

"Then we'll have them ready before your departure," the cutter replied.

"Will we need another fitting?"

"Only if you wish it."

"Then just send the lot when they're ready."

"To the Regent's Park address?"

"Yes, please."

The two changed back into their own clothes and one of them paid their very large bill in euros, then they left.

Stone's jackets were brought out, and he tried them both on. Tiny adjustments were made, then Dino was measured for a topcoat.

"I'm in no rush," Dino said to the cutter. "This is for next fall, really."

"We'll be in New York at the Carlyle in June. We can give you a fitting then."

"Sounds good." Dino gave them a deposit, and he and Stone left the shop. Dino was looking to see if Stone was following, and he ran head-on into a young woman and began apologizing profusely.

"Millie?" Stone asked.

She turned. "Stone Barrington?"

"Yes, and the clumsy one is my friend Dino Bacchetti. Dino, Millie and I were dinner partners last evening."

"Ah," Dino said, "did she have to leave the table with the ladies, too?"

"No, she was important enough to be asked to stay. What brings you to this neighborhood, Millie?"

"I'm staying at the Connaught, just down the block."

"Dino and I are about to get some lunch. Will you join us?"

"Why not? I'm hungry."

"Let's go around the corner to Harry's Bar."

It was a two-minute walk, and a table was available. Stone loved the food there, and he tried not to over-order.

"Well, I get a chance to talk to you," Millie said. "Dame Felicity rather monopolized you at dinner."

"We're old friends, and I hadn't seen her for a while. I apologize for giving you my back. Tell me, was your companion one of Felicity's young men?"

"I'm not quite sure what you mean by that," Millie said.

"Not *that* kind of young man, though it wouldn't surprise me. I meant was he MI6."

She nodded.

"I had the feeling that the two of you were the entertainment for the evening."

"I suppose we were. We've been working with them on something."

"Ah, but of course you can't tell me what."

"Just chasing some Middle Eastern bad guys."

"Speaking of the Middle East, do you know where a place called Dahai is?"

She looked at him sharply. "It's a small sultanate on the southern border of Saudi Arabia. Why do you ask? Has Holly said something to you about it?"

"No, it came up when I was at my tailor's. We were just leaving there when we—Dino—ran into you."

"Came up how? Really, I'm interested."

"There were two young men, brothers, being fitted for some clothes, and the tailor mentioned that he visits Dahai twice a year to see customers."

"Can you describe the brothers?"

"Fairly tall, slim, blond, well dressed, terribly British."

"Twins, by any chance?"

"Yes. How did you know?"

"Are they still in the shop?"

"No, they left ahead of us, perhaps forty-five minutes ago."

"Did they say anything that would give you any idea where they might have been headed?"

"They said they'd be in town for another week and asked that their finished clothes be delivered to a Regent's Park address."

"Did you hear a name?"

"One of them was called David. Oh, and they spoke to each other briefly in a foreign language—Arabic, perhaps."

"Excuse me, please," Millie said, standing up. "Order me the veal, will you?" She walked quickly away from the table, digging out her cell phone.

"What do you suppose that was about?" Dino asked

Millie called Ian.

"Yes?"

"We may have a sighting of Larry and Curly."

"Where?"

"In a tailor's shop, in Mount Street."

"Hayward?"

"Yes, I think so."

"Are they still there?"

"No, they left three-quarters of an hour ago. You remember Stone Barrington?"

"Yes."

"He was there for a fitting. He heard one of them called David, and they asked that their finished clothes be sent to a Regent's Park address."

"How did you learn about this?"

"I'm having lunch with Barrington and a friend right now."

"Where?"

"At Harry's Bar."

"Go back and finish your lunch. Leave this with me." He hung up without further ado.

Millie went back to the table.

"YOU LOOK TROUBLED," Stone said.

"Far from it. You may have just given us a very big break."

"Would you like to tell me how, and what sort of break?"

"You'll have to ask Holly," she replied. "May I have a Bellini, please?" She gave him her best smile. "Now, Dino, tell me about you. Do you practice law with Stone?"

Dino gave her his card. "If you'd ever like a job as an interrogator, call me."

51

IAN RATTLE ran up the stairs to his boss's office and entered without knocking.

Dame Felicity looked up from her desk with an expression of half curiosity, half outrage at the intrusion. "Yeesss?" she drawled.

"We've got a hit on Larry and Curly," he said. He quickly related his conversation with Millie.

"What do you suggest?"

"I suggest I wring the complete address out of that tailor and we descend on the property in force."

"Well, that's subtle," she said. "And it would be unproductive."

"It would break up whatever they're planning," Ian pointed out.

"Break up what? We have no idea what they're planning. I should think that, after what we saw from Washington this morning, you'd see an alternative to a huge bust—one that might tell us what they're up to and perhaps cast a wider net."

"Of course, that's a wonderful idea," Ian said, "but we don't have the technical knowledge to pull that off."

Dame Felicity consulted her computer and glanced at her watch: very early in D.C. She dialed a telephone number.

"This is Epstein," he said, sounding wide awake.

"Good morning, Assistant Director Epstein," she said. "This is Felicity Devonshire in London."

"Good morning, Dame Felicity."

"First, I want to thank you for the brilliant demonstration of your Bureau's surveillance skills that we saw earlier today."

"Thank you—my people worked very hard on that."

"I'm sure they did. Now I must ask you a tremendous favor, and I wanted to come directly to you, rather than your director, which I'm aware is a violation of protocol."

"How may I help you?"

"First, let me tell you that we believe we have discovered the whereabouts of Larry and Curly: they are in London."

"Excellent," Epstein said.

"We know that they expect to be in London for another week, so we believe that we have a few days to discover what they're up to. However, our surveillance skills and equipment are just not up to the job. I wonder if I can persuade you to send your team over here right away to conduct the same sort of surveillance that they did on Moe? We will, of course, provide transport, housing, and all expenses."

"I believe I can make a case for that with my director," Epstein said. "After all, our installations are complete. Now we are monitoring."

"We would very much like to see Special Agent Quentin Phillips and his team here tonight," she said. "I'll call your director and pretend that you and I have not spoken. Then I expect he will call you."

"I'm grateful for the advance warning," Epstein said. "Do you have the director's home number? He won't be up and about just yet."

"I do, thank you. We'll be in touch." She hung up the phone, looked up another number, and dialed it. "Good morning, Ambassador," she said. "This is Felicity Devonshire."

"Good God, Felicity! What time is it?"

"Quite early on your side, I believe. I would not have called were it not urgent."

"All right, what's going on?"

"I believe the Prince and Princess of Wales arrived at Andrews Air Force Base yesterday, in an aircraft of the Queen's Flight, for a three-day visit."

"Yes, that's right. They're upstairs—asleep, I should think."

"Please don't disturb them. On a matter of the utmost importance to our national security, I require their aircraft for the purpose of an immediate flight to London, with a quick turnaround."

"I'm not at all sure that I have the authority to grant that request," the ambassador replied.

"I assure you that by the time the crew arrive at Andrews, all permissions will be in place."

"All right, I'll get in touch with the crew. Oh, and I'd very much appreciate a cable on this subject."

"Of course, Arthur. I'll see that your arse is fully covered." She hung up and buzzed her secretary. "Please get the prime minister on the phone," she said, "and if he's in a meeting, interrupt him. Highest priority." She hung up and waited quietly until she was buzzed back.

"The prime minister's secretary is on the line, Dame Felicity," she said. "She won't put the PM on until she speaks to you."

"Right," Dame Felicity said. She pressed a button. "Margaret, put the PM on *right now*, if you please."

"Yes, Dame Felicity."

"Yes, Felicity," the PM said, "make it quick—half the Cabinet is waiting."

"Prime Minister, we have located Larry and Curly."

"Ah, yes—half the Three Stooges. Excellent."

"We require the assistance of the FBI to install some brilliant new surveillance equipment, and that necessitates our borrowing the Queen's Flight aircraft, now at Andrews Air Force Base, to fly the technicians here, with an immediate return to Andrews."

"Well, that's highly irregular," he replied.

"It's the only way we can have the FBI team at work tomorrow. The Waleses are in Washington for a three-day stay. They'll never know it's gone."

The PM sighed deeply.

"This requires an immediate cable from you to the ambassador, in language that shelters his posterior. This, I assure you, is in the national interest, and of the highest priority."

"Oh, all right, I'll have to get the air minister involved, though. He's waiting for me with the others."

"Please don't let your cable take more than half an hour to arrive in Washington."

"You mean you want it done *instantly*?"

"Thank you *so* much, Prime Minister." Dame Felicity hung up. "Now," she said to Ian, "go to that tailor's shop, and in the gentlest and most discreet manner possible, find out what they know. Call me when you've spoken to them."

"Yes, ma'am," Ian said, then fled the room

Dame Felicity consulted her computer address book again and dialed a number.

"What?" a sleepy American voice demanded.

"Good morning, Director, this is Felicity Devonshire, in London. My apologies for the early hour."

"What time is it?"

"Oh, it's lunchtime over here. I'm sorry to have disturbed your breakfast." That got a laugh. She explained her request in the shortest and most urgent terms.

"Oh, all right," the director said. "I'll call Lev Epstein, who runs that group. How long will you need them?"

"I should think a week," she replied. "Perhaps a day or two longer. We will provide transport, shelter, and all expenses."

"Damn right you will." He hung up.

Five minutes later her secretary buzzed. "A Special Agent Lev Epstein, from Washington. He says you're expecting his call."

"Of course." She pressed the button. "Assistant Director Epstein," she said.

"You apparently lit a fire under the boss," Lev said.

"Not just *your* boss," she replied. "A jet aircraft of the Queen's Flight awaits your team at Andrews Air Force Base," she said. "They will be met on this side and comfortably housed. Please ask them to be prepared to go to work tomorrow morning. Their liaison will be Major Ian Rattle. Will Special Agent Phillips be leading them?"

"Yes, he will, Dame Felicity. I would come myself, but there are pressing matters here."

"How sad," she said. "Perhaps next time." She hung up, satisfied that she had earned her salary that day.

52

IAN RATTLE arrived in Mount Street after an interminable twenty-two-minute trip in heavy traffic. He leaped out of the car, leaving his driver, then, as he approached the door of Hayward, stopped, smoothed down his suit and hair, took a deep breath, and entered the shop.

A woman was hanging a handful of neckties on a rack just inside the door. "May I help you?"

"May I speak with your fitter?" Ian asked.

"He's working in the rear," she said, pointing.

Ian entered the rear room to find a man, a tape measure around his neck, applying a very large pair of scissors to a bolt of cloth. "May I help you, sir?" the man asked.

"You may," Ian said, taking his ID from a pocket as he approached the cutting table and laying it on the tabletop for the man's perusal.

"Ah," the man said. "Whatever I can do."

"It is my understanding that you have clients in the nation of Dahai," Ian said.

"That is so."

"I also understand that two of them, brothers, I believe, were in for a fitting this morning."

"That is so, as well."

"What address in London do you have for them?"

"Regency House, Regent's Park."

"And the names of the two?"

"David and Derek Kimbrough," he said. "I believe they are the sons of Lord Kimbrough, whose house they stay in when in London."

"Have they been your clients for long?"

"They were clients of Douglas Hayward when he was alive and they were at Eton. My employers bought the shop after Mr. Hayward's death, and we have continued to serve them."

"I see. How often do they come to London?"

"Around twice a year," he replied. "We always see them when they're here, and we're in Dahai twice a year to service our clients there."

"Do you have a shop there?"

"No, we work out of a hotel. For the Kimbroughs we call at their home, which is in the grounds of the sultan's palace."

"Does Lord Kimbrough spend time in Dahai?"

"I believe not. He and the boys' mother have lived apart for many years. She apparently has connections to the sultan's court."

"Tell me, do you also have a client called Mahmoud?"

"Yes, two of them—the Sheik Hari Mahmoud and his son, Ali. They maintain a home here."

"May I have that address, please?"

The tailor went to a large leather-bound book and leafed through it. "Here we are," he said. "Malvern House, Cheyne Walk, Chelsea."

"Do you know if he's in town now?"

"If he is, we haven't seen him."

"Thank you so much for your help," Ian said.

"Always happy to oblige MI6."

Ian left the shop, called Dame Felicity, and reported his conversation with the tailor.

"Ah, Lord Kimbrough," she said. "I don't need to look him up in Debrett's *Peerage*—I knew him. He died twenty years ago, and without issue. I would imagine that soon after that the sultan would have acquired his house."

"I believe we should concentrate our efforts on Regent's Park and ignore the property in Belgrave Square. And I believe we should begin outside surveillance of Regency House immediately."

"I agree," she replied. "The FBI team will arrive at RAF Northolt this evening. I would like you to meet them and escort them to the Hyde Park Barracks, headquarters of the Household Cavalry, where they will be housed in some vacant officers' quarters. You might take Millie Martindale with you, since she is acquainted with Quentin Phillips, the team leader."

"As you wish, Dame Felicity."

"Early tomorrow morning, I would like the FBI team to occupy the first-floor conference room here as their operational headquarters. Agent Phillips may use the adjoining office, which is being cleared for him. Please ask our tech people to see that they have whatever of our equipment they may need and to observe as much of their work as possible."

"Of course, ma'am."

"I'm feeling much better about this operation," she said.

"I'm glad, ma'am. So am I." They hung up, and Ian made a call to his number two, and gave the order to begin surveillance of the Regent's Park house. He started to call Millie on his cell phone, then realized she was right around the corner. He walked around to Harry's Bar and entered. He could see Millie, Stone Barrington, and another man at a corner table, where they were just attending to the bill, so he waited in the bar.

MILLIE SPOTTED IAN as they were leaving their table. He greeted them in the bar, and she introduced him to Dino Bacchetti.

"Hello, Mr. Rattle," Stone said, shaking his hand. "Good to see you again."

"It's Ian, please. Millie, may I have a word?"

"Of course."

"Stone, Ian can drop me back at the hotel, after I pick up a package in Mount Street. I wish you a happy flight back to Reykjavik tomorrow." She thanked him for lunch, and they left.

"What's up?" she asked Ian.

"Things are moving very fast." He brought her up to date.

"I don't think it's necessary for me to be at Northolt to meet the team. I have a room at the Connaught for Quentin Phillips," she said, "so you can bring him there after you've quartered the team at Hyde Park Barracks."

"Very good. I'll send a car for him at seven AM tomorrow."

LEV EPSTEIN ARRIVED at his office shortly after seven to find a technician from the monitoring team waiting for him.

"Sir, I've already called Phillips about this, but I think you should know that, shortly before dawn this morning, we observed Ali Mahmoud leaving his apartment in his car. We weren't set up to film him that early, but we followed him, at some distance, to Rock Creek Park."

"What the hell was he doing there at dawn?"

He pulled his car behind some bushes, and we positioned our people so that we could see him remove a large object from the trunk of his car."

"What was it?"

"We watched as he took it to a clearing, along with a case. It turned out to be a drone."

"As in a pilotless aircraft?"

"Not pilotless, sir—Mahmoud was the pilot. The drone was one of those with four propellers—they are highly maneuverable. He did some assembly, which didn't take long, and took a monitor from the case and set that up. Shortly, he was flying the thing, and it went out of our sight line. It must have been electrically powered, because it made little or no noise."

"But you couldn't see where it went?"

"No, sir. Apparently it had a camera aboard, because Mahmoud watched the monitor very carefully as he manipulated the controls. The drone returned after about an hour and landed. He repacked the equipment in his car and drove back to his home, then walked to the embassy."

"So Mahmoud is a drone hobbyist," Epstein muttered to himself.

"Yes, sir, and he appeared to be very proficient in flying the drone. He was very assured in handling it."

"Could the thing be used as a weapon?"

"That doesn't seem likely. It doesn't have the power to carry much in the way of weight—probably only a camera."

"So he wants to spy on something?"

"Possibly."

"Thank you," Epstein said. "Get back to your work."

As he settled behind his desk, Epstein had the feeling that what he had just heard was not a good thing.

QUENTIN PHILLIPS ARRIVED at work and reported to Lev. "What time are you off?"

"We should be at Andrews between ten and eleven."

"Have you heard the report about Mahmoud's activities this morning?"

"No. What's happened?"

Lev told him about Mahmoud and his drone.

"But we've no idea where he flew the thing?"

"None."

"You don't suppose he's just a drone hobbyist?"

"No, I don't, but your tech people say that such a drone could carry no more than a camera."

"And it was electric?"

"Yes, very quiet."

"I'll talk more with the team about it during our flight."

"All right." Lev handed him a printed form. "Draw some pounds and distribute some of them to your team. How many men are you taking?"

"Eight: four operators and four installers."

"Keep me posted. Good luck."

53

MILLIE WAITED for the Connaught bellman to deposit Quentin's luggage in her old bedroom, then she flung her arms around him. "Welcome to London," she said.

"I can see why you put my luggage in here," Quentin said, "but I don't really have to sleep here, do I?"

She kissed him. "You do not. I have other plans for you, beginning with dinner, which I've already ordered."

"I've got to call Lev," he said. "Is there a secure line?"

"The green phone is. It goes through the embassy switchboard."

He kissed her again, then sat down at the desk, picked up the green phone, and asked to be connected to Lev Epstein.

"This is Epstein."

"It's Phillips."

"Are you there?"

"I am, and the team and I talked about Moe and his drone on the way over here."

"Any conclusions?"

"We don't know what he plans to do with it, but we agree, it's too light to carry a weapon or a bomb."

"I already knew that."

"We're all agreed that we have to start surveilling him from the air immediately."

"With what, an Apache helicopter hovering over Dupont Circle?"

"With a drone."

"We don't have any drones, you know that."

"The CIA does. We think they're training with them out at Camp Peary, the Farm. If they are, those things could carry a weapon, like a Hellfire missile. They're doing it all over the Middle East right now."

"Let me understand: You want to position a drone over Washington, D.C., armed with a Hellfire missile? Are you out of your fucking mind?"

"No, no! We just want to use it for surveillance. When Moe flies his drone again, we can see where it goes, then maybe figure out what he plans to do with it. We need an eye in the sky."

Millie tapped him on the shoulder. "I can get it for you, and without the red tape."

"Did I just hear the voice of Ms. Martindale?" Lev asked.

"She says she can get us the drone without the red tape."

"Then tell her to do it! I'm out of this! But don't you arm that thing without my permission!" He hung up.

"Okay," Quentin said. "Get me a drone."

"For surveillance?"

Quentin thought about that. "Multipurpose," he said. "I want something that can hang up there for days, and that can be armed if necessary."

"Explain."

He told her about Moe's drone flying.

Millie kicked him out of the chair, sat down at the desk, picked up the green phone, and dialed Holly's number.

"Hey," Holly said.

"Where are you?"

"Berlin. We just got in from a big dinner. We're off to Rome tomorrow morning."

"Quentin Phillips just arrived with his team, and there's news from D.C." She told her about Moe's drone and what Quentin wanted. "The FBI doesn't have any drones, or at least, any suitable ones, but the Agency does, apparently out at Camp Peary. It's going to take the president to order it."

"What, exactly, does he want?"

"A drone with a camera that can hover for long periods of surveillance and that can be armed later, if it becomes necessary."

"That sounds like two drones to me," Holly said.

"Okay, two drones—one in the air, one on call."

"I'll get back to you," Holly said.

Holly hung up as the doorbell rang. "That will be dinner," Millie said. She opened the door and admitted a waiter with a tray table. When he had gone, she said, "Holly will get back to us."

"Can she really get the president to make that call?"

"If anybody can, it's Holly. Now eat."

They were on dessert when the phone rang, and Millie ran for it. "Hello?"

"Tell Quentin to call Lance Cabot at the following number."

Millie wrote it down. "Got it." But Holly had already hung up.

"Okay," she said to Quentin. "Call Lance Cabot, at this number."

She handed him the pad and gave him the desk chair. "Put him on speaker."

Quentin sat down and asked for the number.

It rang once, then: "Lance Cabot."

"Director Cabot, this is Special Agent Quentin Phillips, FBI."

"Hello, Quentin. I hear you want to borrow my air force."

"Only two drones, sir."

"That is agreeable. I've already given the order to our people at Camp Peary. We're doing this under the condition that only our people operate them. We're not turning them over to you. Understood?"

"Understood."

"The code name for the first drone is 'Stalker,' which will be your surveillance craft. Where do you want it?"

"The Dahai government maintains an apartment building for diplomats off Dupont Circle."

"We know that place. We'll station Stalker at two thousand feet, circling the building. The lenses aboard will bring you in close enough to read the warning label on a pack of cigarettes. My people will give you radio frequencies and phone numbers you can use to request changes in station or to follow a person or vehicle. The video signal will be broadcast from a satellite."

"May we view the images in both Washington and London? I'm in London now."

"It requires a relay, but the short answer is yes."

"What about the second drone?"

"That is code-named 'Condor.' It can be armed with a Gatling gun and/or a Hellfire missile."

"Both, please."

"And it will not leave the ground or fire without a presidential order—that's the president on the phone with me—do you understand?"

"I understand, sir."

"I will now give the order to position Stalker over the embassy apartment building and to establish radio and phone contact with your people in the basement of the Hoover Building."

"Thank you, sir."

"Thank me when it's over—if it works." Lance hung up.

"We're in business," Quentin said.

Millie took him by an ear. "Business later, sex now." She led him to the bedroom.

54

THE FOLLOWING MORNING Stone showered and dressed, then packed his bag; Pat was already packed, he noted. He walked into the sitting room for breakfast to find her at her computer, with a hotel printer on the desk.

"Morning," she said. "Sleep well?"

"Pretty well."

"Are you still worried about Paul Reeves?"

"A little. I wish he'd get it over with."

"Relax, by noon you'll be on your way to Reykjavik." She handed him a sheaf of papers. "Your weather forecast and your flight plan, already filed for noon local. A sunny day, all the way to Goose Bay. I recommend you go all the way today—it'll be worse tomorrow."

Stone looked at the flight plans. "Seven hours in the air: I can do that."

"There's a decent hotel at Goose Bay. I'll book you in."

The phone rang, and Stone picked it up. "It's for you," he said, handing it to Pat.

"Hello? Hi there, how's it going? That's really good news—it's a good-weather day. We'll be at Coventry between ten and eleven. I'll file for twelve. See you then." She hung up. "Good tidings: my client's CJ4 is ready and flight-tested. He's meeting me at Coventry."

"Good for you."

"We'll be in Wichita tonight. I'll fly back to New York tomorrow."

"You'd better come to my house—we don't know what's going on at your place."

"You talked me into it."

Dino and Viv joined them, and breakfast arrived.

THE BELLMAN CAME for their luggage. Dino pointed at two pieces. "Those two go into the second car. My wife is going back to London. The rest go in our Jaguar."

They put Viv into her car and said goodbye, then they loaded their luggage and drove away from Cliveden a little after ten. The weather was superb: warm and sunny with a nice breeze. He chose BBC Three on the radio, and the excellent sound system filled the car with soft classical music.

"I have a feeling we're going to see Reeves at the airport," Stone said.

"So what? At the very worst, you'll get a chance to punch him in the nose. I wouldn't try that with Kevin, though, if he's there."

"If he's there, we'll call the police," Stone said. "Dino, you're in charge of bringing the bobbies down on Kevin Keyes, if he's at the airport."

"I can do that," Dino said.

They arrived at the airport and were buzzed through the security gate. The CJ4 had just landed and was taxiing in; Stone's M2 was just being rolled out of the hangar.

Stone pulled up to his airplane, admiring her once again, and they loaded their luggage while Pat rolled her bag across the ramp toward the CJ4, which had just parked.

A lineman walked up to Stone. "We fueled her yesterday—topped off as you requested."

"Thanks," Stone said. "Is that Mustang still here?"

"No, Mr. Reeves took off half an hour ago."

"Was he alone?"

"His pilot was with him."

"Stone," Pat called out, "will you put the car in the parking lot and leave the keys with the desk inside? Somebody will pick it up."

"Sure, I've got to pay for my fuel and hangar, anyway."

"Anything I can do?" Dino asked.

"Yeah, when I get back, you can turn on the master switch—that's the red one on the left-hand side—and the landing light—that's on the right side. I'll need to check them as part of my pre-flight inspection."

"Got it."

Stone drove the car out, left it in the parking lot, then went inside and handed over the keys and paid his bill. While he was doing that the lineman came inside. "Have we got any string?" he asked.

"Sure," his colleague replied, "there's some on the shelf behind the desk." The lineman got the string and went back outside.

Stone signed the bill and put it in his pocket, then started back to the airplane. Dino was standing halfway between the building and the airplane, and the landing light was not yet turned on. The luggage had been removed from the airplane and was piled next to him. As he got nearer to Dino, he noticed that the ball of string the lineman had asked for was at his feet, and that he was holding the string, which led into the cockpit.

"What are you doing?" Stone asked.

Dino handed him a piece of green-jacketed copper wire about three inches long. "Do you recognize that?" he asked.

"No, where'd you get it?"

"It was on the carpet at the top of the airstair, just inside the door."

"And that caused you to unload the airplane?"

"Call me crazy," Dino said. "We'll see." He tugged hard on the string, and the airplane's landing light came on.

"I don't get—" Stone started to say. Then the front end of the airplane exploded. Stone and Dino dove behind the piled luggage, and small pieces of airplane rained down around them. When they looked up again, the cockpit and everything ahead of it had disappeared. The nose gear, amazingly, was still intact.

Then, slowly, the airplane sat down on her tail, making a crunching noise.

"Holy shit!" Stone said, getting to his feet.

Across the ramp, Pat and her client were cowering next to the CJ4. "Are you two all right?" she shouted.

"Fine," Stone yelled back. "My airplane isn't so good, though." He turned to Dino. "What did you do?"

Dino looked sheepish. "The wire made me suspicious, so I tied some string to the master switch and rigged it so that I could turn it on from here. I guess I didn't really believe that there was a bomb, and I didn't want to call the bomb squad."

"Well, I congratulate you on still being alive—and on saving our luggage, too."

"I'm sorry about the airplane," Dino said.

"That's what insurance is for," Stone replied, and got out his cell phone. "I'd better call them now. You can deal with the cops."

"I think I'll call Sir Martin Beveridge," he said. "It's better to deal with these things from the top down."

THE POLICE WERE there in minutes with a chief inspector in charge, and a van full of men and equipment; they were soon crawling over Stone's M2 like ants.

Stone was about to call his travel agent to book himself and Dino on a flight to New York, when Pat came over. "Listen," she said, "I've talked with my client, and if you like, you and Dino can fly back with us."

"What a great idea!" Stone said. "Saves us a trip to Heathrow and a lot of hassle."

"We've got some very rare favorable winds today, so we'll fly to Presque Isle, Maine, and clear customs there. Do you think you can get a charter to meet you and take you to Teterboro?"

"We can do that," Stone replied. "Where's Presque Isle?"

"Just south of the Canadian border. We can clear customs there much faster than Bangor, where we'd have to mix with commercial passengers."

"Good to know."

Pat pulled him aside, looking embarrassed. "There's something I haven't told you," she said.

"What's that?"

"You're still my attorney, right?"

"Correct."

"I didn't tell you the whole reason why Paul and Kevin have behaved the way they have, but this business with your airplane changes things."

"Go on."

"In the beginning, when they were just trying to frighten me, it was because I know a lot more about Paul's business and his relationship with Kevin than I've told you."

"Tell me now, then."

"I was a part of what they were doing. I flew Paul to various meetings with briefcases full of money, and I knew what it was for. I wasn't exactly a partner, but I was an accomplice."

"I see."

"When Kevin fired those shots at us on Dartmoor, he wasn't warning you, he was warning me, because he thought I might tell you about them. I didn't tell you because I didn't want to testify against them."

"And now?"

"I still don't want to testify against them, but if you advise me to, I will. The bomb on your airplane was a convincer."

"I understand, and I'll keep you as much out of it as I can. The New York DA will be more interested in the murders than in their past."

They rejoined Dino, and the chief inspector approached. "Commissioner," he said to Dino, "my men tell me it was something like half a pound of plastique, wired to the master switch. Very simple, really."

Dino thanked him. "Do you need us for anything else?"

"No, we've talked to everybody. Mr. Barrington, what do you want done with your airplane?"

"My insurance agent will be in touch with you about that," Stone replied. "He's in California and not open yet, but I've left a message for him."

The captain gave him a card. "We've checked, and this Mr. Reeves in the Mustang didn't head for Reykjavik, as you said he might. He filed for Cork. Nothing beyond that. We're still checking."

"I hope you catch up with him," Stone said.

"Mind you, we've nothing to connect him to your airplane, except your suspicions. At least, not yet."

"I understand. Thank you for your help, Captain. We'll be off now." He shook the man's hand, and he and Dino carried their luggage over to the CJ4 and stowed it. Five minutes later, Pat was taxiing the airplane to the runway, with her client in the right cockpit seat and Stone and Dino buckled into passenger seats.

They landed at Shannon, and Stone used the refueling stop to call his insurance agent again. "Larry?"

"Yes, Stone, I got your message. Have you had a problem?"

"You're not going to believe it, Larry."

55

THE MI6 CAR picked up Quentin and Millie at the Connaught at seven AM and drove them to headquarters, where they were escorted to the ground floor and a large conference room, with an office to one side for Quentin. His team was already there, unpacking equipment and dealing with the locals about the voltage differences.

Ian Rattle turned up. "Good morning. When can your people start installing your gear in Regent's Park?"

"Not in broad daylight," Quentin said. "It's a black bag job, and they don't know the territory yet."

"Have a look at our monitors—we've got some aerial shots of the area, and a couple of cameras on the ground."

"Please take away your ground cameras now," Quentin said. "We'll cover all the angles we need, and half our job is not getting spotted. I do want to see the aerial shots, though. For God's sake don't have any more overflights, especially with choppers."

Ian led him over to a large monitor. "Put up the shot from

yesterday afternoon," he said to a tech. An aerial view of a large house surrounded by parkland came into view. "Zoom in to the delivery entrance."

Quentin peered at the closer shot. "I see a delivery truck unloading some large crates," he said.

"Three or four of them."

"Anything longer than, say, four feet?"

"No, there are no air-to-ground missiles in those boxes, if that's what you're thinking, unless they're building them from scratch in the house."

"Doesn't seem likely. Do you have or have access to any drones?"

"Possibly," Ian replied.

"I'd like to know what could be available, by type, range, load, et cetera, and especially hang time."

"I'll see what I can do," Ian said, then excused himself.

"What do you have in mind?" Millie asked him.

"We're going to try for the same level of surveillance we have on the Washington site, but that will depend on how difficult it is to get inside. It would be a great help if you could ask Ian or somebody around here if it's possible to get the plans for this house—maybe from whatever authority issues building permits over here. It's an old house, so it must have been occasionally updated along the way, especially after the sultan bought it. I'd bet that they did a major renovation at that time."

"I'll go find somebody," Millie said.

THE CJ4 TOOK OFF from Shannon and climbed to flight level 400 (forty thousand feet). Stone watched Pat fly for a while from a forward seat and came back to Dino to report. "We've got a twenty-five-knot tailwind," he said.

"Is that unusual?"

"Yes, the prevailing winds are from the west and southwest. I'll call Mike Freeman and ask him to send his Mustang for us."

"Not yet," Dino said. "I want to make some calls first. Have they got a satphone on this crate?"

Stone pointed at it. "Dial zero-one-one, then the area code and number."

Stone tried to relax, but he kept thinking about his ruined airplane. It was as though he'd lost a leg. He was accustomed to flying himself wherever he went and on a moment's notice, and now he was grounded.

Dino hung up the phone. "We got a break," he said.

"What?"

"I had the NYPD flight department run a check on Reeves's airplane. He's filed a report with U.S. Customs saying he'll land in Presque Isle, Maine, at seven this evening."

"That sounds impossible for a Mustang," Stone said, getting out a chart of the North Atlantic. "But maybe he's taking advantage of the tailwinds, too." He did some rough calculations. "From Cork, he could have gone to Santa Maria, in the Azores, then to St. John's, Newfoundland, then Presque Isle. That's stretching his range a lot, but he does have the tailwinds to help."

"Maybe he'll crash into the sea and save us all a lot of trouble," Dino said.

"Hang on a minute," Stone said. He got up, went forward, and tapped Pat on the shoulder. "What's our ETA for Presque Isle?"

She pointed at the top of the multi-function display. "With the time change, six PM Eastern. We're forecast to get even better winds from the southwest as we get closer to the other side."

"Given the winds, could Reeves fly to the Azores, then to St. John's and then to Presque Isle in the Mustang?"

She thought for a minute. "He could very well do that. He departed from Cork that's, let's see, about thirteen hundred miles to Santa Maria, then fourteen hundred to St. John's. Then only about six hundred and fifty to Presque Isle. His range is thirteen hundred, but that's at full cruise. If he pulled power, he'd increase his range, and the winds are even better for that route than they are for ours."

Stone thanked her and returned to his seat. "Reeves can make that schedule," he said.

Dino picked up the satphone and made a call. "Detective Robert Miller," he said, "the commissioner calling. Hello, Bob? It's Dino Bacchetti. Just fine, thanks. I want you to call the flight department and put a hold on our King Air in my name, then get a warrant for Kevin Keyes on the double murder charge and another warrant for a man named Paul Reeves for accessory after the fact. I don't care if the mayor wants the airplane, you get it. Then I want you to fly to Presque Isle, Maine"—he spelled the name—"and I want you there at six PM sharp. After you land, park the airplane so that it's not conspicuous to arriving aircraft. Got it? Stone Barrington and I will be arriving about that time in a Cessna CJ4. Got it?" He listened for a moment. "You got it. See you then." Dino hung up. "Okay, we've got a ride back to Teterboro," he said.

56

QUENTIN WAS at his desk at MI6 when he got a call. "It's Turner at Hoover," a voice said. "Something's up at Mahmoud's residence."

"Tell me, and don't leave anything out."

"There have been two delivery trucks early this morning," Turner said. "One was from an awning company—"

"What the hell is an awning company?"

"They rent tents and the like for outdoor parties, in case of rain."

"Any rain in the local forecast?"

"Not for a week—I checked. We've got a video from the downstairs garage showing them unloading canvas and putting it in the elevator."

"Not outside? Are they expecting rain indoors?"

"Beats me. The second truck delivered air freight—some large crates. I checked with customs, and they were shipped in under diplomatic seal from Dahai. Hey, hang on, have you got a monitor there?"

"Yeah, the one in the office."

A transmission came up on the monitor. "This is from the Agency drone," Turner said. "It's the rooftop of the building."

Quentin watched and saw some men unrolling large pieces of yellow-striped canvas. "They're setting up a tent on the roof?"

"Looks like it. Wait a minute and you'll get a three-sixty view. The drone is orbiting."

Quentin saw the canvas from every angle. "Looks like what you'd see at a funeral, over the grave." They watched as the men set up a metal frame, then hoisted the canvas in place. "Turner, has Mahmoud played with his drone again?"

"Yes, once. The Agency drone wasn't up in time to photograph or follow it."

"Wait, look to the left of the awning," Quentin said. "They're bringing the crates up to the roof." The crates were wheeled under the awning. "Shit. You think they're onto our drone?"

"They couldn't be, we only got it up this morning. They've got reason to think about drones, though, so I think they're just being careful."

"Can we get the Agency drone low enough to see under the awning?"

"No, then the parapet gets in the way."

Quentin went back into the conference room and found the group all staring at the largest monitor.

Ian Rattle was among them. "Hello," he said. "We've got our hands on a drone—don't ask who from." He pointed at the screen. "That's the roof of Regency House," he said.

"Show me the delivery entrance," Quentin said.

"We had a look at it a minute ago," Ian said. "They got a lorry delivery from a marquee company."

"Marquis, like a French aristocrat?"

"No, marquee . . ." He spelled it. "Like a tent. They must be having a garden party."

"It's not a garden party," Quentin said. "They're going to set up the marquee on the roof."

"A roof party?" Ian asked. "It doesn't look like that kind of roof—too industrial."

"Then they're going to bring those crates that we saw earlier up to the roof and unpack them under the marquee."

"We didn't furnish your office with a crystal ball," Ian said. "Where are you getting this?"

"They're doing exactly the same thing in Washington, at the Dahai apartment building."

Ian stared at him. "I don't like it," he said.

"I don't like it, either."

"Can we get one of your black bag boys on the roof tonight?"

"We're better off with the drone," Quentin said. "Tonight, I think there'll be people on the roof."

"What do you think they're doing?"

"My best guess? They're assembling a drone of their own."

Ian seemed speechless. "And what's your best guess as to what they're going to do with it?"

"There are too many things they could do with it," Quentin replied. "The mind boggles."

Millie came into the room. "What's up?"

Quentin told her. "Where is the president?"

"In Rome."

"When does she get back to Washington?"

"Tomorrow afternoon."

"I don't suppose she could add another couple of cities to her tour, could she?"

"It takes weeks, maybe months, to plan that sort of thing."

"I was afraid of that."

Ian was taking all this in. He picked up a phone. "Get me Ten Downing Street," he said, "the PM's private secretary." He waited for a while. "Sir Robert? This is Major Ian Rattle at MI6. Can you tell me, please, what is the PM's schedule for the next few days?" He listened for a minute or so. "He looks to me as though he needs a rest. Do you think you could get him to go down to Chequers for a few days? I see. No, I'll get back to you later today, after I speak to Dame Felicity." He hung up and dialed an extension. "I'd like to come and see her now," he said. "Right." He hung up and turned to Quentin and Millie. "We're seeing her in ten minutes."

TEN MINUTES LATER, Dame Felicity was sitting in an armchair, waiting for them. "Please sit down," she said, "and tell me what's on your mind."

"Quentin?" Ian said.

"No, you," Quentin replied.

"Ma'am," Ian said, "we've come to believe that the Kimbrough twins in London and Ali Mahmoud are assembling drones on the rooftops of their respective buildings."

Dame Felicity thought about that for a moment. "Do you know what kind of drones?"

Ian looked uncomfortable. "Not yet. They're doing the work under the shelter of marquees erected for the purpose."

"Both of them? Simultaneously?"

"Yes, ma'am."

"That is alarming."

"Yes, ma'am."

"Special Agent Phillips, has your surveillance picked up any phone calls or electronic messages that refer to this activity?"

"No, ma'am. I checked with my team in Washington. Mahmoud has gone all quiet, and we don't have our taps here in yet."

Dame Felicity picked up a phone from a table beside her. "Please video-conference me with Director Lance Cabot at the CIA and Assistant Director Lev Epstein at the FBI." She put down the phone. "This is going to take a few minutes," she said. "Special Agent Phillips, while we're waiting, can you give me some idea of what we're dealing with?"

"I'll try, ma'am," Quentin said. He took a deep breath and began.

57

STONE SAT and stared out the airplane window at the North Atlantic far below.

"You're not getting depressed, are you?" Dino asked.

"Not exactly. I'm just thinking about what not having an airplane means, and that's pretty depressing."

"So why don't you get a new one? The process ought to cheer you up. You just told me about the CJ something or other."

"CJ3 Plus," Stone said.

"The one that has exactly the same avionics that your, ah, former plane had?"

"Yes." Stone brightened, and slapped Dino on the knee. "You're a genius," he said.

"All I did was repeat what you told me."

"Exactly." Stone took out his iPhone and looked up the name of the Cessna salesman who had handled the sale of the M2. He put away the iPhone, picked up the satphone, and dialed the number.

"David Hayes."

"Hi, David, it's Stone Barrington."

"Hello, Stone. What can I do for you?"

"Is the new CJ3 Plus certified yet?"

"Almost."

"What does that mean?"

"We're waiting for final approval."

"If I ordered one today, when would it be delivered?"

"Hang on, let me check the printouts."

"See?" Dino said. "You're looking happier already."

David came back on the line. "I'll have to double-check this with the factory, but it looks like about seven weeks. The airplane is already off the line, waiting for an interior and avionics installation. It already has a pretty high spec."

"Read me the list of equipment."

"Well, it's got the Garmin 3000 panel."

"Read me the options installed."

"Okay, it's got an Automatic Direction Finder, which you won't use in the States but is good to have if you want to sell it overseas, Synthetic Vision, provision for high-frequency radios, Garmin datalink, Terrain Awareness Warning System—TAWS A, XM weather and radio, locking fuel caps, and Angle of Attack Indexer. On the interior it's got the refreshment center with optional side-facing seat, sheepskin cockpit seats, dual satphones, Aircell high-speed Internet service—U.S. only, and the Hawthorne interior. You might still be able to change the interior fabrics at this point, and we'll paint the airplane to your specs."

"How much retraining would I need?"

"None. The cockpit is identical to your M2, but you've got seven hundred more miles of range, four hundred and twenty knots of speed, and you can go up to flight level 450."

"Add the HD radio to the list, call the factory and get me a confirmed delivery date and a price. Same paint scheme as the M2."

"I'll do that." Hayes hung up.

"You look downright cheerful now," Dino said. "See what a sat phone call can do?"

"And I wouldn't have to retrain," Stone said happily. He went forward to the cockpit and tapped Pat on the shoulder. "How far out are we?"

"It says here an hour and eight minutes to Presque Isle." Stone thanked her and went back to his seat. "An hour and eight minutes," Stone said.

Dino picked up the satphone, checked the number, and dialed. "Bob? It's the commissioner. Where are you? Good, we'll be in about forty minutes behind you. Listen, I think you'd better get somebody from the Maine State Police out there. We don't want to step on any toes." He listened. "Great, you're thinking ahead." He hung up. "They're going to beat us there," he said. "Looks like all's right with the world."

"Reeves and Keyes are armed, you know," Stone pointed out.

Dino frowned. "You think they're going to want to shoot it out with us?"

"Whataya mean, 'us'? I'm not armed."

"I should have asked Viv for her gun."

"Maybe so. Listen, I think the way to do this is to let U.S. Customs go in first."

"And let them do our dirty work?"

"It's not that, it's that they're expecting customs, so they won't be on their guard. We're probably going to be there before Reeves lands. You can talk with them about it then."

"Okay."

"What am I supposed to do?" Stone asked.

"You're supposed to stay out of the way," Dino said. "I've got two detectives and the Maine State Police for backup. I think we can handle it without your help."

"And you are welcome to do so," Stone said, sitting back in his seat and relaxing.

The satphone rang, and Stone picked it up. "Hello?"

"It's David Hayes. The airplane is yours, if you want it. I added the HD radio in." He quoted a price.

Stone haggled a little, and they came to an agreement. "I'll wire you the deposit tomorrow morning." Stone hung up happy. "I'll have a new CJ3 Plus in seven weeks. You want to come out to Wichita and make the first flight with me?"

"I'd rather make the second flight with you," Dino said. "Or the fifth. Maybe you'll know what you're doing by then."

Shortly, the airplane began to descend. Stone could see a low line of land appearing out of the mist ahead of the wing.

58

QUENTIN REARRANGED HIMSELF in his chair and began. "I've been studying up on this. We can put drones into three categories for our purposes: One, aircraft that are like large, remote control model airplanes that can be launched simply by running with the drone and throwing it. Their payload is fuel—liquid or battery, maybe a small camera. Two, let's call these mid-sized—drones that are like a cross between a flying saucer and a multi-vaned helicopter—usually with four small propellers. These are amazingly maneuverable. I've seen a video with a dozen of them flying in tight formation inside a gymnasium, controlled by a computer. They can be controlled by a man with a joystick, too, and they can carry more payload—a camera and other equipment, even a significant amount of explosives. The operator can control the airplane when it's out of his sight line by watching the camera feed on a monitor. Three, military drones, which can vary from something the size of a very small airplane, all the way up to something that looks like a pilotless jet fighter. These can carry multiple cameras, can stay up for days, and can carry serious armaments like the Hellfire missile. The Hellfire, which was originally intended as an anti-tank weapon, is old technology these days: it weighs about a hundred pounds, and twenty to thirty pounds of that is in two explosive charges—the first designed to penetrate armor, and the second, right behind it, to blow shrapnel everywhere. It's laser-guided: you point it at a target, and it goes directly there, even if the target is moving."

"It seems likely that if Moe, Larry, and Curly use drones, they will be in the middle category. We know that's what Moe has been practicing with in Rock Creek Park—something about three feet in diameter."

"With what sort of payload?" Dame Felicity asked.

"A larger version could carry twenty to thirty pounds," Quentin replied. "Including the camera. The one Moe was operating in the park seemed to be electric, because it was very quiet. His type of drone is excellent for surveillance work—it can fly right up to an office building and hover outside an assigned window."

"If they have an armed drone, how would we deal with it?"

"If it has a gasoline engine, we could bring it down with a heat-seeking rocket. If it has an electric engine . . . well, that's another story. It would be hard to shoot at and hit. Think of how hard it is to swat a fly: they have very fast reactions. The drone could carry a GPS unit that could fly it to selected coordinates, while using a computer-controlled flight path that could zig and zag on its way to the target. The control unit could be no larger than a hardcover book, maybe even a paperback."

"Is there a guided missile small enough to be carried by such a drone?"

"Not that I'm aware of. You'd have to design one from scratch, and that's a time-consuming and expensive operation. But—and here's the rub—if you want to go after a fixed target with a drone, you don't need to fire a missile at it, you can just crash the drone into the target. Without the multiple warheads and electronics of a Hellfire missile, you'd just have the explosive, some shrapnel, and a contact detonator as payload, and with an explosive of twenty to thirty pounds. That's quite a lot of C-4 plastique."

The phone rang, and Dame Felicity picked it up. A monitor came alive with a split-screen image of Lance Cabot and Lev Epstein.

"Good morning, Dame Felicity," Lance said, and Epstein gave a little wave.

"Good morning, gentlemen. I want to thank you both for your participation in this mission, and I want to bring you up to date. From the available evidence in both London and Washington, it would appear that the Three Stooges may be assembling drones, each on the roof of an embassy building here and in Washington. These drones would be large enough to carry a considerable explosive payload, and they are highly maneuverable. The work is being conducted under canvas awnings that hide them from view."

At the invitation of Dame Felicity, Quentin repeated his theory of how the drones might work. When he had finished there was a long silence from everybody on both ends of the conference call.

Finally Lance Cabot said, "This is very worrying."

"Yes, sir," Quentin said. "We can't see what they're doing, and we can't enter these premises to find out because both buildings are embassy properties. We also can't arrest the suspects because they have diplomatic immunity. Not that we have a case that could be prosecuted, anyway, except after the fact of whatever they plan to do."

Lev spoke up. "If we had hard evidence that they plan a terrorist attack of some sort, I would not hesitate to order agents into those buildings and face the consequences later."

"Nor would I," Lance said. "Have you given any thought to what their targets might be?"

Ian spoke up. "I have. If I were a terrorist, I would go for the most important available targets, both from a political and a publicity point of view. In the absence of large airliners to use as weapons, I would go for something more pinpoint."

"Such as?" Lev asked.

"Such as the president of the United States and the prime minister of Great Britain. I've checked: the president will return to Washington from Rome tomorrow afternoon, and the prime minister will be mostly at Number Ten Downing Street for the next three days. The day after tomorrow at nine o'clock AM London time, he will be holding a Cabinet meeting. That would be four AM Washington time, when the president would presumably be in bed asleep, so she won't be surrounded by advisers. However, she is with child, and her assassination would inflame the world."

"They can both be moved to secure locations," Lev said.

"But for how long?" Ian asked. "All these people have to do is wait. They are secure in their physical positions and need be in no rush."

"Then why do you think the day after tomorrow is such a strong possibility?" Dame Felicity asked.

"I'm sorry to have to use the word," Ian said, "but it's a hunch, one based on the earliest moment when it would be advantageous to execute an assassination."

"It sounds like a pretty good hunch to me," Lance said. "Is there a place at Number Ten where the PM and his Cabinet could be made secure?"

"There is such a place," Dame Felicity said. "And I assume that one must be available in the White House, as well."

"I expect so," Lance said. "Quentin, what do you think the chances are of our shooting down their drones with our drones?"

"Somewhere between slim and nil," Quentin replied, "and we can't afford a lack of certainty."

"Neither can we afford the risks associated with firing Gatling guns and air-to-air missiles over densely populated areas," Lance said. "Those bullets and rockets, if they missed, would end up on the ground, and no one could predict where."

"I can suggest a way to get one clean shot at them," Quentin said.

"Please do so," Lance replied.

"I can't speak for MI6, but in Washington we have the possibility of stationing an armed drone above the Dahai building and firing on a drone the second it tried to take off."

"That is a possibility in London, as well," Ian said. "But if something goes wrong, then what?"

"It seems clear to me," Lance said, "that we cannot allow those drones, if that is what they are, to be launched, and that we must use whatever means are at our disposal to see that they are not."

"And face the consequences later?" Dame Felicity asked.

"I'm afraid so," Lance replied.

"We certainly cannot do that without the concurrence of our masters," she said.

"I agree, of course," Lance said. "In the meantime, we must do everything in our power to bolster our case, and it seems inevitable that that will require the laying on of eyes on both of these rooftops, even if the means are extra-legal."

"I agree," Dame Felicity said.

"The question is," Lance pointed out, "shall we ask permission, or shall we just do it and preserve deniability for our superiors?"

"I will have to go to the prime minister," Dame Felicity said.

"Then I will go to the president," Lance Cabot replied. "Shall we conference again when we have done that?"

"Agreed." The conference call ended, and the participants returned to their work.

Millie and Quentin returned to the conference room. "I have to use your office to make a call," she said.

"Go ahead," Quentin replied.

Millie went into the room, closed the door behind her, and called Holly Barker.

59

STONE LOOKED out the window and saw the single runway of Presque Isle airport. As they turned to final approach, he searched the apron beside the runway for any sign of a Mustang and a King Air and saw neither. "Reeves didn't beat us here," he said to Dino.

"Did you see a King Air with NYPD painted on it?"

"No."

"Good."

Pat set down the CJ4 lightly on the runway and braked. A moment later she was taxiing toward a waiting lineman near the FBO. She stopped and waited for the man to chock the nosewheel, then she shut down the engines and turned off the master switch. "Everybody stay on the airplane until customs tells us we can get off," she said, as she made her way out of the cockpit, followed by her client. She opened the cabin door and flipped down the folding stairs, then they both took a seat.

"Good flight," Stone said. "How much fuel did we have left? On landing?"

"Seven hundred pounds," she replied.

"Very good. The winds held, huh?"

"They got better on the last third of the flight."

"You're a lucky pilot."

A man stuck his head inside the door. "Who's the captain?" Holly raised a hand, and he waved her out.

Dino followed her to the door and watched as she went down the stairs to meet them.

"Anything to declare?" The customs man asked.

"Nothing," she replied, handing him a sheet of paper. "Here's our general declaration."

"There are several police officers waiting for you in the FBO," the man said.

"May we go inside?"

"You're cleared. Go ahead."

Dino got down from the airplane, followed by Stone and the client. Dino showed them his ID. "We're expecting two men in a Mustang," he said, "and we're going to arrest them."

"We were notified of only one man, a Paul Reeves," the customs man said.

"There will be another man aboard. You may have to look for him, and you should do so armed, because he will be."

"Whatever you say."

"If you like, my officers and the Maine State Police can handle that part."

"You have more experience of that sort of thing than we do."

"I suggest that you ask Reeves to go inside the FBO with you. After that, we'll approach the airplane."

"As you wish."

They sent their luggage over to the King Air, and Dino beckoned for Stone to follow him inside, where the two NYPD detectives and two Maine State Police officers awaited. Dino told Pat, her client, and Stone to sit down, then he briefed the officers. He looked at his watch. "We expect them in about forty-five minutes, but they could be early. There were tailwinds up there. Let's get suited up for this."

The officers all left the building and came back with flak jackets and assault weapons.

Dino came over to Stone. "This guy Keyes has never seen me, has he?"

"Not on this trip," Stone replied. "But you're on TV from time to time. Maybe he saw you there. If you're thinking of approaching him without the body armor, I wouldn't."

Pat joined them. "You're not going to kill him, are you?" she asked Dino.

"That's not our intention," Dino replied, "but it's really up to him. Were you present when he was arrested in the past?"

She nodded. "Twice."

"Did he go quietly?"

She shook her head. "He went nuts. It took four men to hold him down."

"I guess we'd better be ready for that, then." Dino went to pass the news on to the officers.

STONE WAS DOZING OFF in his chair when the FBO's radio crackled. "Presque Isle traffic: Citation Mustang turning a five-mile final for one-niner."

"There he is," Dino said. "Let's go, guys." He led them out the rear door of the building and they took positions behind parked airplanes as the Mustang turned off the runway and began taxiing toward a lineman, who stood with his hands up, indicating where they should park.

Dino looked at the Mustang as it turned to park. "The window shades are all down on this side of the airplane," he said to his men. "As soon as Reeves is inside the building with the customs officers, we'll approach the airplane from this side and duck under the nose."

STONE WATCHED from a window as the customs men approached the airplane. The door opened and Paul Reeves came down the stairs and handed them a sheet of paper. They indicated that he should follow them inside. They started for the building, and he saw Dino leading the four cops toward the airplane from the other side.

Reeves walked into the FBO building and stopped, staring first at Pat, then at Stone. "What are you doing here?" he demanded.

"We're the reception committee," Stone replied.

DINO DUCKED under the nose of the airplane and approached the door. He stuck his head inside, then quickly withdrew it, then motioned his men to stand behind him. When they were ready, he called out, "Kevin Keyes! This is Bacchetti of the New York Police Department! I have a warrant for your arrest. Put down your weapons and exit the airplane with your hands up!"

Dino was leaning on the airplane, and he felt it move a little.

"Come on out!" he yelled. Then he heard the sound of something metallic hitting the pavement, then the sound of feet on the opposite wing, then the sound of a man running.

"Shit!" Dino said. "I forgot the emergency exit in the rear! He's loose on the other side!" He ran around the airplane just in time to see a man disappear into the woods.

Back in the FBO Stone saw the man, too. "He went out the emergency exit, opposite the toilet," he called back to Pat. "He's on the run!" He looked out the window again. "It's getting dark," he said. "This is not good."

60

HOLLY ANSWERED on the first ring. "Talk fast," she said.

"Holly," Millie replied, "sit down. This is going to take time to explain. Where are you now?"

"In the car with the president."

"This is what has happened, or what we think is happening." She ran through her day as quickly as possible.

"Tell me what you want to do," Holly said when she had finished.

"We need the president's authorization for a surreptitious entry into a building owned by a foreign embassy, and, if the surreptitious part fails, to engage and detain foreigners carrying diplomatic passports."

"Oh, is *that* all?"

"That's all so far," Millie replied.

"Well, I'm going to have to get back to you on that," Holly said, then hung up.

MILLIE WAITED for the better part of an hour for a callback, and when it didn't come she went into the conference room, where Quentin and his team sat around, looking nervous and occasionally monitoring the monitors.

"I take it you spoke to Holly Barker," Quentin said.

"I did."

"And?"

"And she'll get back to us."

"We're losing time," Quentin said. "We've got to do this tonight, if we're going to stop them. We can't be put in a position where our only alternative is to shoot down the drone after it takes off."

"I've explained that to Holly, and I expect she's explaining it to the president right now. If you want to be sure of being ready, I suggest you start planning for both alternatives now."

Quentin stood up. "Okay, everybody, we're going to split into two teams: Ian, how's this? We're sixteen in all—you pick four Brits, and I'll pick four Americans. One of us will plan a black ops rooftop incursion, the other will plan to destroy the drone *after* it flies off the roof. Which operation do you want?"

"I think I'd better take the one that requires live rounds to be fired over London," Ian said. "We can't have Yanks doing that."

"That's good reasoning," Quentin said. "You and your people take the conference room, and my group will meet in my office."

Everybody started to move, but the ringing of Millie's cell phone stopped them.

"Hello?"

"Are you with Quentin?" Holly asked.

"Yes, we're in the conference room with the whole team."

"Put this on speaker, then."

Millie pressed the button. "We're on speaker, Holly."

"We're now at the Rome embassy, and the president has just teleconferenced with Lance Cabot, Lev Epstein, and Dame Felicity. They have confirmed your account of the earlier teleconference as correct in every respect, so congratulations."

"Thank you. What are our instructions?"

"You are to divide yourselves into two teams, each half Brit, half American. Team one, under the command of Quentin Phillips, is to gain surreptitious access to the rooftop of Regency House, there to capture or destroy whatever weapon it finds there, hopefully without being discovered or having to shoot anybody. In the event of the failure of that mission and the launching of a drone or other means of attack, team two, under the command of Ian Rattle, will destroy it the moment it leaves the roof, by *any means deemed necessary*, up to and including RAF aircraft. These operations are to commence at six AM, London time. The Washington operation will commence at one AM, local time. You are to capture and detain Larry and Curly, the twins known as David and Derek Kimbrough, unharmed if at all possible, and transport them, under guard, to RAF Northolt airfield, from where, later in the day, they will be picked up by an aircraft and flown directly to Dahai. Is that all perfectly clear?"

"Yes, Holly," Millie replied.

"I assume you've recorded this conversation?"

Millie looked at Quentin, who nodded.

"Yes."

"Then play it back so that no one can doubt the instructions, then destroy the recording. Any questions?"

"Holly, it's Quentin Phillips. How will the Washington operation be conducted?"

"They will be commanded by Lev Epstein, whose instructions are identical to yours. The Dahai embassy has a sultanate aircraft on the ground at Dulles, and Ali Mahmoud will be placed on that aircraft under armed guard. It will be flown to Northolt, where it will be refueled and take on the twins and be escorted by teams of British and American fighters to the border of Dahai on the Gulf of Aden. The Dahai pilots will be told that if they deviate from that flight plan in any way, their aircraft will be destroyed. Any other questions?"

Quentin shook his head. "No, Holly," Millie replied, and they both hung up. "Well," she said to Quentin, "you read their minds, didn't you?"

"It would seem so," Quentin replied, then he opened the conference room door and called to Ian, "Do you have—either in service or under development—a helicopter that can fly very, very quietly?"

"I thought you might ask," Ian replied. "I have already requisitioned it."

"Thank you," Quentin said, "and please ask them to have two invalid litters aboard."

"Already done."

Quentin smiled and closed the door.

"Do *we* have such an aircraft in or around Washington?" Millie asked.

"You bet your sweet ass we do, and you can also bet that Lev has already commandeered it."

61

DINO BURST into the FBO, huffing and puffing. "What did you tell me on the phone?"

"That Kevin Keyes somehow circled back to the airport, entered Paul Reeves's Mustang, reinstalled the emergency door, and took off in the airplane, headed south."

"Holy shit!" Dino screamed.

"He's not going to get very far," Stone said.

"Why not?"

"Because they flew that airplane from St. John's, Newfoundland, to here, and they have not refueled."

"How far can he get?"

"My guess is he has about a third of the full fuel load. He's unlikely to get any great distance with only that." Stone went to the wall where there was a chart of the state of Maine. "Going south, he could refuel at Bangor, Augusta, or Portland, but I think he'd prefer a smaller airport—say, Bar Harbor, here." He pointed at the field.

"Once refueled, then the world is his oyster, or at least the country is. Funny, I had thought he'd head for Canada, which is only a few miles, but I suppose he had other plans."

Dino turned to a Maine policeman. "Will you get on the horn and get that airplane met at Bar Harbor—also at Bangor, Augusta, and Portland, just in case?"

"Yes, sir, Commissioner," the cop said, and dug out his phone.

Stone dug out his own phone. "We may be able to track him," he said, opening an app. He entered the tail number of Reeves's airplane and waited for a moment. "There he is," he said. "This is called FlightAware, and it shows him headed dead straight for Bar Harbor and nearly halfway there. I'd say you've got about twenty minutes before he lands, and it will take him half an hour to refuel and take off again."

The Maine cop put away his phone. "My people from the Ellsworth station will be there in ten or twelve minutes. I told them no sirens, no lights."

Stone turned to him. "It might be a good idea to call the FBO at Bar Harbor—Columbia Air Services—and tell them to have trouble with the fuel truck. It might be a good time to drive it to the fuel farm and refill the tank, slowly."

"Is there radar at Bar Harbor Airport?" Dino asked.

"No, not unless they've installed it since the last time I was there, last summer."

"Bob, call our pilots and tell them to get the engines started. We're going after Keyes."

"I'm going to hand you off to the captain at that end," the Maine cop said, handing him a slip of paper. "Here's his cell number. If you've got a satphone, you can call him on the way."

Dino pumped his hand and thanked him. "Let's go!" he yelled, and he, his two detectives, and Stone ran for the King Air, the engines of which were already running.

In the air, Dino made contact with the police on the other end, then hung up. "They're already at the airport," he said. "You know, I should thank Keyes—this is going to be a lot easier than chasing him around the Maine woods with bloodhounds."

"I hope you're right," Stone said. "We're getting lower—we must be about to land." He looked out the window. It was dark, now, but the ramp was well lit. "There's the airport, and there's a Mustang on the ramp. No fuel truck present." They turned onto final approach, and he lost sight of the ramp.

They touched down and made the first turnoff. "Tell your pilot to taxi up behind the Mustang," Stone said to Dino, and he went to pass that on to the pilot.

Stone got a better look at the Mustang as they made the turn behind it. The cabin door was open and the stairs extended. No one was on the ramp near it. "He's probably in the FBO," Stone said. He followed Dino and his men, assault weapons at the ready, as they entered the FBO, to be greeted by a Maine State Police officers.

"I'm Everson," the man said. "We've been here for ten minutes, and we can't find him."

Stone went to the counter. "Did the pilot of the Mustang on the ramp rent a car?" he asked the woman in charge.

"No, but rental cars are over at the main terminal, next door. When he heard it was going to take a while to refuel him, he went over there."

"Lead the way," Dino said to the captain, who did so, his men hot on his heels. They poured out of the building and down some stairs, then ran up a short hill toward the terminal and its parking lot. As they did, a car pulled out of the rental spaces and headed toward them.

"That's Kevin Keyes at the wheel," Stone shouted, and the car came to a stop, short of half a dozen assault rifles pointed at it. A cop opened the driver's door, collared the driver, and yanked him onto the pavement. In a moment he was cuffed and bent over the hood, as he was searched for weapons. Two handguns were found.

Stone walked over to the car, bent over, and looked into Keyes's face. "Ah, Kevin, we meet at last," he said. "I just wanted to let you know that you've spent your last day on earth as a free man. One way or another, you're going to die in prison."

"Put him on our airplane," Dino said to the cops. "Bob, show the captain the warrant and the paperwork."

"Did you refuel at Presque Isle?" Stone asked.

"Yep."

"Then you can make it to Teterboro easily on what you've got."

"We'll take off just as soon as this guy is cuffed into a seat next to his buddy," Dino said.

STONE WAS WAKENED from a sound sleep as they touched down at Teterboro Airport, in New Jersey. An NYPD van pulled up to the airplane, and the prisoners were transferred and driven away.

Dino made a dusting motion with his hands. "I'm glad to be rid of those two," he said.

"No more you than I," Stone replied, getting into Dino's SUV and settling in. "Wake me when we're home." By the time they had driven off the ramp, he was asleep again.

62

MILLIE AND QUENTIN'S team crowded into a small briefing room at RAF Northolt. A large-scale map was pinned to the wall, and a red circle was drawn around a house bordering Regent's Park. Everyone was in black battle dress, full body armor with helmets, including Millie.

The helicopter pilot held a pointer. "This is the plan," he said. "We're going to reach this point down the road from the house at a hundred feet, no lights. Our machine is very quiet, but we'll follow the road as we descend, so that any noise we make will sound like traffic on the ground. Just about here, we'll hover. At that point we'll lower you to a visual altitude of about ten feet above the parapet, then we'll inch toward the house sideways and play a red spotlight on the roof, so as not to interfere with the night vision goggles."

"Any weapons backup?" Quentin asked.

"A man with a mounted, silenced, heavy assault rifle will stand in the doorway, ready to take out anybody you say. You'll be in radio contact with your headset, and you will make that call. If anybody points a weapon at you, our gunner won't wait."

"How long to get to the house?"

"We will arrive above the house at precisely five AM," the pilot said. "It is my understanding that the lady is coming along as an unarmed observer and will be strapped into her seat at all times. Are we clear on that?"

"Perfectly clear," Millie replied.

"You will all remain hooked up at all times, until you enter the building. We'll give you slack. Your headsets will work inside the house, so try and keep us posted on your progress. Another thing," the pilot said, "my orders are, if anything lifts off that roof and begins to fly away, I'm to get the hell out of there in a hurry, because there will be incoming. We'll snatch you as quickly as we can, but you're going to get a ride while dangling, until we can get you winched up. If you're still in the house, a van will be parked in the street to take you away, but we can't help you get out of the house."

"Right," Quentin said.

The pilot consulted his watch. "Time to saddle up."

The men filed out of the building onto the tarmac, where the matte black helicopter awaited, its rotors turning. Millie climbed in first, and an airman belted her into a five-point harness that held her tightly in her seat. "Just turn the knob to release," the man said, tightening the straps, "but not until we're on the ground." Millie nodded.

Quentin and his men hooked onto their cables and sat in the open doors on both sides of the chopper, their feet dangling. They had had only one rehearsal, and Quentin was grateful for that.

The machine lifted off and climbed to a thousand feet, then

turned and headed toward London. Two minutes out from their objective and descending, the sound of the helicopter was reduced to a low whirr.

THERE WAS a little light in the east, and Quentin could see the park. Then they were down to under a hundred feet, and he saw a man walking his dog. The man didn't even look up, and that pleased Quentin.

The helicopter came to a stop, hovering, and descended slowly. The rooftop was a hundred feet away, and Quentin could make out the yellow-striped awning. A crewman knocked on his helmet, and he pushed off into space.

IN WASHINGTON, Lev Epstein, fully suited out, stood in the door of the helicopter and stared at the striped awning a hundred feet away. He slapped the team leader on the helmet, and he and they pushed out the door and started down, each controlling his own cable with a remote control. Lev knew he was too old and too fat to go with them, but he still wanted to.

They touched the roof and ran toward the tent, paying out wire. Lev saw no one else on the roof.

ONE FLOOR DOWN, in the penthouse apartment, Ali Mahmoud's eyelids fluttered. He thought he had heard a soft thump above him, but it might have been a dream. He tried to go back to sleep, but his brain replayed the thump. He swung his feet over the side of the bed, opened a drawer, and removed a .45 semiautomatic pistol—loaded, one in the chamber and cocked. He got into his slippers, thumbed the safety down, and padded across his bedroom, into the living room, and out the door into the hallway. The stairway door was a few feet away. He opened the door and listened. There seemed to be some sort of shuffling going on above him. Had one of his people gone up there to check things again? He started up the stairs and as he did, he heard a ratcheting noise from the roof. At the top of the stairs, he put his hand on the door handle, pushed it slowly down, and opened it, taking the final step onto the roof. There were dark shapes moving around, and the canopy was gone. He raised his pistol, but as he did he felt cold steel against his right temple.

"Shhhh," someone said, putting a hand over his mouth, and his gun was taken from his hand. Something stabbed him in the side of the neck, and he went limp. He felt the sensation of being carried before he passed out.

IN LONDON, the red spotlight came on, and Quentin saw two elongated lumps on the roof, between him and the awning. Then one of the lumps sat up, and both of them disappeared under a wave of heavy men. Two men in sleeping bags, he thought to himself. They were held down until the drugs had been administered, and he stepped forward for a look. Blond hair protruded from the bag. He switched on his flashlight and got a look, then at the other one. He spoke into his microphone. "Lower litters," he said. He turned and watched them come down, then saw them, loaded, go up again and disappear into the helicopter.

When he turned around, the awning had been removed and he

was staring at a spidery-looking beast about six feet in diameter with six rotors, each about eighteen inches long, and a pod underneath the thing. His explosives man was on his back, inching under the machine with a flashlight. After a moment, he came out with a piece of wire and a small cylinder in his hand.

"Detonator removed," the man whispered into his microphone, then stood up and looked at the drone. "We're never going to get this thing into the helicopter—it's too big."

Quentin lifted one leg of the thing and was surprised at how light it was. He unhooked his cable, looped it around one of the machine's legs twice, and clipped it to itself. "Pilot, this is number one. It's too big to go inside—we're going to have to carry it dangling."

"Roger," the pilot replied.

Quentin pressed his remote control, the cable tightened, and the machine lifted off the roof and began to rise. When it was six feet below the chopper, he pressed the button again, and it hung there, suspended. "Number one to crew, I need another cable."

The litter carrying the twins was lifted aboard and secured, then Quentin was winched up and helped inside. "Count off," he said. The men stated their numbers. "Pilot, let's get out of here," he said.

The helicopter rotated ninety degrees and began to climb. Quentin sat down beside Millie, unclipped his cable, and fastened his seat harness. "Hi there," he said.

She put a hand on his cheek. "Welcome back," she replied.

IN WASHINGTON, Lev leaned out of the helicopter and peered at the thing dangling below them as they flew over the rooftops of the city and began climbing. He hadn't expected it to be so big. He made his way over to the litter and looked at the unconscious Ali Mahmoud in silk pajamas, strapped into it. "All right," he said into the headset, "let's head for Dulles."

FORTY MINUTES LATER at the military terminal the chopper descended by inches until the drone could be unhooked and removed to a hangar, then the litter was carried to the waiting jet. The sleeping Mahmoud was removed from the litter, strapped into a seat, and handcuffed to the armrest, across from where the two Dahai pilots sat, opposite the two CIA guards who would accompany them to London. One of them reclined the prisoner's seat, then put a blanket over him and a pillow behind his head. "Sleep tight," he said.

Up front in the cockpit, two CIA officers were completing their checklists. Lev tapped one of the guards on the shoulder. "When he wakes up, tell him that he has been declared persona non grata by the secretary of state of the United States of America. His embassy will be notified."

Lev left the airplane and walked back toward the hangar, unbuckling gear and handing it to one of his men. Inside, the others were gathered around the drone. "It's big, isn't it?" one of them said.

"Bigger than we planned for," Lev replied. He looked back and watched as the Dahai jet taxied away. He got out his cell phone and pressed a button.

"This is Phillips."

"It's Lev. Mission complete here. How about you?"

"All is well."

"The airplane is taking off now. It will be there in about seven hours. You got the twins?"

"That part was easy—they were sleeping on the roof, next to the drone."

"Well done, Special Agent. You're going to do well out of this."

"Thanks, but not as well as you, sir."

Lev laughed. "Let's not get ahead of ourselves. When are you coming home?"

"Can I have a couple of days?"

"We'll teleconference at three PM London time for debriefing. After that, you can take as much time as you want."

MILLIE CALLED HOLLY, who was already up. "It's done," she said. "On both ends—all of it. The airplane is on its way to London."

"That is perfectly wonderful," Holly said. "When are you coming back?"

"Can I take a couple of days?"

"Sure. I'll see what I can do about an aircraft for you two."

"You're a good boss."

"You're a good kid." They hung up.

AT LANGLEY, Lance Cabot thanked Lev Epstein, then sat, sipping coffee and waiting for his call to his Yemen station chief to go through. Finally, the phone rang. "Yes?"

"It's Carter, Director."

"Scramble."

"I am scrambled."

"Ah, Carter. Tell me about your contact with the leader of the Dahai Freedom Brigade—what's his name?"

"We're not sure, but he answers to Habbib. A good man, sir. If they're ever able to dislodge the sultan, he'll be in line for the leadership."

"I believe we supplied him with a dozen Russian SA-7 shoulder-fired missiles a few weeks ago."

"We did, sir."

"What sort of guidance system?"

"Laser-operated, sir. You lock on, then let it go."

"Range?"

"Six miles target detection, four miles engagement range, up to twenty thousand feet."

"Can you get in touch with your man?"

"We also supplied him with an encrypted cell phone."

"Ring him up and tell him there will be an irresistible target arriving at Dahai International at seven this evening, local time. It's a G-450, painted white, tail number Delta Alpha 004. I believe the wind is forecast from the north today, so the flight will fly the ILS 36 approach. The initial approach fix is out over the sea, about six miles from the threshold of runway 36 and four miles from the beach. We'd like it to fall in deep water."

"Can I tell him who's aboard?"

"Three of the sultan's favorites."

"He'll like that. Shall I offer him an incentive?"

"Tell him if he hits the mark, we'll wire a million dollars to whatever account he likes."

"Consider it done, sir."

"I knew you'd say that. Oh, and tell him not to shoot down an airliner, will you?"

"I'll tell him to take along his binoculars."

"And tell him to be sure to issue a statement saying that the Brigade takes responsibility. We want him to have all the credit."

"I'll see that he does, sir."

"Thank you, Carter." Lance hung up and poured himself another cup of coffee.

63

IT WAS BROAD DAYLIGHT when Millie closed the curtains in her suite at the Connaught and climbed into bed with Quentin. "You'd better still be awake," she said, snuggling up to him.

"Wide awake," he said, fondling a breast and kissing her.

"You didn't want to stay and see the Dahai jet off?"

"Ian can take care of that. I'm right where I want to be." He rolled over on top of her. "We have until two-thirty, when the car comes to take us to MI6 for our debriefing teleconference."

"Then we'd better get started," she said, guiding him inside her.

IT WAS AFTER MIDNIGHT before Stone crawled into bed, tired enough to be glad he was alone. He fell immediately into a contented sleep.

HE WOKE at six-thirty and ordered breakfast, then got into a hot shower. He was eating breakfast in bed at seven, when he turned on the *CBS Morning News*. A banner was spread across the screen: BREAKING NEWS!

Charlie Rose came on. "Good morning. In just a moment we'll be going to the James Brady Briefing Room at the White House, where the president will be making what we are told will be an extraordinary announcement. Nora O'Donnell, do you have any idea what this is about?"

"Charlie, I hope we're going to hear that the Middle East negotiations have been successfully concluded. Wait, here we go."

The White House press secretary stepped to the podium. "Ladies and gentlemen," he said gravely, "the president."

Then Will Lee entered from stage left, dressed casually in khaki trousers, an open-necked plaid shirt, and a blue blazer. "Sorry, wrong president," he said, getting a big laugh. "Ladies and gentlemen, it falls to me to make an announcement never before heard at the White House. This morning, a little after five-thirty AM, the president of the United States gave birth to a son."

The room was on its feet, clapping and cheering.

When the noise had died down Will continued. "He will be named, oddly enough, William Henry Lee the Fifth, continuing a tradition that began with my great-grandfather. He will be called, in the family, Will Henry, after *his* great-grandfather. In spite of being a few weeks premature, he weighed six pounds nine ounces."

"Who delivered him?" someone in the front row asked.

"I'm afraid this was a very hurried process," Will said. "I was awakened from a sound sleep a little late in the game by the president, who asked me to call the doctor. I had hardly finished the call when events took a sudden turn. Assisted by Secret Service Agent Frances Buchannan, who in a previous existence was a registered nurse, I called upon my experience in college, when during two summers I worked as an EMT, and I delivered the boy myself. By the time the doctor arrived, the process was essentially complete."

More applause, cheering, and stomping.

Will got them quieted down. "Mother and child are resting comfortably, and now I must return to my duties as President Mom. More bulletins to come."

Will left the podium to cheering, and a photograph of Kate and Will Henry was projected onto a large screen.

Stone found himself grinning and clapping.

AUTHOR'S NOTE

I am happy to hear from readers, but you should know that if you write to me in care of my publisher, three to six months will pass before I receive your letter, and when it finally arrives it will be one among many, and I will not be able to reply.

However, if you have access to the Internet, you may visit my website at www.stuartwoods.com, where there is a button for sending me e-mail. So far, I have been able to reply to all my e-mail, and I will continue to try to do so.

If you send me an e-mail and do not receive a reply, it is probably because you are among an alarming number of people who have entered their e-mail address incorrectly in their mail software. I have many of my replies returned as undeliverable.

Remember: e-mail, reply; snail mail, no reply.

When you e-mail, please do not send attachments, as I never open these. They can take twenty minutes to download, and they often contain viruses.

AUTHOR'S NOTE

Please do not place me on your mailing lists for funny stories, prayers, political causes, charitable fund-raising, petitions, or sentimental claptrap. I get enough of that from people I already know. Generally speaking, when I get e-mail addressed to a large number of people, I immediately delete it without reading it.

Please do not send me your ideas for a book, as I have a policy of writing only what I myself invent. If you send me story ideas, I will immediately delete them without reading them. If you have a good idea for a book, write it yourself, but I will not be able to advise you on how to get it published. Buy a copy of *Writer's Market* at any bookstore; that will tell you how.

Anyone with a request concerning events or appearances may e-mail it to me or send it to: Publicity Department, Penguin Group (USA), 375 Hudson Street, New York, NY 10014.

Those ambitious folk who wish to buy film, dramatic, or television rights to my books should contact Matthew Snyder, Creative Artists Agency, 9830 Wilshire Boulevard, Beverly Hills, CA 98212-1825.

Those who wish to make offers for rights of a literary nature should contact Anne Sibbald, Janklow & Nesbit, 445 Park Avenue, New York, NY 10022. (Note: This is not an invitation for you to send her your manuscript or to solicit her to be your agent.)

If you want to know if I will be signing books in your city, please visit my website, www.stuartwoods.com, where the tour schedule will be published a month or so in advance. If you wish me to do a book signing in your locality, ask your favorite bookseller to contact his Penguin representative or the Penguin publicity department with the request.

If you find typographical or editorial errors in my book and feel an irresistible urge to tell someone, please write to Sara Minnich at Penguin's address above. Do not e-mail your discoveries to me, as I will already have learned about them from others.

A list of my published works appears in the front of this book and on my website. All the novels are still in print in paperback and can be found at or ordered from any bookstore. If you wish to obtain hardcover copies of earlier novels or of the two nonfiction books, a good used-book store or one of the online bookstores can help you find them. Otherwise, you will have to go to a great many garage sales.

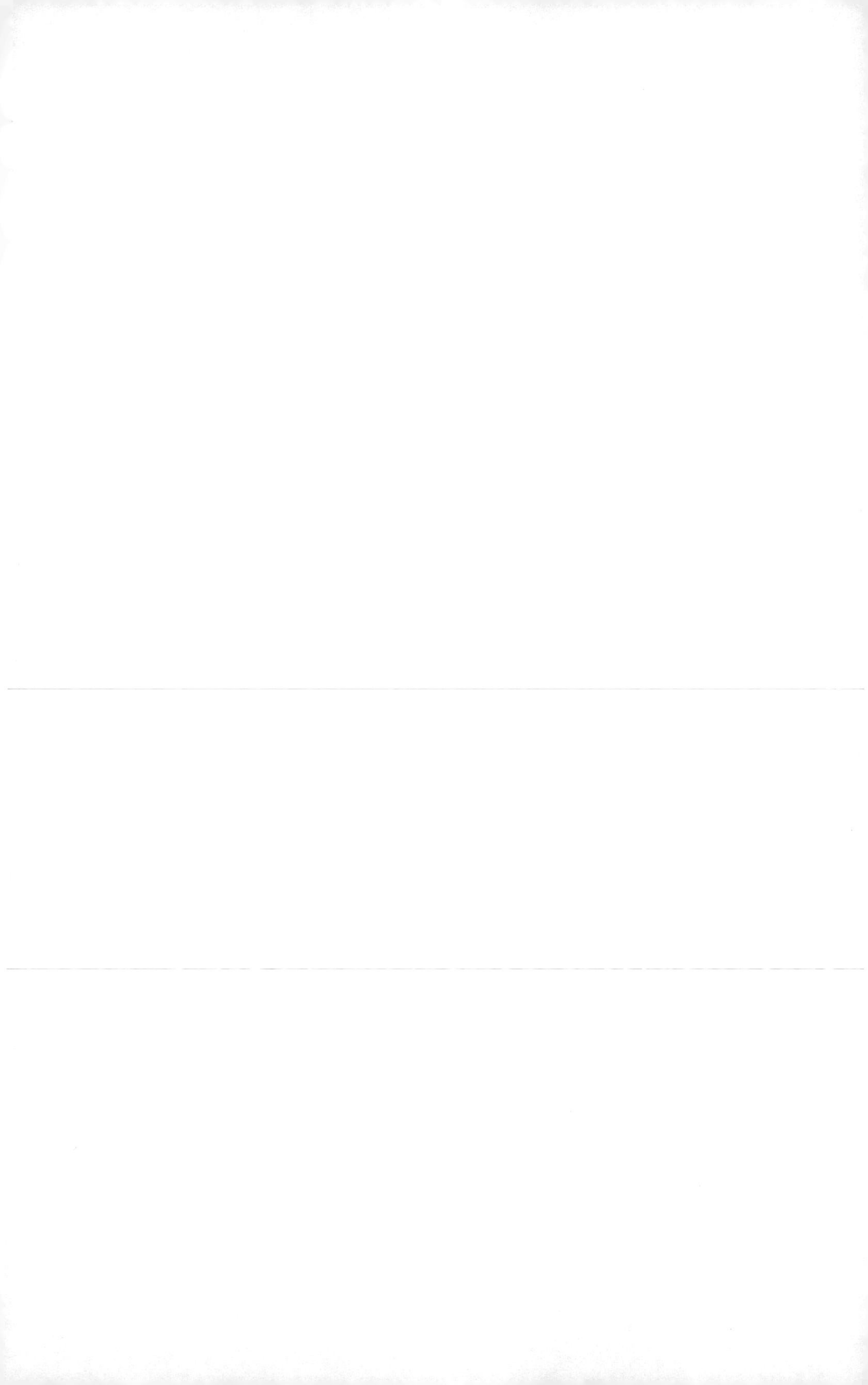

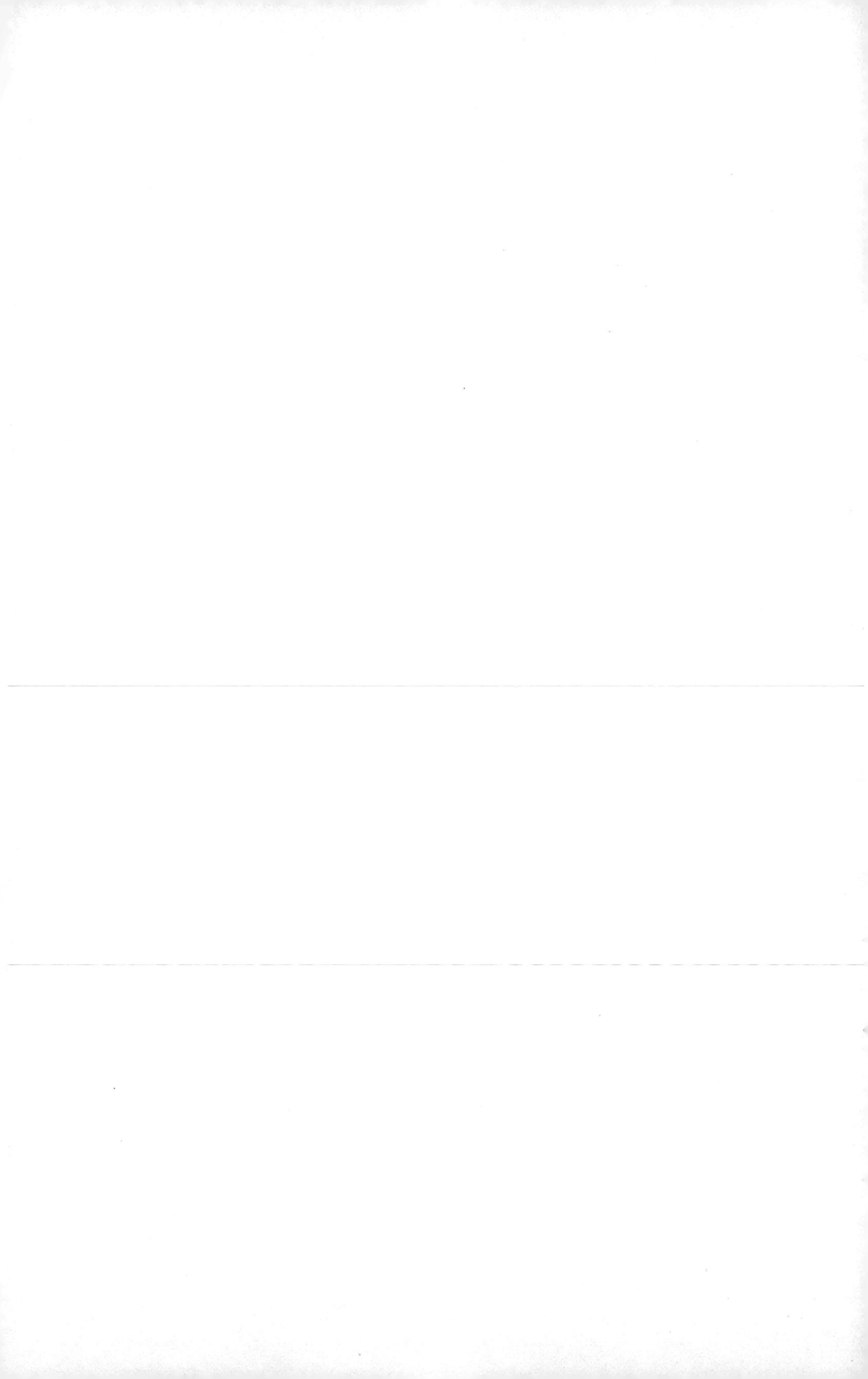

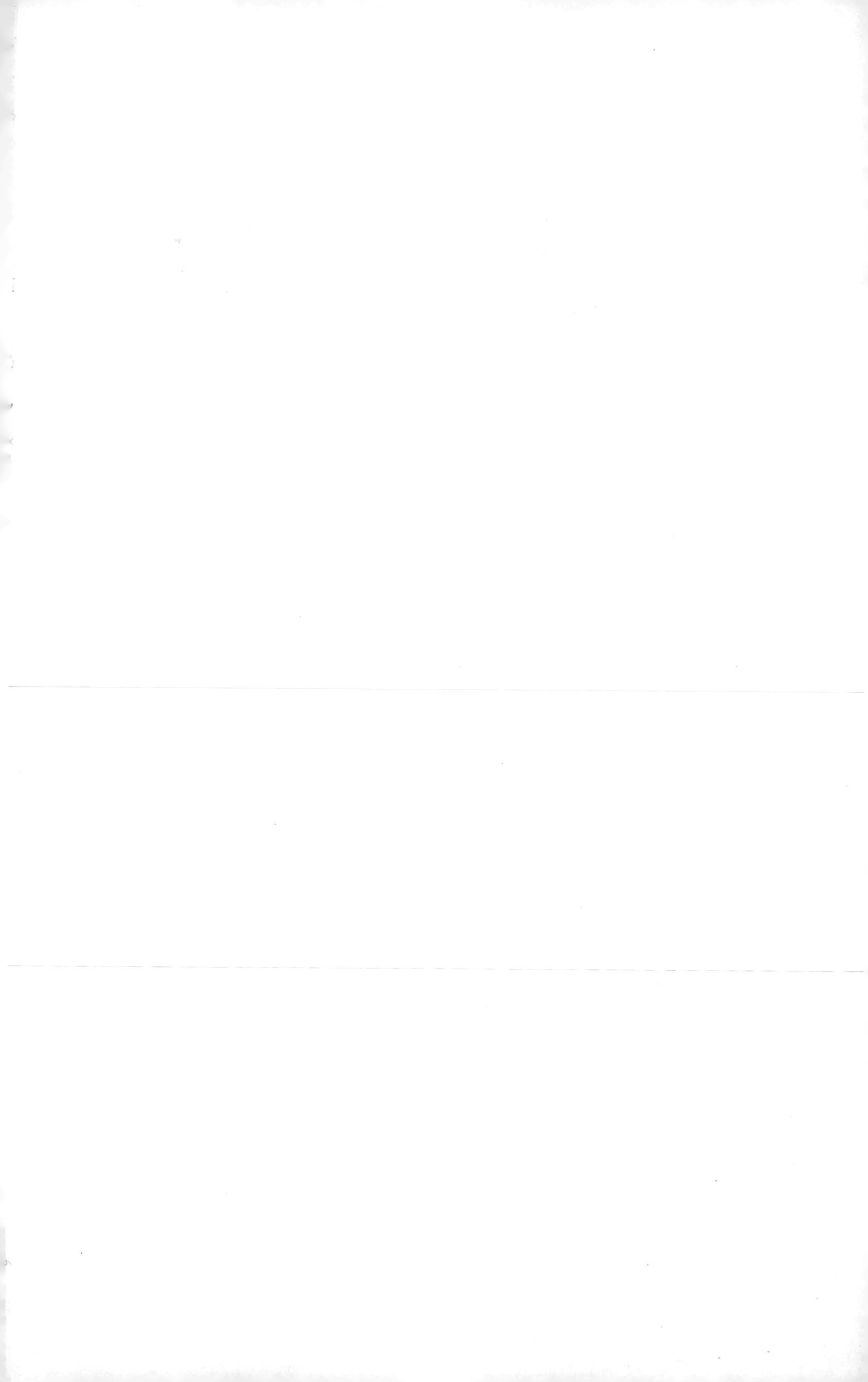